Best Short Stories

of Arthur Conan Doyle

CONTENTS

The Brown Hand..5
The Terror of Blue John Gap..................................19
The Captain of the Pole-Star...............................34
The Great Kleinplatz Experiment......................55
The Man from Archangel.......................................69
The Ring of Thoth...89
Lot No. 249..105
The Case of Lady Sannox....................................135
The Horror of the Heights..................................144
The Surgeon of Gaster Fell................................158

THE BROWN HAND

Every one knows that Sir Dominick Holden, the famous Indian surgeon, made me his heir, and that his death changed me in an hour from a hard-working and impecunious medical man to a well-to-do landed proprietor. Many know also that there were at least five people between the inheritance and me, and that Sir Dominick's selection appeared to be altogether arbitrary and whimsical. I can assure them, however, that they are quite mistaken, and that, although I only knew Sir Dominick in the closing years of his life, there were none the less very real reasons why he should show his goodwill towards me. As a matter of fact, though I say it myself, no man ever did more for another than I did for my Indian uncle. I cannot expect the story to be believed, but it is so singular that I should feel that it was a breach of duty if I did not put it upon record--so here it is, and your belief or incredulity is your own affair.

Sir Dominick Holden, C.B., K.C.S.I., and I don't know what besides, was the most distinguished Indian surgeon of his day. In the Army originally, he afterwards settled down into civil practice in Bombay, and visited as a consultant every part of India. His name is best remembered in connection with the Oriental Hospital, which he founded and supported. The time came, however, when his iron constitution began to show signs of the long strain to which he had subjected it, and his brother practitioners (who were not, perhaps, entirely disinterested upon the point) were unanimous in recommending him to return to England. He held on so long as he could, but at last he developed nervous symptoms of a very pronounced character, and so came back, a broken man, to his native county of Wiltshire. He bought a considerable estate with an ancient manor-house upon the edge of Salisbury Plain, and devoted his old age to the study of Comparative Pathology, which had been his learned hobby all his life, and in which he was a foremost authority.

We of the family were, as may be imagined, much excited by the news of the return of this rich and childless uncle to England. On his part, although by no means exuberant in his hospitality, he showed some sense of his duty to his relations, and each of us in turn had an invitation to visit him. From the accounts of my cousins it appeared to be a melancholy business, and it was with mixed feelings that I at last received my own summons to appear at Rodenhurst. My wife was so carefully excluded in the invitation that my first impulse was to refuse it, but the interests of the children had to be considered, and so, with her consent, I set out one October afternoon upon my visit to Wiltshire, with little thought of what that visit was to entail.

My uncle's estate was situated where the arable land of the plains begins to swell upwards into the rounded chalk hills which are characteristic of the county. As I drove from Dinton Station in the waning light of that autumn day, I was impressed by the weird nature of the scenery. The few scattered cottages of the peasants were so dwarfed by the huge evidences of prehistoric life, that the present appeared to be a dream and the past to be the obtrusive and masterful reality. The road wound through the valleys, formed by a succession of grassy hills, and the summit of each was cut and carved into the most elaborate fortifications, some circular, and some square, but all on a scale which has defied the winds and the rains of many centuries. Some call them Roman and some British, but their true origin and the reasons for this particular tract of country being so interlaced with entrenchments have never been finally made clear. Here and there on the long, smooth, olive-coloured slopes there rose small rounded barrows or tumuli. Beneath them lie the cremated ashes of the race which cut so deeply into the hills, but their graves tell us nothing save that a jar full of dust represents the man who once laboured under the sun.

It was through this weird country that I approached my uncle's residence of Rodenhurst, and the house was, as I found, in due keeping with its surroundings. Two broken and weather-stained pillars, each surmounted by a mutilated heraldic emblem, flanked the entrance to a neglected drive. A cold wind whistled through the elms which lined it, and the air was full of the drifting leaves. At the far end, under the gloomy arch of trees, a single yellow lamp burned steadily. In the dim half-light of the coming night I saw a long, low building stretching out two irregular wings, with deep eaves, a sloping gambrel roof, and walls which were criss-crossed with timber balks in the fashion of the Tudors. The cheery light of a fire flickered in the broad, latticed window to the left of the low-porched door, and this, as it proved, marked the study of my uncle, for it was thither that I was led by his butler in order to make my host's acquaintance.

He was cowering over his fire, for the moist chill of an English autumn had set him shivering. His lamp was unlit, and I only saw the red glow of the embers beating upon a huge, craggy face, with a Red Indian nose and cheek, and deep furrows and seams from eye to chin, the sinister marks of hidden volcanic fires. He sprang up at my entrance with something of an old-world courtesy and welcomed me warmly to Rodenhurst. At the same time I was conscious, as the lamp was carried in, that it was a very critical pair of light-blue eyes which looked out at me from under shaggy eyebrows, like scouts beneath a bush, and that this outlandish uncle of mine was carefully reading off my character with all the ease of a practised observer and an experienced man of the world.

For my part I looked at him, and looked again, for I had never seen a man whose appearance was more fitted to hold one's attention. His figure was the framework of a giant, but he had fallen away until his coat dangled straight down in a shocking fashion from a pair of broad and bony shoulders. All his limbs were huge and yet emaciated, and I could not take my gaze from his knobby wrists, and long, gnarled hands. But his eyes--those peering light-blue eyes--they were the most arrestive of any of his peculiarities. It was not their colour alone, nor was it the ambush of hair in which they lurked; but it was the expression which I read in them. For the appearance and bearing of the man were masterful, and one expected a certain corresponding arrogance in his eyes, but instead of that I read the look which tells of a spirit cowed and crushed, the furtive, expectant look of the dog whose master has taken the whip from the rack. I formed my own medical diagnosis upon one glance at those critical and yet appealing eyes. I believed that he was stricken with some mortal ailment, that he knew himself to be exposed to sudden death, and that he lived in terror of it. Such was my judgment--a false one, as the event showed; but I mention it that it may help you to realise the look which I read in his eyes.

My uncle's welcome was, as I have said, a courteous one, and in an hour or so I found myself seated between him and his wife at a comfortable dinner, with curious pungent delicacies upon the table, and a stealthy, quick-eyed Oriental waiter behind his chair. The old couple had come round to that tragic imitation of the dawn of life when husband and wife, having lost or scattered all those who were their intimates, find themselves face to face and alone once more, their work done, and the end nearing fast. Those who have reached that stage in sweetness and love, who can change their winter into a gentle Indian summer, have come as victors through the ordeal of life.

Lady Holden was a small, alert woman with a kindly eye, and her expression as she glanced at him was a certificate of character to her husband. And yet, though I read a mutual love in their glances, I read also mutual horror, and recognised in her face some reflection of that stealthy fear which I had detected in his. Their talk was sometimes merry and sometimes sad, but there was a forced note in their merriment and a naturalness in their sadness which told me that a heavy heart beat upon either side of me.

We were sitting over our first glass of wine, and the servants had left the room, when the conversation took a turn which produced a remarkable effect upon my host and hostess. I cannot recall what it was which started the topic of the supernatural, but it ended in my showing them that the abnormal in psychical experiences was a subject to which I had, like many neurologists, devoted a great deal of attention. I concluded by narrating my experiences when, as a member of the Psychical Research Society, I had formed one of a committee of three who spent the night in a haunted house. Our adventures were neither exciting nor convincing, but, such as it was, the story appeared to interest my auditors in a remarkable degree. They listened with an eager silence, and I caught a look of intelligence between them which I could not understand. Lady Holden immediately afterwards rose and left the room.

Sir Dominick pushed the cigar-box over to me, and we smoked for some little time in silence. That huge bony hand of his was twitching as he raised it with his cheroot to his lips, and I felt that the man's nerves were vibrating like fiddle-strings. My instincts told me that he was on the verge of some intimate confidence, and I feared to speak lest I should interrupt it. At last he turned towards me with a spasmodic gesture like a man who throws his last scruple to the winds.

"From the little that I have seen of you it appears to me, Dr. Hardacre," said he, "that you are the very man I have wanted to meet."

"I am delighted to hear it, sir."

"Your head seems to be cool and steady. You will acquit me of any desire to flatter you, for the circumstances are too serious to permit of insincerities. You have some special knowledge upon these subjects, and you evidently view them from that philosophical standpoint which robs them of all vulgar terror. I presume that the sight of an apparition would not seriously discompose you?"

"I think not, sir."

"Would even interest you, perhaps?"

"Most intensely."

"As a psychical observer, you would probably investigate it in as impersonal a fashion as an astronomer investigates a wandering comet?"

"Precisely."

He gave a heavy sigh.

"Believe me, Dr. Hardacre, there was a time when I could have spoken as you do now. My nerve was a by-word in India. Even the Mutiny never shook it for an instant. And yet you see what I am reduced to--the most timorous man, perhaps, in all this county of Wiltshire. Do not speak too bravely upon this subject, or you may find yourself subjected to as long-drawn a test as I am--a test which can only end in the madhouse or the grave."

I waited patiently until he should see fit to go farther in his confidence. His preamble had, I need not say, filled me with interest and expectation.

"For some years, Dr. Hardacre," he continued, "my life and that of my wife have been made miserable by a cause which is so grotesque that it borders upon the ludicrous. And yet familiarity has never made it more easy to bear--on the contrary, as time passes my nerves become more worn and shattered by the constant attrition. If you have no physical fears, Dr. Hardacre, I should very much value your opinion upon this phenomenon which troubles us so."

"For what it is worth my opinion is entirely at your service. May I ask the nature of the phenomenon?"

"I think that your experiences will have a higher evidential value if you are not told in advance what you may expect to encounter. You are yourself aware of the quibbles of unconscious cerebration and subjective impressions with which a scientific sceptic may throw a doubt upon your statement. It would be as well to guard against them in advance."

"What shall I do, then?"

"I will tell you. Would you mind following me this way?" He led me out of the dining-room and down a long passage until we came to a terminal door. Inside there was a large bare room fitted as a laboratory, with numerous scientific instruments and bottles. A shelf ran along one side, upon which there stood a long line of glass jars containing pathological and anatomical specimens.

"You see that I still dabble in some of my old studies," said Sir Dominick. "These jars are the remains of what was once a most excellent collection, but unfortunately I lost the greater part of them when my house was burned down in Bombay in '92. It was a most unfortunate affair for me--in more ways than one. I had examples of many rare conditions, and my splenic collection was probably unique. These are the survivors."

I glanced over them, and saw that they really were of a very great value and rarity from a pathological point of view: bloated organs, gaping cysts, distorted bones, odious parasites--a singular exhibition of the products of India.

"There is, as you see, a small settee here," said my host. "It was far from our intention to offer a guest so meagre an accommodation, but since affairs have taken this turn, it would be a great kindness upon your part if you would consent to spend the night in this apartment. I beg that you will not hesitate to let me know if the idea should be at all repugnant to you."

"On the contrary," I said, "it is most acceptable."

"My own room is the second on the left, so that if you should feel that you are in need of company a call would always bring me to your side."

"I trust that I shall not be compelled to disturb you."

"It is unlikely that I shall be asleep. I do not sleep much. Do not hesitate to summon me."

And so with this agreement we joined Lady Holden in the drawing-room and talked of lighter things.

It was no affectation upon my part to say that the prospect of my night's adventure was an agreeable one. I had no pretence to greater physical courage than my neighbours, but familiarity with a subject robs it of those vague and undefined terrors which are the most appalling to the imaginative mind. The human brain is capable of only one strong emotion at a time, and if it be filled with curiosity or scientific enthusiasm, there is no room for fear. It is true that I had my uncle's assurance that he had himself originally taken this point of view, but I reflected that the breakdown of his nervous system might be due to his forty years in India as much as to any psychical experiences which had befallen him. I at least was sound in nerve and brain, and it was with something of the pleasurable thrill of anticipation with which the sportsman takes his position beside the haunt of his game that I shut the laboratory door behind me, and partially undressing, lay down upon the rug-covered settee.

It was not an ideal atmosphere for a bedroom. The air was heavy with many chemical odours, that of methylated spirit predominating. Nor were the decorations of my chamber very sedative. The odious line of glass jars with their relics of disease and suffering stretched in front of my very eyes. There was no blind to the window, and a three-quarter moon streamed its white light into the room, tracing a silver square with filigree lattices upon the opposite wall. When I had extinguished my candle this one bright patch in the midst of the general gloom had certainly an eerie and discomposing aspect. A rigid and absolute silence reigned throughout the old house, so that the low swish of the branches in the garden came softly and smoothly to my ears. It may have been the hypnotic lullaby of this gentle susurrus, or it may have been the result of my tiring day, but after many dozings and many efforts to regain my clearness of perception, I fell at last into a deep and dreamless sleep.

 I was awakened by some sound in the room, and I instantly raised myself upon my elbow on the couch. Some hours had passed, for the square patch upon the wall had slid downwards and sideways until it lay obliquely at the end of my bed. The rest of the room was in deep shadow. At first I could see nothing, presently, as my eyes became accustomed to the faint light, I was aware, with a thrill which all my scientific absorption could not entirely prevent, that something was moving slowly along the line of the wall. A gentle, shuffling sound, as of soft slippers, came to my ears, and I dimly discerned a human figure walking stealthily from the direction of the door. As it emerged into the patch of moonlight I saw very clearly what it was and how it was employed. It was a man, short and squat, dressed in some sort of dark-grey gown, which hung straight from his shoulders to his feet. The moon shone upon the side of his face, and I saw that it was chocolate-brown in colour, with a ball of black hair like a woman's at the back of his head. He walked slowly, and his eyes were cast upwards towards the line of bottles which contained those gruesome remnants of humanity. He seemed to examine each jar with attention, and then to pass on to the next. When he had come to the end of the line, immediately opposite my bed, he stopped, faced me, threw up his hands with a gesture of despair, and vanished from my sight.

 I have said that he threw up his hands, but I should have said his arms, for as he assumed that attitude of despair I observed a singular peculiarity about his appearance. He had only one hand! As the sleeves drooped down from the upflung arms I saw the left plainly, but the right ended in a knobby and unsightly stump. In every other way his appearance was so natural, and I had both seen and heard him so clearly, that I could easily have believed that he was an Indian servant of Sir Dominick's who had come into my room in search of something. It was only his sudden disappearance which suggested anything more sinister to me. As it was I sprang from my couch, lit a candle, and examined the whole room carefully. There were no signs of my visitor, and I was forced to conclude that there had really been something outside the normal laws of Nature in his appearance. I lay awake for the remainder of the night, but nothing else occurred to disturb me.

I am an early riser, but my uncle was an even earlier one, for I found him pacing up and down the lawn at the side of the house. He ran towards me in his eagerness when he saw me come out from the door.

"Well, well!" he cried. "Did you see him?"

"An Indian with one hand?"

"Precisely."

"Yes, I saw him"--and I told him all that occurred. When I had finished, he led the way into his study. "We have a little time before breakfast," said he. "It will suffice to give you an explanation of this extraordinary affair--so far as I can explain that which is essentially inexplicable. In the first place, when I tell you that for four years I have never passed one single night, either in Bombay, aboard ship, or here in England without my sleep being broken by this fellow, you will understand why it is that I am a wreck of my former self. His programme is always the same. He appears by my bedside, shakes me roughly by the shoulder, passes from my room into the laboratory, walks slowly along the line of my bottles, and then vanishes. For more than a thousand times he has gone through the same routine."

"What does he want?"

"He wants his hand."

"His hand?"

"Yes, it came about in this way. I was summoned to Peshawur for a consultation some ten years ago, and while there I was asked to look at the hand of a native who was passing through with an Afghan caravan. The fellow came from some mountain tribe living away at the back of beyond somewhere on the other side of Kaffiristan. He talked a bastard Pushtoo, and it was all I could do to understand him. He was suffering from a soft sarcomatous swelling of one of the metacarpal joints, and I made him realise that it was only by losing his hand that he could hope to save his life. After much persuasion he consented to the operation, and he asked me, when it was over, what fee I demanded. The poor fellow was almost a beggar, so that the idea of a fee was absurd, but I answered in jest that my fee should be his hand, and that I proposed to add it to my pathological collection.

"To my surprise he demurred very much to the suggestion, and he explained that according to his religion it was an all-important matter that the body should be reunited after death, and so make a perfect dwelling for the spirit. The belief is, of course, an old one, and the mummies of the Egyptians arose from an analogous superstition. I answered him that his hand was already off, and asked him how he intended to preserve it. He replied that he would pickle it in salt and carry it about with him. I suggested that it might be safer in my keeping than his, and that I had better means than salt for preserving it. On realising that I really intended to carefully keep it, his opposition vanished instantly. 'But remember, sahib,' said he, 'I shall want it back when I am dead.' I laughed at the remark, and so the matter ended. I returned to my practice, and he no doubt in the course of time was able to continue his journey to Afghanistan.

"Well, as I told you last night, I had a bad fire in my house at Bombay. Half of it was burned down, and, among other things, my pathological collection was largely destroyed. What you see are the poor remains of it. The hand of the hillman went with the rest, but I gave the matter no particular thought at the time. That was six years ago.

"Four years ago--two years after the fire--I was awakened one night by a furious tugging at my sleeve. I sat up under the impression that my favourite mastiff was trying to arouse me. Instead of this, I saw my Indian patient of long ago, dressed in the long grey gown which was the badge of his people. He was holding up his stump and looking reproachfully at me. He then went over to my bottles, which at that time I kept in my room, and he examined them carefully, after which he gave a gesture of anger and vanished. I realised that he had just died, and that he had come to claim my promise that I should keep his limb in safety for him.

"Well, there you have it all, Dr. Hardacre. Every night at the same hour for four years this performance has been repeated. It is a simple thing in itself, but it has worn me out like water dropping on a stone. It has brought a vile insomnia with it, for I cannot sleep now for the expectation of his coming. It has poisoned my old age and that of my wife, who has been the sharer in this great trouble. But there is the breakfast gong, and she will be waiting impatiently to know how it fared with you last night. We are both much indebted to you for your gallantry, for it takes something from the weight of our misfortune when we share it, even for a single night, with a friend, and it reassures us as to our sanity, which we are sometimes driven to question."

This was the curious narrative which Sir Dominick confided to me--a story which to many would have appeared to be a grotesque impossibility, but which, after my experience of the night before, and my previous knowledge of such things, I was prepared to accept as an absolute fact. I thought deeply over the matter, and brought the whole range of my reading and experience to bear upon it. After breakfast, I surprised my host and hostess by announcing that I was returning to London by the next train.

"My dear doctor," cried Sir Dominick in great distress, "you make me feel that I have been guilty of a gross breach of hospitality in intruding this unfortunate matter upon you. I should have borne my own burden."

"It is, indeed, that matter which is taking me to London," I answered; "but you are mistaken, I assure you, if you think that my experience of last night was an unpleasant one to me. On the contrary, I am about to ask your permission to return in the evening and spend one more night in your laboratory. I am very eager to see this visitor once again."

My uncle was exceedingly anxious to know what I was about to do, but my fears of raising false hopes prevented me from telling him. I was back in my own consulting-room a little after luncheon, and was confirming my memory of a passage in a recent book upon occultism which had arrested my attention when I had read it.

"In the case of earth-bound spirits," said my authority, "some one dominant idea obsessing them at the hour of death is sufficient to hold them in this material world. They are the amphibia of this life and of the next, capable of passing from one to the other as the turtle passes from land to water. The causes which may bind a soul so strongly to a life which its body has abandoned are any violent emotion. Avarice, revenge, anxiety, love, and pity have all been known to have this effect. As a rule it springs from some unfulfilled wish, and when the wish has been fulfilled the material bond relaxes. There are many cases upon record which show the singular persistence of these visitors, and also their disappearance when their wishes have been fulfilled, or in some cases when a reasonable compromise has been effected."

"A reasonable compromise effected"--those were the words which I had brooded over all the morning, and which I now verified in the original. No actual atonement could be made here--but a reasonable compromise! I made my way as fast as a train could take me to the Shadwell Seamen's Hospital, where my old friend Jack Hewett was house-surgeon. Without explaining the situation I made him understand what it was that I wanted.

"A brown man's hand!" said he, in amazement. "What in the world do you want that for?"

"Never mind. I'll tell you some day. I know that your wards are full of Indians."

"I should think so. But a hand----" He thought a little and then struck a bell.

"Travers," said he to a student-dresser, "what became of the hands of the Lascar which we took off yesterday? I mean the fellow from the East India Dock who got caught in the steam winch."

"They are in the post-mortem room, sir."

"Just pack one of them in antiseptics and give it to Dr. Hardacre."

And so I found myself back at Rodenhurst before dinner with this curious outcome of my day in town. I still said nothing to Sir Dominick, but I slept that night in the laboratory, and I placed the Lascar's hand in one of the glass jars at the end of my couch.

So interested was I in the result of my experiment that sleep was out of the question. I sat with a shaded lamp beside me and waited patiently for my visitor. This time I saw him clearly from the first. He appeared beside the door, nebulous for an instant, and then hardening into as distinct an outline as any living man. The slippers beneath his grey gown were red and heelless, which accounted for the low, shuffling sound which he made as he walked. As on the previous night he passed slowly along the line of bottles until he paused before that which contained the hand. He reached up to it, his whole figure quivering with expectation, took it down, examined it eagerly, and then, with a face which was convulsed with disappointment, he hurled it down on the floor. There was a crash which resounded through the house, and when I looked up the mutilated Indian had disappeared. A moment later my door flew open and Sir Dominick rushed in.

"You are not hurt?" he cried.

"No--but deeply disappointed."

He looked in astonishment at the splinters of glass, and the brown hand lying upon the floor.

"Good God!" he cried. "What is this?"

I told him my idea and its wretched sequel. He listened intently, but shook his head.

"It was well thought of," said he, "but I fear that there is no such easy end to my sufferings. But one thing I now insist upon. It is that you shall never again upon any pretext occupy this room. My fears that something might have happened to you--when I heard that crash--have been the most acute of all the agonies which I have undergone. I will not expose myself to a repetition of it."

He allowed me, however, to spend the remainder of the night where I was, and I lay there worrying over the problem and lamenting my own failure. With the first light of morning there was the Lascar's hand still lying upon the floor to remind me of my fiasco. I lay looking at it--and as I lay suddenly an idea flew like a bullet through my head and brought me quivering with excitement out of my couch. I raised the grim relic from where it had fallen. Yes, it was indeed so. The hand was the left hand of the Lascar.

By the first train I was on my way to town, and hurried at once to the Seamen's Hospital. I remembered that both hands of the Lascar had been amputated, but I was terrified lest the precious organ which I was in search of might have been already consumed in the crematory. My suspense was soon ended. It had still been preserved in the post-mortem room. And so I returned to Rodenhurst in the evening with my mission accomplished and the material for a fresh experiment.

But Sir Dominick Holden would not hear of my occupying the laboratory again. To all my entreaties he turned a deaf ear. It offended his sense of hospitality, and he could no longer permit it. I left the hand, therefore, as I had done its fellow the night before, and I occupied a comfortable bedroom in another portion of the house, some distance from the scene of my adventures.

But in spite of that my sleep was not destined to be uninterrupted. In the dead of night my host burst into my room, a lamp in his hand. His huge gaunt figure was enveloped in a loose dressing-gown, and his whole appearance might certainly have seemed more formidable to a weak-nerved man than that of the Indian of the night before. But it was not his entrance so much as his expression which amazed me. He had turned suddenly younger by twenty years at the least. His eyes were shining, his features radiant, and he waved one hand in triumph over his head. I sat up astounded, staring sleepily at this extraordinary visitor. But his words soon drove the sleep from my eyes.

"We have done it! We have succeeded!" he shouted. "My dear Hardacre, how can I ever in this world repay you?"

"You don't mean to say that it is all right?"

"Indeed I do. I was sure that you would not mind being awakened to hear such blessed news."

"Mind! I should think not indeed. But is it really certain?"

"I have no doubt whatever upon the point. I owe you such a debt, my dear nephew, as I have never owed a man before, and never expected to. What can I possibly do for you that is commensurate? Providence must have sent you to my rescue. You have saved both my reason and my life, for another six months of this must have seen me either in a cell or a coffin. And my wife--it was wearing her out before my eyes. Never could I have believed that any human being could have lifted this burden off me." He seized my hand and wrung it in his bony grip.

"It was only an experiment--a forlorn hope--but I am delighted from my heart that it has succeeded. But how do you know that it is all right? Have you seen something?"

He seated himself at the foot of my bed.

"I have seen enough," said he. "It satisfies me that I shall be troubled no more. What has passed is easily told. You know that at a certain hour this creature always comes to me. To-night he arrived at the usual time, and aroused me with even more violence than is his custom. I can only surmise that his disappointment of last night increased the bitterness of his anger against me. He looked angrily at me, and then went on his usual round. But in a few minutes I saw him, for the first time since this persecution began, return to my chamber. He was smiling. I saw the gleam of his white teeth through the dim light. He stood facing me at the end of my bed, and three times he made the low Eastern salaam which is their solemn leave-taking. And the third time that he bowed he raised his arms over his head, and I saw his two hands outstretched in the air. So he vanished, and, as I believe, for ever."

* * * * *

So that is the curious experience which won me the affection and the gratitude of my celebrated uncle, the famous Indian surgeon. His anticipations were realised, and never again was he disturbed by the visits of the restless hillman in search of his lost member. Sir Dominick and Lady Holden spent a very happy old age, unclouded, so far as I know, by any trouble, and they finally died during the great influenza epidemic within a few weeks of each other. In his lifetime he always turned to me for advice in everything which concerned that English life of which he knew so little; and I aided him also in the purchase and development of his estates. It was no great surprise to me, therefore, that I found myself eventually promoted over the heads of five exasperated cousins, and changed in a single day from a hard-working country doctor into the head of an important Wiltshire family. I at least have reason to bless the memory of the man with the brown hand, and the day when I was fortunate enough to relieve Rodenhurst of his unwelcome presence.

THE TERROR OF BLUE JOHN GAP

The following narrative was found among the papers of Dr. James Hardcastle, who died of phthisis on February 4th, 1908, at 36, Upper Coventry Flats, South Kensington. Those who knew him best, while refusing to express an opinion upon this particular statement, are unanimous in asserting that he was a man of a sober and scientific turn of mind, absolutely devoid of imagination, and most unlikely to invent any abnormal series of events. The paper was contained in an envelope, which was docketed, "A Short Account of the Circumstances which occurred near Miss Allerton's Farm in North-West Derbyshire in the Spring of Last Year." The envelope was sealed, and on the other side was written in pencil--

DEAR SEATON,--

"It may interest, and perhaps pain you, to know that the incredulity with which you met my story has prevented me from ever opening my mouth upon the subject again. I leave this record after my death, and perhaps strangers may be found to have more confidence in me than my friend."

Inquiry has failed to elicit who this Seaton may have been. I may add that the visit of the deceased to Allerton's Farm, and the general nature of the alarm there, apart from his particular explanation, have been absolutely established. With this foreword I append his account exactly as he left it. It is in the form of a diary, some entries in which have been expanded, while a few have been erased.

April 17.--Already I feel the benefit of this wonderful upland air. The farm of the Allertons lies fourteen hundred and twenty feet above sea-level, so it may well be a bracing climate. Beyond the usual morning cough I have very little discomfort, and, what with the fresh milk and the home-grown mutton, I have every chance of putting on weight. I think Saunderson will be pleased.

The two Miss Allertons are charmingly quaint and kind, two dear little hard-working old maids, who are ready to lavish all the heart which might have gone out to husband and to children upon an invalid stranger. Truly, the old maid is a most useful person, one of the reserve forces of the community. They talk of the superfluous woman, but what would the poor superfluous man do without her kindly presence? By the way, in their simplicity they very quickly let out the reason why Saunderson recommended their farm. The Professor rose from the ranks himself, and I believe that in his youth he was not above scaring crows in these very fields.

It is a most lonely spot, and the walks are picturesque in the extreme. The farm consists of grazing land lying at the bottom of an irregular valley. On each side are the fantastic limestone hills, formed of rock so soft that you can break it away with your hands. All this country is hollow. Could you strike it with some gigantic hammer it would boom like a drum, or possibly cave in altogether and expose some huge subterranean sea. A great sea there must surely be, for on all sides the streams run into the mountain itself, never to reappear. There are gaps everywhere amid the rocks, and when you pass through them you find yourself in great caverns, which wind down into the bowels of the earth. I have a small bicycle lamp, and it is a perpetual joy to me to carry it into these weird solitudes, and to see the wonderful silver and black effect when I throw its light upon the stalactites which drape the lofty roofs. Shut off the lamp, and you are in the blackest darkness. Turn it on, and it is a scene from the Arabian Nights.

But there is one of these strange openings in the earth which has a special interest, for it is the handiwork, not of nature, but of man. I had never heard of Blue John when I came to these parts. It is the name given to a peculiar mineral of a beautiful purple shade, which is only found at one or two places in the world. It is so rare that an ordinary vase of Blue John would be valued at a great price. The Romans, with that extraordinary instinct of theirs, discovered that it was to be found in this valley, and sank a horizontal shaft deep into the mountain side. The opening of their mine has been called Blue John Gap, a clean-cut arch in the rock, the mouth all overgrown with bushes. It is a goodly passage which the Roman miners have cut, and it intersects some of the great water-worn caves, so that if you enter Blue John Gap you would do well to mark your steps and to have a good store of candles, or you may never make your way back to the daylight again. I have not yet gone deeply into it, but this very day I stood at the mouth of the arched tunnel, and peering down into the black recesses beyond, I vowed that when my health returned I would devote some holiday to exploring those mysterious depths and finding out for myself how far the Roman had penetrated into the Derbyshire hills.

Strange how superstitious these countrymen are! I should have thought better of young Armitage, for he is a man of some education and character, and a very fine fellow for his station in life. I was standing at the Blue John Gap when he came across the field to me.

"Well, doctor," said he, "you're not afraid, anyhow."

"Afraid!" I answered. "Afraid of what?"

"Of it," said he, with a jerk of his thumb towards the black vault, "of the Terror that lives in the Blue John Cave."

How absurdly easy it is for a legend to arise in a lonely countryside! I examined him as to the reasons for his weird belief. It seems that from time to time sheep have been missing from the fields, carried bodily away, according to Armitage. That they could have wandered away of their own accord and disappeared among the mountains was an explanation to which he would not listen. On one occasion a pool of blood had been found, and some tufts of wool. That also, I pointed out, could be explained in a perfectly natural way. Further, the nights upon which sheep disappeared were invariably very dark, cloudy nights with no moon. This I met with the obvious retort that those were the nights which a commonplace sheep-stealer would naturally choose for his work. On one occasion a gap had been made in a wall, and some of the stones scattered for a considerable distance. Human agency again, in my opinion. Finally, Armitage clinched all his arguments by telling me that he had actually heard the Creature-- indeed, that anyone could hear it who remained long enough at the Gap. It was a distant roaring of an immense volume. I could not but smile at this, knowing, as I do, the strange reverberations which come out of an underground water system running amid the chasms of a limestone formation. My incredulity annoyed Armitage so that he turned and left me with some abruptness.

And now comes the queer point about the whole business. I was still standing near the mouth of the cave turning over in my mind the various statements of Armitage, and reflecting how readily they could be explained away, when suddenly, from the depth of the tunnel beside me, there issued a most extraordinary sound. How shall I describe it? First of all, it seemed to be a great distance away, far down in the bowels of the earth. Secondly, in spite of this suggestion of distance, it was very loud. Lastly, it was not a boom, nor a crash, such as one would associate with falling water or tumbling rock, but it was a high whine, tremulous and vibrating, almost like the whinnying of a horse. It was certainly a most remarkable experience, and one which for a moment, I must admit, gave a new significance to Armitage's words. I waited by the Blue John Gap for half an hour or more, but there was no return of the sound, so at last I wandered back to the farmhouse, rather mystified by what had occurred. Decidedly I shall explore that cavern when my strength is restored. Of course, Armitage's explanation is too absurd for discussion, and yet that sound was certainly very strange. It still rings in my ears as I write.

April 20.--In the last three days I have made several expeditions to the Blue John Gap, and have even penetrated some short distance, but my bicycle lantern is so small and weak that I dare not trust myself very far. I shall do the thing more systematically. I have heard no sound at all, and could almost believe that I had been the victim of some hallucination suggested, perhaps, by Armitage's conversation. Of course, the whole idea is absurd, and yet I must confess that those bushes at the entrance of the cave do present an appearance as if some heavy creature had forced its way through them. I begin to be keenly interested. I have said nothing to the Miss Allertons, for they are quite superstitious enough already, but I have bought some candles, and mean to investigate for myself.

I observed this morning that among the numerous tufts of sheep's wool which lay among the bushes near the cavern there was one which was smeared with blood. Of course, my reason tells me that if sheep wander into such rocky places they are likely to injure themselves, and yet somehow that splash of crimson gave me a sudden shock, and for a moment I found myself shrinking back in horror from the old Roman arch. A fetid breath seemed to ooze from the black depths into which I peered. Could it indeed be possible that some nameless thing, some dreadful presence, was lurking down yonder? I should have been incapable of such feelings in the days of my strength, but one grows more nervous and fanciful when one's health is shaken.

For the moment I weakened in my resolution, and was ready to leave the secret of the old mine, if one exists, for ever unsolved. But tonight my interest has returned and my nerves grown more steady. Tomorrow I trust that I shall have gone more deeply into this matter.

April 22.--Let me try and set down as accurately as I can my extraordinary experience of yesterday. I started in the afternoon, and made my way to the Blue John Gap. I confess that my misgivings returned as I gazed into its depths, and I wished that I had brought a companion to share my exploration. Finally, with a return of resolution, I lit my candle, pushed my way through the briars, and descended into the rocky shaft.

It went down at an acute angle for some fifty feet, the floor being covered with broken stone. Thence there extended a long, straight passage cut in the solid rock. I am no geologist, but the lining of this corridor was certainly of some harder material than limestone, for there were points where I could actually see the tool-marks which the old miners had left in their excavation, as fresh as if they had been done yesterday. Down this strange, old- world corridor I stumbled, my feeble flame throwing a dim circle of light around me, which made the shadows beyond the more threatening and obscure. Finally, I came to a spot where the Roman tunnel opened into a water-worn cavern--a huge hall, hung with long white icicles of lime deposit. From this central chamber I could dimly perceive that a number of passages worn by the subterranean streams wound away into the depths of the earth. I was standing there wondering whether I had better return, or whether I dare venture farther into this dangerous labyrinth, when my eyes fell upon something at my feet which strongly arrested my attention.

The greater part of the floor of the cavern was covered with boulders of rock or with hard incrustations of lime, but at this particular point there had been a drip from the distant roof, which had left a patch of soft mud. In the very centre of this there was a huge mark--an ill-defined blotch, deep, broad and irregular, as if a great boulder had fallen upon it. No loose stone lay near, however, nor was there anything to account for the impression. It was far too large to be caused by any possible animal, and besides, there was only the one, and the patch of mud was of such a size that no reasonable stride could have covered it. As I rose from the examination of that singular mark and then looked round into the black shadows which hemmed me in, I must confess that I felt for a moment a most unpleasant sinking of my heart, and that, do what I could, the candle trembled in my outstretched hand.

I soon recovered my nerve, however, when I reflected how absurd it was to associate so huge and shapeless a mark with the track of any known animal. Even an elephant could not have produced it. I determined, therefore, that I would not be scared by vague and senseless fears from carrying out my exploration. Before proceeding, I took good note of a curious rock formation in the wall by which I could recognize the entrance of the Roman tunnel. The precaution was very necessary, for the great cave, so far as I could see it, was intersected by passages. Having made sure of my position, and reassured myself by examining my spare candles and my matches, I advanced slowly over the rocky and uneven surface of the cavern.

And now I come to the point where I met with such sudden and desperate disaster. A stream, some twenty feet broad, ran across my path, and I walked for some little distance along the bank to find a spot where I could cross dry-shod. Finally, I came to a place where a single flat boulder lay near the centre, which I could reach in a stride. As it chanced, however, the rock had been cut away and made top-heavy by the rush of the stream, so that it tilted over as I landed on it and shot me into the ice-cold water. My candle went out, and I found myself floundering about in utter and absolute darkness.

I staggered to my feet again, more amused than alarmed by my adventure. The candle had fallen from my hand, and was lost in the stream, but I had two others in my pocket, so that it was of no importance. I got one of them ready, and drew out my box of matches to light it. Only then did I realize my position. The box had been soaked in my fall into the river. It was impossible to strike the matches.

A cold hand seemed to close round my heart as I realized my position. The darkness was opaque and horrible. It was so utter one put one's hand up to one's face as if to press off something solid. I stood still, and by an effort I steadied myself. I tried to reconstruct in my mind a map of the floor of the cavern as I had last seen it. Alas! the bearings which had impressed themselves upon my mind were high on the wall, and not to be found by touch. Still, I remembered in a general way how the sides were situated, and I hoped that by groping my way along them I should at last come to the opening of the Roman tunnel. Moving very slowly, and continually striking against the rocks, I set out on this desperate quest.

But I very soon realized how impossible it was. In that black, velvety darkness one lost all one's bearings in an instant. Before I had made a dozen paces, I was utterly bewildered as to my whereabouts. The rippling of the stream, which was the one sound audible, showed me where it lay, but the moment that I left its bank I was utterly lost. The idea of finding my way back in absolute darkness through that limestone labyrinth was clearly an impossible one.

I sat down upon a boulder and reflected upon my unfortunate plight. I had not told anyone that I proposed to come to the Blue John mine, and it was unlikely that a search party would come after me. Therefore I must trust to my own resources to get clear of the danger. There was only one hope, and that was that the matches might dry. When I fell into the river, only half of me had got thoroughly wet. My left shoulder had remained above the water. I took the box of matches, therefore, and put it into my left armpit. The moist air of the cavern might possibly be counteracted by the heat of my body, but even so, I knew that I could not hope to get a light for many hours. Meanwhile there was nothing for it but to wait.

By good luck I had slipped several biscuits into my pocket before I left the farm-house. These I now devoured, and washed them down with a draught from that wretched stream which had been the cause of all my misfortunes. Then I felt about for a comfortable seat among the rocks, and, having discovered a place where I could get a support for my back, I stretched out my legs and settled myself down to wait. I was wretchedly damp and cold, but I tried to cheer myself with the reflection that modern science prescribed open windows and walks in all weather for my disease. Gradually, lulled by the monotonous gurgle of the stream, and by the absolute darkness, I sank into an uneasy slumber.

How long this lasted I cannot say. It may have been for an hour, it may have been for several. Suddenly I sat up on my rock couch, with every nerve thrilling and every sense acutely on the alert. Beyond all doubt I had heard a sound--some sound very distinct from the gurgling of the waters. It had passed, but the reverberation of it still lingered in my ear. Was it a search party? They would most certainly have shouted, and vague as this sound was which had wakened me, it was very distinct from the human voice. I sat palpitating and hardly daring to breathe. There it was again! And again! Now it had become continuous. It was a tread --yes, surely it was the tread of some living creature. But what a tread it was! It gave one the impression of enormous weight carried upon sponge-like feet, which gave forth a muffled but ear-filling sound. The darkness was as complete as ever, but the tread was regular and decisive. And it was coming beyond all question in my direction.

My skin grew cold, and my hair stood on end as I listened to that steady and ponderous footfall. There was some creature there, and surely by the speed of its advance, it was one which could see in the dark. I crouched low on my rock and tried to blend myself into it. The steps grew nearer still, then stopped, and presently I was aware of a loud lapping and gurgling. The creature was drinking at the stream. Then again there was silence, broken by a succession of long sniffs and snorts of tremendous volume and energy. Had it caught the scent of me? My own nostrils were filled by a low fetid odour, mephitic and abominable. Then I heard the steps again. They were on my side of the stream now. The stones rattled within a few yards of where I lay.

Hardly daring to breathe, I crouched upon my rock. Then the steps drew away. I heard the splash as it returned across the river, and the sound died away into the distance in the direction from which it had come.

For a long time I lay upon the rock, too much horrified to move. I thought of the sound which I had heard coming from the depths of the cave, of Armitage's fears, of the strange impression in the mud, and now came this final and absolute proof that there was indeed some inconceivable monster, something utterly unearthly and dreadful, which lurked in the hollow of the mountain. Of its nature or form I could frame no conception, save that it was both light-footed and gigantic. The combat between my reason, which told me that such things could not be, and my senses, which told me that they were, raged within me as I lay. Finally, I was almost ready to persuade myself that this experience had been part of some evil dream, and that my abnormal condition might have conjured up an hallucination. But there remained one final experience which removed the last possibility of doubt from my mind.

I had taken my matches from my armpit and felt them. They seemed perfectly hard and dry. Stooping down into a crevice of the rocks, I tried one of them. To my delight it took fire at once. I lit the candle, and, with a terrified backward glance into the obscure depths of the cavern, I hurried in the direction of the Roman passage. As I did so I passed the patch of mud on which I had seen the huge imprint. Now I stood astonished before it, for there were three similar imprints upon its surface, enormous in size, irregular in outline, of a depth which indicated the ponderous weight which had left them. Then a great terror surged over me. Stooping and shading my candle with my hand, I ran in a frenzy of fear to the rocky archway, hastened up it, and never stopped until, with weary feet and panting lungs, I rushed up the final slope of stones, broke through the tangle of briars, and flung myself exhausted upon the soft grass under the peaceful light of the stars. It was three in the morning when I reached the farm- house, and today I am all unstrung and quivering after my terrific adventure. As yet I have told no one. I must move warily in the matter. What would the poor lonely women, or the uneducated yokels here think of it if I were to tell them my experience? Let me go to someone who can understand and advise.

April 25.--I was laid up in bed for two days after my incredible adventure in the cavern. I use the adjective with a very definite meaning, for I have had an experience since which has shocked me almost as much as the other. I have said that I was looking round for someone who could advise me. There is a Dr. Mark Johnson who practices some few miles away, to whom I had a note of recommendation from Professor Saunderson. To him I drove, when I was strong enough to get about, and I recounted to him my whole strange experience. He listened intently, and then carefully examined me, paying special attention to my reflexes and to the pupils of my eyes. When he had finished, he refused to discuss my adventure, saying that it was entirely beyond him, but he gave me the card of a Mr. Picton at Castleton, with the advice that I should instantly go to him and tell him the story exactly as I had done to himself. He was, according to my adviser, the very man who was pre-eminently suited to help me. I went on to the station, therefore, and made my way to the little town, which is some ten miles away. Mr. Picton appeared to be a man of importance, as his brass plate was displayed upon the door of a considerable building on the outskirts of the town. I was about to ring his bell, when some misgiving came into my mind, and, crossing to a neighbouring shop, I asked the man behind the counter if he could tell me anything of Mr. Picton. "Why," said he, "he is the best mad doctor in Derbyshire, and yonder is his asylum." You can imagine that it was not long before I had shaken the dust of Castleton from my feet and returned to the farm, cursing all unimaginative pedants who cannot conceive that there may be things in creation which have never yet chanced to come across their mole's vision. After all, now that I am cooler, I can afford to admit that I have been no more sympathetic to Armitage than Dr. Johnson has been to me.

April 27. When I was a student I had the reputation of being a man of courage and enterprise. I remember that when there was a ghost-hunt at Coltbridge it was I who sat up in the haunted house. Is it advancing years (after all, I am only thirty-five), or is it this physical malady which has caused degeneration? Certainly my heart quails when I think of that horrible cavern in the hill, and the certainty that it has some monstrous occupant. What shall I do? There is not an hour in the day that I do not debate the question. If I say nothing, then the mystery remains unsolved. If I do say anything, then I have the alternative of mad alarm over the whole countryside, or of absolute incredulity which may end in consigning me to an asylum. On the whole, I think that my best course is to wait, and to prepare for some expedition which shall be more deliberate and better thought out than the last. As a first step I have been to Castleton and obtained a few essentials--a large acetylene lantern for one thing, and a good double-barrelled sporting rifle for another. The latter I have hired, but I have bought a dozen heavy game cartridges, which would bring down a rhinoceros. Now I am ready for my troglodyte friend. Give me better health and a little spate of energy, and I shall try conclusions with him yet. But who and what is he? Ah! there is the question which stands between me and my sleep. How many theories do I form, only to discard each in turn! It is all so utterly unthinkable. And yet the cry, the footmark, the tread in the cavern--no reasoning can get past these I think of the old- world legends of dragons and of other monsters. Were they, perhaps, not such fairy-tales as we have thought? Can it be that there is some fact which underlies them, and am I, of all mortals, the one who is chosen to expose it?

May 3.--For several days I have been laid up by the vagaries of an English spring, and during those days there have been developments, the true and sinister meaning of which no one can appreciate save myself. I may say that we have had cloudy and moonless nights of late, which according to my information were the seasons upon which sheep disappeared. Well, sheep have disappeared. Two of Miss Allerton's, one of old Pearson's of the Cat Walk, and one of Mrs. Moulton's. Four in all during three nights. No trace is left of them at all, and the countryside is buzzing with rumours of gipsies and of sheep-stealers.

But there is something more serious than that. Young Armitage has disappeared also. He left his moorland cottage early on Wednesday night and has never been heard of since. He was an unattached man, so there is less sensation than would otherwise be the case. The popular explanation is that he owes money, and has found a situation in some other part of the country, whence he will presently write for his belongings. But I have grave misgivings. Is it not much more likely that the recent tragedy of the sheep has caused him to take some steps which may have ended in his own destruction? He may, for example, have lain in wait for the creature and been carried off by it into the recesses of the mountains. What an inconceivable fate for a civilized Englishman of the twentieth century! And yet I feel that it is possible and even probable. But in that case, how far am I answerable both for his death and for any other mishap which may occur? Surely with the knowledge I already possess it must be my duty to see that something is done, or if necessary to do it myself. It must be the latter, for this morning I went down to the local police-station and told my story. The inspector entered it all in a large book and bowed me out with commendable gravity, but I heard a burst of laughter before I had got down his garden path. No doubt he was recounting my adventure to his family.

June 10.--I am writing this, propped up in bed, six weeks after my last entry in this journal. I have gone through a terrible shock both to mind and body, arising from such an experience as has seldom befallen a human being before. But I have attained my end. The danger from the Terror which dwells in the Blue John Gap has passed never to return. Thus much at least I, a broken invalid, have done for the common good. Let me now recount what occurred as clearly as I may.

The night of Friday, May 3rd, was dark and cloudy--the very night for the monster to walk. About eleven o'clock I went from the farm-house with my lantern and my rifle, having first left a note upon the table of my bedroom in which I said that, if I were missing, search should be made for me in the direction of the Gap. I made my way to the mouth of the Roman shaft, and, having perched myself among the rocks close to the opening, I shut off my lantern and waited patiently with my loaded rifle ready to my hand.

It was a melancholy vigil. All down the winding valley I could see the scattered lights of the farm-houses, and the church clock of Chapel-le-Dale tolling the hours came faintly to my ears. These tokens of my fellow-men served only to make my own position seem the more lonely, and to call for a greater effort to overcome the terror which tempted me continually to get back to the farm, and abandon for ever this dangerous quest. And yet there lies deep in every man a rooted self-respect which makes it hard for him to turn back from that which he has once undertaken. This feeling of personal pride was my salvation now, and it was that alone which held me fast when every instinct of my nature was dragging me away. I am glad now that I had the strength. In spite of all that is has cost me, my manhood is at least above reproach.

Twelve o'clock struck in the distant church, then one, then two. It was the darkest hour of the night. The clouds were drifting low, and there was not a star in the sky. An owl was hooting somewhere among the rocks, but no other sound, save the gentle sough of the wind, came to my ears. And then suddenly I heard it! From far away down the tunnel came those muffled steps, so soft and yet so ponderous. I heard also the rattle of stones as they gave way under that giant tread. They drew nearer. They were close upon me. I heard the crashing of the bushes round the entrance, and then dimly through the darkness I was conscious of the loom of some enormous shape, some monstrous inchoate creature, passing swiftly and very silently out from the tunnel. I was paralysed with fear and amazement. Long as I had waited, now that it had actually come I was unprepared for the shock. I lay motionless and breathless, whilst the great dark mass whisked by me and was swallowed up in the night.

But now I nerved myself for its return. No sound came from the sleeping countryside to tell of the horror which was loose. In no way could I judge how far off it was, what it was doing, or when it might be back. But not a second time should my nerve fail me, not a second time should it pass unchallenged. I swore it between my clenched teeth as I laid my cocked rifle across the rock.

And yet it nearly happened. There was no warning of approach now as the creature passed over the grass. Suddenly, like a dark, drifting shadow, the huge bulk loomed up once more before me, making for the entrance of the cave. Again came that paralysis of volition which held my crooked forefinger impotent upon the trigger. But with a desperate effort I shook it off. Even as the brushwood rustled, and the monstrous beast blended with the shadow of the Gap, I fired at the retreating form. In the blaze of the gun I caught a glimpse of a great shaggy mass, something with rough and bristling hair of a withered grey colour, fading away to white in its lower parts, the huge body supported upon short, thick, curving legs. I had just that glance, and then I heard the rattle of the stones as the creature tore down into its burrow. In an instant, with a triumphant revulsion of feeling, I had cast my fears to the wind, and uncovering my powerful lantern, with my rifle in my hand, I sprang down from my rock and rushed after the monster down the old Roman shaft.

My splendid lamp cast a brilliant flood of vivid light in front of me, very different from the yellow glimmer which had aided me down the same passage only twelve days before. As I ran, I saw the great beast lurching along before me, its huge bulk filling up the whole space from wall to wall. Its hair looked like coarse faded oakum, and hung down in long, dense masses which swayed as it moved. It was like an enormous unclipped sheep in its fleece, but in size it was far larger than the largest elephant, and its breadth seemed to be nearly as great as its height. It fills me with amazement now to think that I should have dared to follow such a horror into the bowels of the earth, but when one's blood is up, and when one's quarry seems to be flying, the old primeval hunting- spirit awakes and prudence is cast to the wind. Rifle in hand, I ran at the top of my speed upon the trail of the monster.

I had seen that the creature was swift. Now I was to find out to my cost that it was also very cunning. I had imagined that it was in panic flight, and that I had only to pursue it. The idea that it might turn upon me never entered my excited brain. I have already explained that the passage down which I was racing opened into a great central cave. Into this I rushed, fearful lest I should lose all trace of the beast. But he had turned upon his own traces, and in a moment we were face to face.

That picture, seen in the brilliant white light of the lantern, is etched for ever upon my brain. He had reared up on his hind legs as a bear would do, and stood above me, enormous, menacing-- such a creature as no nightmare had ever brought to my imagination. I have said that he reared like a bear, and there was something bear-like--if one could conceive a bear which was ten-fold the bulk of any bear seen upon earth--in his whole pose and attitude, in his great crooked forelegs with their ivory-white claws, in his rugged skin, and in his red, gaping mouth, fringed with monstrous fangs. Only in one point did he differ from the bear, or from any other creature which walks the earth, and even at that supreme moment a shudder of horror passed over me as I observed that the eyes which glistened in the glow of my lantern were huge, projecting bulbs, white and sightless. For a moment his great paws swung over my head. The next he fell forward upon me, I and my broken lantern crashed to the earth, and I remember no more.

When I came to myself I was back in the farm-house of the Allertons. Two days had passed since my terrible adventure in the Blue John Gap. It seems that I had lain all night in the cave insensible from concussion of the brain, with my left arm and two ribs badly fractured. In the morning my note had been found, a search party of a dozen farmers assembled, and I had been tracked down and carried back to my bedroom, where I had lain in high delirium ever since. There was, it seems, no sign of the creature, and no bloodstain which would show that my bullet had found him as he passed. Save for my own plight and the marks upon the mud, there was nothing to prove that what I said was true.

Six weeks have now elapsed, and I am able to sit out once more in the sunshine. Just opposite me is the steep hillside, grey with shaly rock, and yonder on its flank is the dark cleft which marks the opening of the Blue John Gap. But it is no longer a source of terror. Never again through that ill-omened tunnel shall any strange shape flit out into the world of men. The educated and the scientific, the Dr.

Johnsons and the like, may smile at my narrative, but the poorer folk of the countryside had never a doubt as to its truth. On the day after my recovering consciousness they assembled in their hundreds round the Blue John Gap. As the Castleton Courier said:

"It was useless for our correspondent, or for any of the adventurous gentlemen who had come from Matlock, Buxton, and other parts, to offer to descend, to explore the cave to the end, and to finally test the extraordinary narrative of Dr. James Hardcastle. The country people had taken the matter into their own hands, and from an early hour of the morning they had worked hard in stopping up the entrance of the tunnel. There is a sharp slope where the shaft begins, and great boulders, rolled along by many willing hands, were thrust down it until the Gap was absolutely sealed. So ends the episode which has caused such excitement throughout the country. Local opinion is fiercely divided upon the subject. On the one hand are those who point to Dr. Hardcastle's impaired health, and to the possibility of cerebral lesions of tubercular origin giving rise to strange hallucinations. Some idee fixe, according to these gentlemen, caused the doctor to wander down the tunnel, and a fall among the rocks was sufficient to account for his injuries. On the other hand, a legend of a strange creature in the Gap has existed for some months back, and the farmers look upon Dr. Hardcastle's narrative and his personal injuries as a final corroboration. So the matter stands, and so the matter will continue to stand, for no definite solution seems to us to be now possible. It transcends human wit to give any scientific explanation which could cover the alleged facts."

Perhaps before the Courier published these words they would have been wise to send their representative to me. I have thought the matter out, as no one else has occasion to do, and it is possible that I might have removed some of the more obvious difficulties of the narrative and brought it one degree nearer to scientific acceptance. Let me then write down the only explanation which seems to me to elucidate what I know to my cost to have been a series of facts. My theory may seem to be wildly improbable, but at least no one can venture to say that it is impossible.

My view is--and it was formed, as is shown by my diary, before my personal adventure--that in this part of England there is a vast subterranean lake or sea, which is fed by the great number of streams which pass down through the limestone. Where there is a large collection of water there must also be some evaporation, mists or rain, and a possibility of vegetation. This in turn suggests that there may be animal life, arising, as the vegetable life would also do, from those seeds and types which had been introduced at an early period of the world's history, when communication with the outer air was more easy. This place had then developed a fauna and flora of its own, including such monsters as the one which I had seen, which may well have been the old cave-bear, enormously enlarged and modified by its new environment. For countless aeons the internal and the external creation had kept apart, growing steadily away from each other. Then there had come some rift in the depths of the mountain which had enabled one creature to wander up and, by means of the Roman tunnel, to reach the open air. Like all subterranean life, it had lost the power of sight, but this had no doubt been compensated for by nature in other directions. Certainly it had some means of finding its way about, and of hunting down the sheep upon the hillside. As to its choice of dark nights, it is part of my theory that light was painful to those great white eyeballs, and that it was only a pitch-black world which it could tolerate. Perhaps, indeed, it was the glare of my lantern which saved my life at that awful moment when we were face to face. So I read the riddle. I leave these facts behind me, and if you can explain them, do so; or if you choose to doubt them, do so. Neither your belief nor your incredulity can alter them, nor affect one whose task is nearly over.

So ended the strange narrative of Dr. James Hardcastle.

THE CAPTAIN OF THE "POLE-STAR"

[Being an extract from the singular journal of JOHN M`ALISTER RAY, student of medicine.]

September 11th.--Lat. 81 degrees 40' N.; long. 2 degrees E. Still lying-to amid enormous ice fields. The one which stretches away to the north of us, and to which our ice-anchor is attached, cannot be smaller than an English county. To the right and left unbroken sheets extend to the horizon. This morning the mate reported that there were signs of pack ice to the southward. Should this form of sufficient thickness to bar our return, we shall be in a position of danger, as the food, I hear, is already running somewhat short. It is late in the season, and the nights are beginning to reappear.

This morning I saw a star twinkling just over the fore-yard, the first since the beginning of May. There is considerable discontent among the crew, many of whom are anxious to get back home to be in time for the herring season, when labour always commands a high price upon the Scotch coast. As yet their displeasure is only signified by sullen countenances and black looks, but I heard from the second mate this afternoon that they contemplated sending a deputation to the Captain to explain their grievance. I much doubt how he will receive it, as he is a man of fierce temper, and very sensitive about anything approaching to an infringement of his rights. I shall venture after dinner to say a few words to him upon the subject. I have always found that he will tolerate from me what he would resent from any other member of the crew. Amsterdam Island, at the north-west corner of Spitzbergen, is visible upon our starboard quarter--a rugged line of volcanic rocks, intersected by white seams, which represent glaciers. It is curious to think that at the present moment there is probably no human being nearer to us than the Danish settlements in the south of Greenland--a good nine hundred miles as the crow flies. A captain takes a great responsibility upon himself when he risks his vessel under such circumstances. No whaler has ever remained in these latitudes till so advanced a period of the year.

9 P.M,--I have spoken to Captain Craigie, and though the result has been hardly satisfactory, I am bound to say that he listened to

what I had to say very quietly and even deferentially. When I had finished he put on that air of iron determination which I have frequently observed upon his face, and paced rapidly backwards and forwards across the narrow cabin for some minutes. At first I feared that I had seriously offended him, but he dispelled the idea by sitting down again, and putting his hand upon my arm with a gesture which almost amounted to a caress. There was a depth of tenderness too in his wild dark eyes which surprised me considerably. "Look here, Doctor," he said, "I'm sorry I ever took you--I am indeed--and I would give fifty pounds this minute to see you standing safe upon the Dundee quay. It's hit or miss with me this time. There are fish to the north of us. How dare you shake your head, sir, when I tell you I saw them blowing from the masthead?"--this in a sudden burst of fury, though I was not conscious of having shown any signs of doubt. "Two-and-twenty fish in as many minutes as I am a living man, and not one under ten foot.[1] Now, Doctor, do you think I can leave the country when there is only one infernal strip of ice between me and my fortune? If it came on to blow from the north to-morrow we could fill the ship and be away before the frost could catch us. If it came on to blow from the south--well, I suppose the men are paid for risking their lives, and as for myself it matters but little to me, for I have more to bind me to the other world than to this one. I confess that I am sorry for you, though. I wish I had old Angus Tait who was with me last voyage, for he was a man that would never be missed, and you--you said once that you were engaged, did you not?"

[1] *A whale is measured among whalers not by the length of its body, but by the length of its whalebone.*

"Yes," I answered, snapping the spring of the locket which hung from my watch-chain, and holding up the little vignette of Flora.

"Curse you!" he yelled, springing out of his seat, with his very beard bristling with passion. "What is your happiness to me? What have I to do with her that you must dangle her photograph before my eyes?" I almost thought that he was about to strike me in the frenzy of his rage, but with another imprecation he dashed open the door of the cabin and rushed out upon deck, leaving me considerably astonished at his extraordinary violence. It is the first time that he has ever shown me anything but courtesy and kindness. I can hear him pacing excitedly up and down overhead as I write these lines.

I should like to give a sketch of the character of this man, but it seems presumptuous to attempt such a thing upon paper, when the idea in my own mind is at best a vague and uncertain one. Several times I have thought that I grasped the clue which might explain it, but only to be disappointed by his presenting himself in some new light which would upset all my conclusions. It may be that no human eye but my own shall ever rest upon these lines, yet as a psychological study I shall attempt to leave some record of Captain Nicholas Craigie.

A man's outer case generally gives some indication of the soul within. The Captain is tall and well-formed, with dark, handsome face, and a curious way of twitching his limbs, which may arise from nervousness, or be simply an outcome of his excessive energy. His jaw and whole cast of countenance is manly and resolute, but the eyes are the distinctive feature of his face. They are of the very darkest hazel, bright and eager, with a singular mixture of recklessness in their expression, and of something else which I have sometimes thought was more allied with horror than any other emotion. Generally the former predominated, but on occasions, and more particularly when he was thoughtfully inclined, the look of fear would spread and deepen until it imparted a new character to his whole countenance. It is at these times that he is most subject to tempestuous fits of anger, and he seems to be aware of it, for I have known him lock himself up so that no one might approach him until his dark hour was passed. He sleeps badly, and I have heard him shouting during the night, but his cabin is some little distance from mine, and I could never distinguish the words which he said.

This is one phase of his character, and the most disagreeable one. It is only through my close association with him, thrown together as we are day after day, that I have observed it. Otherwise he is an agreeable companion, well-read and entertaining, and as gallant a seaman as ever trod a deck. I shall not easily forget the way in which he handled the ship when we were caught by a gale among the loose ice at the beginning of April. I have never seen him so cheerful, and even hilarious, as he was that night, as he paced backwards and forwards upon the bridge amid the flashing of the lightning and the howling of the wind. He has told me several times that the thought of death was a pleasant one to him, which is a sad thing for a young man to say; he cannot be much more than thirty, though his hair and moustache are already slightly grizzled. Some great sorrow must have overtaken him and blighted his whole life. Perhaps I should be the same if I lost my Flora-- God knows! I think if it were not for her that I should care very little whether the wind blew from the north or the south to-morrow.

There, I hear him come down the companion, and he has locked himself up in his room, which shows that he is still in an unamiable mood. And so to bed, as old Pepys would say, for the candle is burning down (we have to use them now since the nights are closing in), and the steward has turned in, so there are no hopes of another one.

September 12th.--Calm, clear day, and still lying in the same position. What wind there is comes from the south-east, but it is very slight. Captain is in a better humour, and apologised to me at breakfast for his rudeness. He still looks somewhat distrait, however, and retains that wild look in his eyes which in a Highlander would mean that he was "fey"--at least so our chief engineer remarked to me, and he has some reputation among the Celtic portion of our crew as a seer and expounder of omens.

It is strange that superstition should have obtained such mastery over this hard-headed and practical race. I could not have believed to what an extent it is carried had I not observed it for myself. We have had a perfect epidemic of it this voyage, until I have felt inclined to serve out rations of sedatives and nerve- tonics with the Saturday allowance of grog. The first symptom of it was that shortly after leaving Shetland the men at the wheel used to complain that they heard plaintive cries and screams in the wake of the ship, as if something were following it and were unable to overtake it. This fiction has been kept up during the whole voyage, and on dark nights at the beginning of the seal-fishing it was only with great difficulty that men could be induced to do their spell. No doubt what they heard was either the creaking of the rudder-chains, or the cry of some passing sea-bird. I have been fetched out of bed several times to listen to it, but I need hardly say that I was never able to distinguish anything unnatural.

The men, however, are so absurdly positive upon the subject that it is hopeless to argue with them. I mentioned the matter to the Captain once, but to my surprise he took it very gravely, and indeed appeared to be considerably disturbed by what I told him. I should have thought that he at least would have been above such vulgar delusions.

All this disquisition upon superstition leads me up to the fact that Mr. Manson, our second mate, saw a ghost last night--or, at least, says that he did, which of course is the same thing. It is quite refreshing to have some new topic of conversation after the eternal routine of bears and whales which has served us for so many months. Manson swears the ship is haunted, and that he would not stay in her a day if he had any other place to go to. Indeed the fellow is honestly frightened, and I had to give him some chloral and bromide of potassium this morning to steady him down. He seemed quite indignant when I suggested that he had been having an extra glass the night before, and I was obliged to pacify him by keeping as grave a countenance as possible during his story, which he certainly narrated in a very straight-forward and matter- of-fact way.

"I was on the bridge," he said, "about four bells in the middle watch, just when the night was at its darkest. There was a bit of a moon, but the clouds were blowing across it so that you couldn't see far from the ship. John M`Leod, the harpooner, came aft from the foc'sle-head and reported a strange noise on the starboard bow.

I went forrard and we both heard it, sometimes like a bairn crying and sometimes like a wench in pain. I've been seventeen years to the country and I never heard seal, old or young, make a sound like that. As we were standing there on the foc'sle-head the moon came out from behind a cloud, and we both saw a sort of white figure moving across the ice field in the same direction that we had heard the cries. We lost sight of it for a while, but it came back on the port bow, and we could just make it out like a shadow on the ice. I sent a hand aft for the rifles, and M`Leod and I went down on to the pack, thinking that maybe it might be a bear. When we got on the ice I lost sight of M`Leod, but I pushed on in the direction where I could still hear the cries. I followed them for a mile or maybe more, and then running round a hummock I came right on to the top of it standing and waiting for me seemingly. I don't know what it was. It wasn't a bear any way. It was tall and white and straight, and if it wasn't a man nor a woman, I'll stake my davy it was something worse. I made for the ship as hard as I could run, and precious glad I was to find myself aboard. I signed articles to do my duty by the ship, and on the ship I'll stay, but you don't catch me on the ice again after sundown."

That is his story, given as far as I can in his own words. I fancy what he saw must, in spite of his denial, have been a young bear erect upon its hind legs, an attitude which they often assume when alarmed. In the uncertain light this would bear a resemblance to a human figure, especially to a man whose nerves were already somewhat shaken. Whatever it may have been, the occurrence is unfortunate, for it has produced a most unpleasant effect upon the crew. Their looks are more sullen than before, and their discontent more open. The double grievance of being debarred from the herring fishing and of being detained in what they choose to call a haunted vessel, may lead them to do something rash. Even the harpooners, who are the oldest and steadiest among them, are joining in the general agitation.

Apart from this absurd outbreak of superstition, things are looking rather more cheerful. The pack which was forming to the south of us has partly cleared away, and the water is so warm as to lead me to believe that we are lying in one of those branches of the gulf- stream which run up between Greenland and Spitzbergen. There are numerous small Medusse and sealemons about the ship, with abundance of shrimps, so that there is every possibility of "fish" being sighted. Indeed one was seen blowing about dinner-time, but in such a position that it was impossible for the boats to follow it.

September 13th.--Had an interesting conversation with the chief mate, Mr. Milne, upon the bridge. It seems that our Captain is as great an enigma to the seamen, and even to the owners of the vessel, as he has been to me. Mr. Milne tells me that when the ship is paid off, upon returning from a voyage, Captain Craigie disappears, and is not seen again until the approach of another season, when he walks quietly into the office of the company, and asks whether his services will be required. He has no friend in Dundee, nor does any one pretend to be acquainted with his early history. His position depends entirely upon his skill as a seaman, and the name for courage and coolness which he had earned in the capacity of mate, before being entrusted with a separate command. The unanimous opinion seems to be that he is not a Scotchman, and that his name is an assumed one. Mr. Milne thinks that he has devoted himself to whaling simply for the reason that it is the most dangerous occupation which he could select, and that he courts death in every possible manner. He mentioned several instances of this, one of which is rather curious, if true. It seems that on one occasion he did not put in an appearance at the office, and a substitute had to be selected in his place. That was at the time of the last Russian and Turkish war. When he turned up again next spring he had a puckered wound in the side of his neck which he used to endeavour to conceal with his cravat. Whether the mate's inference that he had been engaged in the war is true or not I cannot say. It was certainly a strange coincidence.

The wind is veering round in an easterly direction, but is still very slight. I think the ice is lying closer than it did yesterday. As far as the eye can reach on every side there is one wide expanse of spotless white, only broken by an occasional rift or the dark shadow of a hummock. To the south there is the narrow lane of blue water which is our sole means of escape, and which is closing up every day. The

Captain is taking a heavy responsibility upon himself. I hear that the tank of potatoes has been finished, and even the biscuits are running short, but he preserves the same impassible countenance, and spends the greater part of the day at the crow's nest, sweeping the horizon with his glass. His manner is very variable, and he seems to avoid my society, but there has been no repetition of the violence which he showed the other night.

7.30 P.M.--My deliberate opinion is that we are commanded by a madman. Nothing else can account for the extraordinary vagaries of Captain Craigie. It is fortunate that I have kept this journal of our voyage, as it will serve to justify us in case we have to put him under any sort of restraint, a step which I should only consent to as a last resource. Curiously enough it was he himself who suggested lunacy and not mere eccentricity as the secret of his strange conduct. He was standing upon the bridge about an hour ago, peering as usual through his glass, while I was walking up and down the quarterdeck. The majority of the men were below at their tea, for the watches have not been regularly kept of late. Tired of walking, I leaned against the bulwarks, and admired the mellow glow cast by the sinking sun upon the great ice fields which surround us. I was suddenly aroused from the reverie into which I had fallen by a hoarse voice at my elbow, and starting round I found that the Captain had descended and was standing by my side. He was staring out over the ice with an expression in which horror, surprise, and something approaching to joy were contending for the mastery. In spite of the cold, great drops of perspiration were coursing down his forehead, and he was evidently fearfully excited.

His limbs twitched like those of a man upon the verge of an epileptic fit, and the lines about his mouth were drawn and hard.

"Look!" he gasped, seizing me by the wrist, but still keeping his eyes upon the distant ice, and moving his head slowly in a horizontal direction, as if following some object which was moving across the field of vision. "Look! There, man, there! Between the hummocks! Now coming out from behind the far one! You see her--you MUST see her! There still! Flying from me, by God, flying from me--and gone!"

He uttered the last two words in a whisper of concentrated agony which shall never fade from my remembrance. Clinging to the ratlines he endeavoured to climb up upon the top of the bulwarks as if in the hope of obtaining a last glance at the departing object. His strength was not equal to the attempt, however, and he staggered back against the saloon skylights, where he leaned panting and exhausted. His face was so livid that I expected him to become unconscious, so lost no time in leading him down the companion, and stretching him upon one of the sofas in the cabin. I then poured him out some brandy, which I held to his lips, and which had a wonderful effect upon him, bringing the blood back into his white face and steadying his poor shaking limbs. He raised himself up upon his elbow, and looking round to see that we were alone, he beckoned to me to come and sit beside him.

"You saw it, didn't you?" he asked, still in the same subdued awesome tone so foreign to the nature of the man.

"No, I saw nothing."

His head sank back again upon the cushions. "No, he wouldn't without the glass," he murmured. "He couldn't. It was the glass that showed her to me, and then the eyes of love--the eyes of love.

I say, Doc, don't let the steward in! He'll think I'm mad. Just bolt the door, will you!"

I rose and did what he had commanded.

He lay quiet for a while, lost in thought apparently, and then raised himself up upon his elbow again, and asked for some more brandy.

"You don't think I am, do you, Doc?" he asked, as I was putting the bottle back into the after-locker. "Tell me now, as man to man, do you think that I am mad?"

"I think you have something on your mind," I answered, "which is exciting you and doing you a good deal of harm."

"Right there, lad!" he cried, his eyes sparkling from the effects of the brandy. "Plenty on my mind--plenty! But I can work out the latitude and the longitude, and I can handle my sextant and manage my logarithms. You couldn't prove me mad in a court of law, could you, now?" It was curious to hear the man lying back and coolly arguing out the question of his own sanity.

"Perhaps not," I said; "but still I think you would be wise to get home as soon as you can, and settle down to a quiet life for a while."

"Get home, eh?" he muttered, with a sneer upon his face. "One word for me and two for yourself, lad. Settle down with Flora--pretty little Flora. Are bad dreams signs of madness?"

"Sometimes," I answered.

"What else? What would be the first symptoms?"

"Pains in the head, noises in the ears flashes before the eyes, delusions"----

"Ah! what about them?" he interrupted. "What would you call a delusion?"

"Seeing a thing which is not there is a delusion."

"But she WAS there!" he groaned to himself. "She WAS there!" and rising, he unbolted the door and walked with slow and uncertain steps to his own cabin, where I have no doubt that he will remain until to-morrow morning. His system seems to have received a terrible shock, whatever it may have been that he imagined himself to have seen. The man becomes a greater mystery every day, though I fear that the solution which he has himself suggested is the correct one, and that his reason is affected. I do not think that a guilty conscience has anything to do with his behaviour. The idea is a popular one among the officers, and, I believe, the crew; but I have seen nothing to support it. He has not the air of a guilty man, but of one who has had terrible usage at the hands of fortune, and who should be regarded as a martyr rather than a criminal.

The wind is veering round to the south to-night. God help us if it blocks that narrow pass which is our only road to safety! Situated as we are on the edge of the main Arctic pack, or the "barrier" as it is called by the whalers, any wind from the north has the effect of shredding out the ice around us and allowing our escape, while a wind from the south blows up all the loose ice behind us and hems us in between two packs. God help us, I say again!

September 14th.--Sunday, and a day of rest. My fears have been confirmed, and the thin strip of blue water has disappeared from the southward. Nothing but the great motionless ice fields around us, with their weird hummocks and fantastic pinnacles. There is a deathly silence over their wide expanse which is horrible. No lapping of the waves now, no cries of seagulls or straining of sails, but one deep universal silence in which the murmurs of the seamen, and the creak of their boots upon the white shining deck, seem discordant and out of place. Our only visitor was an Arctic fox, a rare animal upon the pack, though common enough upon the land. He did not come near the ship, however, but after surveying us from a distance fled rapidly across the ice. This was curious conduct, as they generally know nothing of man, and being of an inquisitive nature, become so familiar that they are easily captured. Incredible as it may seem, even this little incident produced a bad effect upon the crew. "Yon puir beastie kens mair, ay, an' sees mair nor you nor me!" was the comment of one of the leading harpooners, and the others nodded their acquiescence. It is vain to attempt to argue against such puerile superstition. They have made up their minds that there is a curse upon the ship, and nothing will ever persuade them to the contrary.

The Captain remained in seclusion all day except for about half an hour in the afternoon, when he came out upon the quarterdeck. I observed that he kept his eye fixed upon the spot where the vision of yesterday had appeared, and was quite prepared for another outburst, but none such came. He did not seem to see me although I was standing close beside him. Divine service was read as usual by the chief engineer. It is a curious thing that in whaling vessels the Church of England Prayer-book is always employed, although there is never a member of that Church among either officers or crew. Our men are all Roman Catholics or Presbyterians, the former predominating. Since a ritual is used which is foreign to both, neither can complain that the other is preferred to them, and they listen with all attention and devotion, so that the system has something to recommend it.

A glorious sunset, which made the great fields of ice look like a lake of blood. I have never seen a finer and at the same time more weird effect. Wind is veering round. If it will blow twenty-four hours from the north all will yet be well.

September 15th.--To-day is Flora's birthday. Dear lass! it is well that she cannot see her boy, as she used to call me, shut up among the ice fields with a crazy captain and a few weeks' provisions. No doubt she scans the shipping list in the Scotsman every morning to see if we are reported from Shetland. I have to set an example to the men and look cheery and unconcerned; but God knows, my heart is very heavy at times.

The thermometer is at nineteen Fahrenheit to-day. There is but little wind, and what there is comes from an unfavourable quarter. Captain is in an excellent humour; I think he imagines he has seen some other omen or vision, poor fellow, during the night, for he came into my room early in the morning, and stooping down over my bunk, whispered, "It wasn't a delusion, Doc; it's all right!" After breakfast he asked me to find out how much food was left, which the second mate and I proceeded to do. It is even less than we had expected. Forward they have half a tank full of biscuits, three barrels of salt meat, and a very limited supply of coffee beans and sugar. In the after-hold and lockers there are a good many luxuries, such as tinned salmon, soups, haricot mutton, &c., but they will go a very short way among a crew of fifty men. There are two barrels of flour in the store-room, and an unlimited supply of tobacco. Altogether there is about enough to keep the men on half rations for eighteen or twenty days--certainly not more. When we reported the state of things to the Captain, he ordered all hands to be piped, and addressed them from the quarterdeck. I never saw him to better advantage. With his tall, well-knit figure, and dark animated face, he seemed a man born to command, and he discussed the situation in a cool sailor-like way which showed that while appreciating the danger he had an eye for every loophole of escape.

"My lads," he said, "no doubt you think I brought you into this fix, if it is a fix, and maybe some of you feel bitter against me on account of it. But you must remember that for many a season no ship that comes to the country has brought in as much oil-money as the old Pole-Star, and every one of you has had his share of it. You can leave your wives behind you in comfort while other poor fellows come back to find their lasses on the parish. If you have to thank me for the one you have to thank me for the other, and we may call it quits. We've tried a bold venture before this and succeeded, so now that we've tried one and failed we've no cause to cry out about it. If the worst comes to the worst, we can make the land across the ice, and lay in a stock of seals which will keep us alive until the spring. It won't come to that, though, for you'll see the Scotch coast again before three weeks are out. At present every man must go on half rations, share and share alike, and no favour to any. Keep up your hearts and you'll pull through this as you've pulled through many a danger before." These few simple words of his had a wonderful effect upon the crew. His former unpopularity was forgotten, and the old harpooner whom I have already mentioned for his superstition, led off three cheers, which were heartily joined in by all hands.

September 16th.--The wind has veered round to the north during the night, and the ice shows some symptoms of opening out. The men are in a good humour in spite of the short allowance upon which they have been placed. Steam is kept up in the engine-room, that there may be no delay should an opportunity for escape present itself. The Captain is in exuberant spirits, though he still retains that wild "fey" expression which I have already remarked upon. This burst of cheerfulness puzzles me more than his former gloom. I cannot understand it. I think I mentioned in an early part of this journal that one of his oddities is that he never permits any person to enter his cabin, but insists upon making his own bed, such as it is, and performing every other office for himself. To my surprise he handed me the key to-day and requested me to go down there and take the time by his chronometer while he measured the altitude of the sun at noon. It is a bare little room, containing a washing-stand and a few books, but little else in the way of luxury, except some pictures upon the walls. The majority of these are small cheap oleographs, but there was one water-colour sketch of the head of a young lady which arrested my attention. It was evidently a portrait, and not one of those fancy types of female beauty which sailors particularly affect. No artist could have evolved from his own mind such a curious mixture of character and weakness. The languid, dreamy eyes, with their drooping lashes, and the broad, low brow, unruffled by thought or care, were in strong contrast with the clean-cut, prominent jaw, and the resolute set of the lower lip. Underneath it in one of the corners was written, "M. B., aet. 19." That any one in the short space of nineteen years of existence could develop such strength of will as was stamped upon her face seemed to me at the time to be well-nigh incredible. She must have been an extraordinary woman. Her features have thrown such a glamour over me that, though I had but a fleeting glance at them, I could, were I a draughtsman, reproduce them line for line upon this page of the journal. I wonder what part she has played in our Captain's life. He has hung her picture at the end of his berth, so that his eyes continually rest upon it. Were he a less reserved man I should make some remark upon the subject. Of the other things in his cabin there was nothing worthy of mention-- uniform coats, a camp- stool, small looking-glass, tobacco-box, and numerous pipes, including an oriental hookah--which, by-the-bye, gives some colour to Mr. Milne's story about his participation in the war, though the connection may seem rather a distant one.

11.20 P.M.--Captain just gone to bed after a long and interesting conversation on general topics. When he chooses he can be a most fascinating companion, being remarkably well-read, and having the power of expressing his opinion forcibly without appearing to be dogmatic. I hate to have my intellectual toes trod upon. He spoke about the nature of the soul, and sketched out the views of Aristotle and Plato upon the subject in a masterly manner. He seems to have a leaning for metempsychosis and the doctrines of Pythagoras. In discussing them we touched upon modern spiritualism, and I made some joking allusion to the impostures of Slade, upon which, to my surprise, he warned me most impressively against confusing the innocent with the guilty, and argued that it would be as logical to brand Christianity as an error because Judas, who professed that religion, was a villain. He shortly afterwards bade me good-night and retired to his room.

The wind is freshening up, and blows steadily from the north. The nights are as dark now as they are in England. I hope to-morrow may set us free from our frozen fetters.

September 17th.--The Bogie again. Thank Heaven that I have strong nerves! The superstition of these poor fellows, and the circumstantial accounts which they give, with the utmost earnestness and self-conviction, would horrify any man not accustomed to their ways. There are many versions of the matter, but the sum-total of them all is that something uncanny has been flitting round the ship all night, and that Sandie M`Donald of Peterhead and "lang" Peter Williamson of Shetland saw it, as also did Mr. Milne on the bridge-- so, having three witnesses, they can make a better case of it than the second mate did. I spoke to Milne after breakfast, and told him that he should be above such nonsense, and that as an officer he ought to set the men a better example. He shook his weatherbeaten head ominously, but answered with characteristic caution, "Mebbe aye, mebbe na, Doctor," he said; "I didna ca' it a ghaist. I canna' say I preen my faith in sea-bogles an' the like, though there's a mony as claims to ha' seen a' that and waur. I'm no easy feared, but maybe your ain bluid would run a bit cauld, mun, if instead o' speerin' aboot it in daylicht ye were wi' me last night, an' seed an awfu' like shape, white an' gruesome, whiles here, whiles there, an' it greetin' and ca'ing in the darkness like a bit lambie that hae lost its mither. Ye would na' be sae ready to put it a' doon to auld wives' clavers then, I'm thinkin'." I saw it was hopeless to reason with him, so contented myself with begging him as a personal favour to call me up the next time the spectre appeared--a request to which he acceded with many ejaculations expressive of his hopes that such an opportunity might never arise.

As I had hoped, the white desert behind us has become broken by many thin streaks of water which intersect it in all directions. Our latitude to-day was 80 degrees 52' N., which shows that there is a strong southerly drift upon the pack. Should the wind continue favourable it will break up as rapidly as it formed. At present we can do nothing but smoke and wait and hope for the best. I am rapidly becoming a fatalist. When dealing with such uncertain factors as wind and ice a man can be nothing else. Perhaps it was the wind and sand of the Arabian deserts which gave the minds of the original followers of Mahomet their tendency to bow to kismet.

These spectral alarms have a very bad effect upon the Captain. I feared that it might excite his sensitive mind, and endeavoured to conceal the absurd story from him, but unfortunately he overheard one of the men making an allusion to it, and insisted upon being informed about it. As I had expected, it brought out all his latent lunacy in an exaggerated form. I can hardly believe that this is the same man who discoursed philosophy last night with the most critical acumen and coolest judgment. He is pacing backwards and forwards upon the quarterdeck like a caged tiger, stopping now and again to throw out his hands with a yearning gesture, and stare impatiently out over the ice. He keeps up a continual mutter to himself, and once he called out, "But a little time, love--but a little time!" Poor fellow, it is sad to see a gallant seaman and accomplished gentleman reduced to such a pass, and to think that imagination and delusion can cow a mind to which real danger was but the salt of life. Was ever a man in such a position as I, between a demented captain and a ghost-seeing mate? I sometimes think I am the only really sane man aboard the vessel--except perhaps the second engineer, who is a kind of ruminant, and would care nothing for all the fiends in the Red Sea so long as they would leave him alone and not disarrange his tools.

The ice is still opening rapidly, and there is every probability of our being able to make a start to-morrow morning. They will think I am inventing when I tell them at home all the strange things that have befallen me.

12 P.M.--I have been a good deal startled, though I feel steadier now, thanks to a stiff glass of brandy. I am hardly myself yet, however, as this handwriting will testify. The fact is, that I have gone through a very strange experience, and am beginning to doubt whether I was justified in branding every one on board as madmen because they professed to have seen things which did not seem reasonable to my understanding. Pshaw! I am a fool to let such a trifle unnerve me; and yet, coming as it does after all these alarms, it has an additional significance, for I cannot doubt either Mr. Manson's story or that of the mate, now that I have experienced that which I used formerly to scoff at.

After all it was nothing very alarming--a mere sound, and that was all. I cannot expect that any one reading this, if any one ever should read it, will sympathise with my feelings, or realise the effect which it produced upon me at the time. Supper was over, and I had gone on deck to have a quiet pipe before turning in. The night was very dark-- so dark that, standing under the quarter-boat, I was unable to see the officer upon the bridge. I think I have already mentioned the extraordinary silence which prevails in these frozen seas. In other parts of the world, be they ever so barren, there is some slight vibration of the air--some faint hum, be it from the distant haunts of men, or from the leaves of the trees, or the wings of the birds, or even the faint rustle of the grass that covers the ground. One may not actively perceive the sound, and yet if it were withdrawn it would be missed. It is only here in these Arctic seas that stark, unfathomable stillness obtrudes itself upon you in all its gruesome reality. You find your tympanum straining to catch some little murmur, and dwelling eagerly upon every accidental sound within the vessel. In this state I was leaning against the bulwarks when there arose from the ice almost directly underneath me a cry, sharp and shrill, upon the silent air of the night, beginning, as it seemed to me, at a note such as prima donna never reached, and mounting from that ever higher and higher until it culminated in a long wail of agony, which might have been the last cry of a lost soul. The ghastly scream is still ringing in my ears. Grief, unutterable grief, seemed to be expressed in it, and a great longing, and yet through it all there was an occasional wild note of exultation. It shrilled out from close beside me, and yet as I glared into the darkness I could discern nothing. I waited some little time, but without hearing any repetition of the sound, so I came below, more shaken than I have ever been in my life before. As I came down the companion I met Mr. Milne coming up to relieve the watch. "Weel, Doctor," he said, "maybe that's auld wives' clavers tae? Did ye no hear it skirling? Maybe that's a supersteetion? What d'ye think o't noo?" I was obliged to apologise to the honest fellow, and acknowledge that I was as puzzled by it as he was. Perhaps to-morrow things may look different. At present I dare hardly write all that I think. Reading it again in days to come, when I have shaken off all these associations, I should despise myself for having been so weak.

September 18th.--Passed a restless and uneasy night, still haunted by that strange sound. The Captain does not look as if he had had much repose either, for his face is haggard and his eyes bloodshot. I have not told him of my adventure of last night, nor shall I. He is already restless and excited, standing up, sitting down, and apparently utterly unable to keep still.

A fine lead appeared in the pack this morning, as I had expected, and we were able to cast off our ice-anchor, and steam about twelve miles in a west-sou'-westerly direction. We were then brought to a halt by a great floe as massive as any which we have left behind us. It bars our progress completely, so we can do nothing but anchor again and wait until it breaks up, which it will probably do within twenty-four hours, if the wind holds. Several bladder-nosed seals were seen swimming in the water, and one was shot, an immense creature more than eleven feet long. They are fierce, pugnacious animals, and are said to be more than a match for a bear. Fortunately they are slow and clumsy in their movements, so that there is little danger in attacking them upon the ice.

The Captain evidently does not think we have seen the last of our troubles, though why he should take a gloomy view of the situation is more than I can fathom, since every one else on board considers that we have had a miraculous escape, and are sure now to reach the open sea.

"I suppose you think it's all right now, Doctor?" he said, as we sat together after dinner.

"I hope so," I answered.

"We mustn't be too sure--and yet no doubt you are right. We'll all be in the arms of our own true loves before long, lad, won't we? But we mustn't be too sure--we mustn't be too sure."

He sat silent a little, swinging his leg thoughtfully backwards and forwards. "Look here," he continued; "it's a dangerous place this, even at its best--a treacherous, dangerous place. I have known men cut off very suddenly in a land like this. A slip would do it sometimes--a single slip, and down you go through a crack, and only a bubble on the green water to show where it was that you sank. It's a queer thing," he continued with a nervous laugh, "but all the years I've been in this country I never once thought of making a will--not that I have anything to leave in particular, but still when a man is exposed to danger he should have everything arranged and ready--don't you think so?"

"Certainly," I answered, wondering what on earth he was driving at.

"He feels better for knowing it's all settled," he went on. "Now if anything should ever befall me, I hope that you will look after things for me. There is very little in the cabin, but such as it is I should like it to be sold, and the money divided in the same proportion as the oil-money among the crew. The chronometer I wish you to keep yourself as some slight remembrance of our voyage. Of course all this is a mere precaution, but I thought I would take the opportunity of speaking to you about it. I suppose I might rely upon you if there were any necessity?"

"Most assuredly," I answered; "and since you are taking this step, I may as well"----

"You! you!" he interrupted. "YOU'RE all right. What the devil is the matter with YOU? There, I didn't mean to be peppery, but I don't like to hear a young fellow, that has hardly began life, speculating about death. Go up on deck and get some fresh air into your lungs instead of talking nonsense in the cabin, and encouraging me to do the same."

The more I think of this conversation of ours the less do I like it. Why should the man be settling his affairs at the very time when we seem to be emerging from all danger? There must be some method in his madness. Can it be that he contemplates suicide? I remember that upon one occasion he spoke in a deeply reverent manner of the heinousness of the crime of self-destruction. I shall keep my eye upon him, however, and though I cannot obtrude upon the privacy of his cabin, I shall at least make a point of remaining on deck as long as he stays up.

Mr. Milne pooh-poohs my fears, and says it is only the "skipper's little way." He himself takes a very rosy view of the situation. According to him we shall be out of the ice by the day after to-morrow, pass Jan Meyen two days after that, and sight Shetland in little more than a week. I hope he may not be too sanguine. His opinion may be fairly balanced against the gloomy precautions of the Captain, for he is an old and experienced seaman, and weighs his words well before uttering them.

. . . . . .

The long-impending catastrophe has come at last. I hardly know what to write about it. The Captain is gone. He may come back to us again alive, but I fear me--I fear me. It is now seven o'clock of the morning of the 19th of September. I have spent the whole night traversing the great ice-floe in front of us with a party of seamen in the hope of coming upon some trace of him, but in vain. I shall try to give some account of the circumstances which attended upon his disappearance. Should any one ever chance to read the words which I put down, I trust they will remember that I do not write from conjecture or from hearsay, but that I, a sane and educated man, am describing accurately what actually occurred before my very eyes. My inferences are my own, but I shall be answerable for the facts.

The Captain remained in excellent spirits after the conversation which I have recorded. He appeared to be nervous and impatient, however, frequently changing his position, and moving his limbs in an aimless choreic way which is characteristic of him at times. In a quarter of an hour he went upon deck seven times, only to descend after a few hurried paces. I followed him each time, for there was something about his face which confirmed my resolution of not letting him out of my sight. He seemed to observe the effect which his movements had produced, for he endeavoured by an over-done hilarity, laughing boisterously at the very smallest of jokes, to quiet my apprehensions.

After supper he went on to the poop once more, and I with him. The night was dark and very still, save for the melancholy soughing of the wind among the spars. A thick cloud was coming up from the northwest, and the ragged tentacles which it threw out in front of it were drifting across the face of the moon, which only shone now and again through a rift in the wrack. The Captain paced rapidly backwards and forwards, and then seeing me still dogging him, he came across and hinted that he thought I should be better below-- which, I need hardly say, had the effect of strengthening my resolution to remain on deck.

I think he forgot about my presence after this, for he stood silently leaning over the taffrail, and peering out across the great desert of snow, part of which lay in shadow, while part glittered mistily in the moonlight. Several times I could see by his movements that he was referring to his watch, and once he muttered a short sentence, of which I could only catch the one word "ready." I confess to having felt an eerie feeling creeping over me as I watched the loom of his tall figure through the darkness, and noted how completely he fulfilled the idea of a man who is keeping a tryst. A tryst with whom? Some vague perception began to dawn upon me as I pieced one fact with another, but I was utterly unprepared for the sequel.

By the sudden intensity of his attitude I felt that he saw something. I crept up behind him. He was staring with an eager questioning gaze at what seemed to be a wreath of mist, blown swiftly in a line with the ship. It was a dim, nebulous body, devoid of shape, sometimes more, sometimes less apparent, as the light fell on it. The moon was dimmed in its brilliancy at the moment by a canopy of thinnest cloud, like the coating of an anemone.

"Coming, lass, coming," cried the skipper, in a voice of unfathomable tenderness and compassion, like one who soothes a beloved one by some favour long looked for, and as pleasant to bestow as to receive.

What followed happened in an instant. I had no power to interfere.

He gave one spring to the top of the bulwarks, and another which took him on to the ice, almost to the feet of the pale misty figure. He held out his hands as if to clasp it, and so ran into the darkness with outstretched arms and loving words. I still stood rigid and motionless, straining my eyes after his retreating form, until his voice died away in the distance. I never thought to see him again, but at that moment the moon shone out brilliantly through a chink in the cloudy heaven, and illuminated the great field of ice. Then I saw his dark figure already a very long way off, running with prodigious speed across the frozen plain. That was the last glimpse which we caught of him--perhaps the last we ever shall. A party was organised to follow him, and I accompanied them, but the men's hearts were not in the work, and nothing was found. Another will be formed within a few hours. I can hardly believe I have not been dreaming, or suffering from some hideous nightmare, as I write these things down.

7.30 P.M.--Just returned dead beat and utterly tired out from a second unsuccessful search for the Captain. The floe is of enormous extent, for though we have traversed at least twenty miles of its surface, there has been no sign of its coming to an end. The frost has been so severe of late that the overlying snow is frozen as hard as granite, otherwise we might have had the footsteps to guide us. The crew are anxious that we should cast off and steam round the floe and so to the southward, for the ice has opened up during the night, and the sea is visible upon the horizon. They argue that Captain Craigie is certainly dead, and that we are all risking our lives to no purpose by remaining when we have an opportunity of escape. Mr. Milne and I have had the greatest difficulty in persuading them to wait until tomorrow night, and have been compelled to promise that we will not under any circumstances delay our departure longer than that. We propose therefore to take a few hours' sleep, and then to start upon a final search.

September 20th, evening.--I crossed the ice this morning with a party of men exploring the southern part of the floe, while Mr. Milne went off in a northerly direction. We pushed on for ten or twelve miles without seeing a trace of any living thing except a single bird, which fluttered a great way over our heads, and which by its flight I should judge to have been a falcon. The southern extremity of the ice field tapered away into a long narrow spit which projected out into the sea. When we came to the base of this promontory, the men halted, but I begged them to continue to the extreme end of it, that we might have the satisfaction of knowing that no possible chance had been neglected.

We had hardly gone a hundred yards before M`Donald of Peterhead cried out that he saw something in front of us, and began to run. We all got a glimpse of it and ran too. At first it was only a vague darkness against the white ice, but as we raced along together it took the shape of a man, and eventually of the man of whom we were in search. He was lying face downwards upon a frozen bank. Many little crystals of ice and feathers of snow had drifted on to him as he lay, and sparkled upon his dark seaman's jacket. As we came up some wandering puff of wind caught these tiny flakes in its vortex, and they whirled up into the air, partially descended again, and then, caught once more in the current, sped rapidly away in the direction of the sea. To my eyes it seemed but a snow-drift, but many of my companions averred that it started up in the shape of a woman, stooped over the corpse and kissed it, and then hurried away across the floe. I have learned never to ridicule any man's opinion, however strange it may seem. Sure it is that Captain Nicholas Craigie had met with no painful end, for there was a bright smile upon his blue pinched features, and his hands were still outstretched as though grasping at the strange visitor which had summoned him away into the dim world that lies beyond the grave.

We buried him the same afternoon with the ship's ensign around him, and a thirty-two pound shot at his feet. I read the burial service, while the rough sailors wept like children, for there were many who owed much to his kind heart, and who showed now the affection which his strange ways had repelled during his lifetime. He went off the grating with a dull, sullen splash, and as I looked into the green water I saw him go down, down, down until he was but a little flickering patch of white hanging upon the outskirts of eternal darkness. Then even that faded away, and he was gone. There he shall lie, with his secret and his sorrows and his mystery all still buried in his breast, until that great day when the sea shall give up its dead, and Nicholas Craigie come out from among the ice with the smile upon his face, and his stiffened arms outstretched in greeting. I pray that his lot may be a happier one in that life than it has been in this.

I shall not continue my journal. Our road to home lies plain and clear before us, and the great ice field will soon be but a remembrance of the past. It will be some time before I get over the shock produced by recent events. When I began this record of our voyage I little thought of how I should be compelled to finish it. I am writing these final words in the lonely cabin, still starting at times and fancying I hear the quick nervous step of the dead man upon the deck above me.

I entered his cabin to-night, as was my duty, to make a list of his effects in order that they might be entered in the official log. All was as it had been upon my previous visit, save that the picture which I have described as having hung at the end of his bed had been cut out of its frame, as with a knife, and was gone. With this last link in a strange chain of evidence I close my diary of the voyage of the Pole-Star.

[NOTE by Dr. John M'Alister Ray, senior.--I have read over the strange events connected with the death of the Captain of the Pole-Star, as narrated in the journal of my son. That everything occurred exactly as he describes it I have the fullest confidence, and, indeed, the most positive certainty, for I know him to be a strong-nerved and unimaginative man, with the strictest regard for veracity. Still, the story is, on the face of it, so vague and so improbable, that I was long opposed to its publication. Within the last few days, however, I have had independent testimony upon the subject which throws a new light upon it. I had run down to Edinburgh to attend a meeting of the British Medical Association, when I chanced to come across Dr. P----, an old college chum of mine, now practising at Saltash, in Devonshire. Upon my telling him of this experience of my son's, he declared to me that he was familiar with the man, and proceeded, to my no small surprise, to give me a description of him, which tallied remarkably well with that given in the journal, except that he depicted him as a younger man. According to his account, he had been engaged to a young lady of singular beauty residing upon the Cornish coast. During his absence at sea his betrothed had died under circumstances of peculiar horror.]

THE GREAT KEINPLATZ EXPERIMENT

Of all the sciences which have puzzled the sons of men, none had such an attraction for the learned Professor von Baumgarten as those which relate to psychology and the ill-defined relations between mind and matter. A celebrated anatomist, a profound chemist, and one of the first physiologists in Europe, it was a relief for him to turn from these subjects and to bring his varied knowledge to bear upon the study of the soul and the mysterious relationship of spirits. At first, when as a young man he began to dip into the secrets of mesmerism, his mind seemed to be wandering in a strange land where all was chaos and darkness, save that here and there some great unexplainable and disconnected fact loomed out in front of him. As the years passed, however, and as the worthy Professor's stock of knowledge increased, for knowledge begets knowledge as money bears interest, much which had seemed strange and unaccountable began to take another shape in his eyes. New trains of reasoning became familiar to him, and he perceived connecting links where all had been incomprehensible and startling.

By experiments which extended over twenty years, he obtained a basis of facts upon which it was his ambition to build up a new exact science which should embrace mesmerism, spiritualism, and all cognate subjects. In this he was much helped by his intimate knowledge of the more intricate parts of animal physiology which treat of nerve currents and the working of the brain; for Alexis von Baumgarten was Regius Professor of Physiology at the University of Keinplatz, and had all the resources of the laboratory to aid him in his profound researches.

Professor von Baumgarten was tall and thin, with a hatchet face and steel-grey eyes, which were singularly bright and penetrating. Much thought had furrowed his forehead and contracted his heavy eyebrows, so that he appeared to wear a perpetual frown, which often misled people as to his character, for though austere he was tender-hearted. He was popular among the students, who would gather round him after his lectures and listen eagerly to his strange theories. Often he would call for volunteers from amongst them in order to conduct some experiment, so that eventually there was hardly a lad in the class who had not, at one time or another, been thrown into a mesmeric trance by his Professor.

Of all these young devotees of science there was none who equalled in enthusiasm Fritz von Hartmann. It had often seemed strange to his fellow-students that wild, reckless Fritz, as dashing a young fellow as ever hailed from the Rhinelands, should devote the time and trouble which he did in reading up abstruse works and in assisting the Professor in his strange experiments. The fact was, however, that Fritz was a knowing and long-headed fellow. Months before he had lost his heart to young Elise, the blue-eyed, yellow-haired daughter of the lecturer. Although he had succeeded in learning from her lips that she was not indifferent to his suit, he had never dared to announce himself to her family as a formal suitor. Hence he would have found it a difficult matter to see his young lady had he not adopted the expedient of making himself useful to the Professor. By this means he frequently was asked to the old man's house, where he willingly submitted to be experimented upon in any way as long as there was a chance of his receiving one bright glance from the eyes of Elise or one touch of her little hand.

Young Fritz von Hartmann was a handsome lad enough. There were broad acres, too, which would descend to him when his father died. To many he would have seemed an eligible suitor; but Madame frowned upon his presence in the house, and lectured the Professor at times on his allowing such a wolf to prowl around their lamb. To tell the truth, Fritz had an evil name in Keinplatz. Never was there a riot or a duel, or any other mischief afoot, but the young Rhinelander figured as a ringleader in it. No one used more free and violent language, no one drank more, no one played cards more habitually, no one was more idle, save in the one solitary subject.

No wonder, then, that the good Frau Professorin gathered her Fraulein under her wing, and resented the attentions of such a mauvais sujet. As to the worthy lecturer, he was too much engrossed by his strange studies to form an opinion upon the subject one way or the other.

For many years there was one question which had continually obtruded itself upon his thoughts. All his experiments and his theories turned upon a single point. A hundred times a day the Professor asked himself whether it was possible for the human spirit to exist apart from the body for a time and then to return to it once again. When the possibility first suggested itself to him his scientific mind had revolted from it. It clashed too violently with preconceived ideas and the prejudices of his early training. Gradually, however, as he proceeded farther and farther along the pathway of original research, his mind shook off its old fetters and became ready to face any conclusion which could reconcile the facts. There were many things which made him believe that it was possible for mind to exist apart from matter. At last it occurred to him that by a daring and original experiment the question might be definitely decided.

"It is evident," he remarked in his celebrated article upon invisible entities, which appeared in the Keinplatz wochenliche Medicalschrift about this time, and which surprised the whole scientific world--"it is evident that under certain conditions the soul or mind does separate itself from the body. In the case of a mesmerised person, the body lies in a cataleptic condition, but the spirit has left it. Perhaps you reply that the soul is there, but in a dormant condition. I answer that this is not so, otherwise how can one account for the condition of clairvoyance, which has fallen into disrepute through the knavery of certain scoundrels, but which can easily be shown to be an undoubted fact. I have been able myself, with a sensitive subject, to obtain an accurate description of what was going on in another room or another house. How can such knowledge be accounted for on any hypothesis save that the soul of the subject has left the body and is wandering through space? For a moment it is recalled by the voice of the operator and says what it has seen, and then wings its way once more through the air. Since the spirit is by its very nature invisible, we cannot see these comings and goings, but we see their effect in the body of the subject, now rigid and inert, now struggling to narrate impressions which could never have come to it by natural means. There is only one way which I can see by which the fact can be demonstrated. Although we in the flesh are unable to see these spirits, yet our own spirits, could we separate them from the body, would be conscious of the presence of others. It is my intention, therefore, shortly to mesmerise one of my pupils. I shall then mesmerise myself in a manner which has become easy to me. After that, if my theory holds good, my spirit will have no difficulty in meeting and communing with the spirit of my pupil, both being separated from the body. I hope to be able to communicate the result of this interesting experiment in an early number of the Keinplatz wochenliche Medicalschrilt."

When the good Professor finally fulfilled his promise, and published an account of what occurred, the narrative was so extraordinary that it was received with general incredulity. The tone of some of the papers was so offensive in their comments upon the matter that the angry savant declared that he would never open his mouth again or refer to the subject in any way--a promise which he has faithfully kept. This narrative has been compiled, however, from the most authentic sources, and the events cited in it may be relied upon as substantially correct.

It happened, then, that shortly after the time when Professor von Baumgarten conceived the idea of the above-mentioned experiment, he was walking thoughtfully homewards after a long day in the laboratory, when he met a crowd of roystering students who had just streamed out from a beer-house. At the head of them, half-intoxicated and very noisy, was young Fritz von Hartmann. The Professor would have passed them, but his pupil ran across and intercepted him.

"Heh! my worthy master," he said, taking the old man by the sleeve, and leading him down the road with him. "There is something that I have to say to you, and it is easier for me to say it now, when the good beer is humming in my head, than at another time."

"What is it, then, Fritz?" the physiologist asked, looking at him in mild surprise.

"I hear, mein herr, that you are about to do some wondrous experiment in which you hope to take a man's soul out of his body, and then to put it back again. Is it not so?"

"It is true, Fritz."

"And have you considered, my dear sir, that you may have some difficulty in finding some one on whom to try this? Potztausend! Suppose that the soul went out and would not come back. That would be a bad business. Who is to take the risk?"

"But, Fritz," the Professor cried, very much startled by this view of the matter, "I had relied upon your assistance in the attempt. Surely you will not desert me. Consider the honour and glory."

"Consider the fiddlesticks!" the student cried angrily. "Am I to be paid always thus? Did I not stand two hours upon a glass insulator while you poured electricity into my body? Have you not stimulated my phrenic nerves, besides ruining my digestion with a galvanic current round my stomach? Four-and-thirty times you have mesmerised me, and what have I got from all this? Nothing. And now you wish to take my soul out, as you would take the works from a watch. It is more than flesh and blood can stand."

"Dear, dear!" the Professor cried in great distress. "That is very true, Fritz. I never thought of it before. If you can but suggest how I can compensate you, you will find me ready and willing."

"Then listen," said Fritz solemnly. "If you will pledge your word that after this experiment I may have the hand of your daughter, then I am willing to assist you; but if not, I shall have nothing to do with it. These are my only terms."

"And what would my daughter say to this?" the Professor exclaimed, after a pause of astonishment.

"Elise would welcome it," the young man replied. "We have loved each other long."

"Then she shall be yours," the physiologist said with decision, "for you are a good-hearted young man, and one of the best neurotic subjects that I have ever known--that is when you are not under the influence of alcohol. My experiment is to be performed upon the fourth of next month. You will attend at the physiological laboratory at twelve o'clock. It will be a great occasion, Fritz. Von Gruben is coming from Jena, and Hinterstein from Basle. The chief men of science of all South Germany will be there."

"I shall be punctual," the student said briefly; and so the two parted. The Professor plodded homeward, thinking of the great coming event, while the young man staggered along after his noisy companions, with his mind full of the blue-eyed Elise, and of the bargain which he had concluded with her father.

The Professor did not exaggerate when he spoke of the widespread interest excited by his novel psychophysiological experiment. Long before the hour had arrived the room was filled by a galaxy of talent. Besides the celebrities whom he had mentioned, there had come from London the great Professor Lurcher, who had just established his reputation by a remarkable treatise upon cerebral centres. Several great lights of the Spiritualistic body had also come a long distance to be present, as had a Swedenborgian minister, who considered that the proceedings might throw some light upon the doctrines of the Rosy Cross.

There was considerable applause from this eminent assembly upon the appearance of Professor von Baumgarten and his subject upon the platform. The lecturer, in a few well-chosen words, explained what his views were, and how he proposed to test them. "I hold," he said, "that when a person is under the influence of mesmerism, his spirit is for the time released from his body, and I challenge any one to put forward any other hypothesis which will account for the fact of clairvoyance. I therefore hope that upon mesmerising my young friend here, and then putting myself into a trance, our spirits may be able to commune together, though our bodies lie still and inert. After a time nature will resume her sway, our spirits will return into our respective bodies, and all will be as before. With your kind permission, we shall now proceed to attempt the experiment."

The applause was renewed at this speech, and the audience settled down in expectant silence. With a few rapid passes the Professor mesmerised the young man, who sank back in his chair, pale and rigid. He then took a bright globe of glass from his pocket, and by concentrating his gaze upon it and making a strong mental effort, he succeeded in throwing himself into the same condition. It was a strange and impressive sight to see the old man and the young sitting together in the same cataleptic condition. Whither, then, had their souls fled? That was the question which presented itself to each and every one of the spectators.

Five minutes passed, and then ten, and then fifteen, and then fifteen more, while the Professor and his pupil sat stiff and stark upon the platform. During that time not a sound was heard from the assembled savants, but every eye was bent upon the two pale faces, in search of the first signs of returning consciousness. Nearly an hour had elapsed before the patient watchers were rewarded. A faint flush came back to the cheeks of Professor von Baumgarten. The soul was coming back once more to its earthly tenement. Suddenly he stretched out his long thin arms, as one awaking from sleep, and rubbing his eyes, stood up from his chair and gazed about him as though he hardly realised where he was. "Tausend Teufel!" he exclaimed, rapping out a tremendous South German oath, to the great astonishment of his audience and to the disgust of the Swedenborgian. "Where the Henker am I then, and what in thunder has occurred? Oh yes, I remember now. One of these nonsensical mesmeric experiments. There is no result this time, for I remember nothing at all since I became unconscious; so you have had all your long journeys for nothing, my learned friends, and a very good joke too; "at which the Regius Professor of Physiology burst into a roar of laughter and slapped his thigh in a highly indecorous fashion. The audience were so enraged at this unseemly behaviour on the part of their host, that there might have been a considerable disturbance, had it not been for the judicious interference of young Fritz von Hartmann, who had now recovered from his lethargy. Stepping to the front of the platform, the young man apologised for the conduct of his companion. "I am sorry to say," he said, "that he is a harum-scarum sort of fellow, although he appeared so grave at the commencement of this experiment. He is still suffering from mesmeric reaction, and is hardly accountable for his words. As to the experiment itself, I do not consider it to be a failure. It is very possible that our spirits may have been communing in space during this hour; but, unfortunately, our gross bodily memory is distinct from our spirit, and we cannot recall what has occurred. My energies shall now be devoted to devising some means by which spirits may be able to recollect what occurs to them in their free state, and I trust that when I have worked this out, I may have the pleasure of meeting you all once again in this hall, and demonstrating to you the result." This address, coming from so young a student, caused considerable astonishment among the audience, and some were inclined to be offended, thinking that he assumed rather too much importance. The majority, however, looked upon him as a young man of great promise, and many comparisons were made as they left the hall between his dignified conduct and the levity of his professor, who during the above remarks was laughing heartily in a corner, by no means abashed at the failure of the experiment.

Now although all these learned men were filing out of the lecture-room under the impression that they had seen nothing of note, as a matter of fact one of the most wonderful things in the whole history of the world had just occurred before their very eyes Professor von Baumgarten had been so far correct in his theory that both his spirit and that of his pupil had been for a time absent from his body. But here a strange and unforeseen complication had occurred. In their return the spirit of Fritz von Hartmann had entered into the body of Alexis von Baumgarten, and that of Alexis von Baumgarten had taken up its abode in the frame of Fritz von Hartmann. Hence the slang and scurrility which issued from the lips of the serious Professor, and hence also the weighty words and grave statements which fell from the careless student. It was an unprecedented event, yet no one knew of it, least of all those whom it concerned.

The body of the Professor, feeling conscious suddenly of a great dryness about the back of the throat, sallied out into the street, still chuckling to himself over the result of the experiment, for the soul of Fritz within was reckless at the thought of the bride whom he had won so easily. His first impulse was to go up to the house and see her, but on second thoughts he came to the conclusion that it would be best to stay away until Madame Baumgarten should be informed by her husband of the agreement which had been made. He therefore made his way down to the Graner Mann, which was one of the favourite trysting-places of the wilder students, and ran, boisterously waving his cane in the air, into the little parlour, where sat Spiegler and Muller and half a dozen other boon companions.

"Ha, ha! my boys," he shouted. "I knew I should find you here. Drink up, every one of you, and call for what you like, for I'm going to stand treat to-day."

Had the green man who is depicted upon the signpost of that well-known inn suddenly marched into the room and called for a bottle of wine, the students could not have been more amazed than they were by this unexpected entry of their revered professor. They were so astonished that for a minute or two they glared at him in utter bewilderment without being able to make any reply to his hearty invitation.

"Donner und Blitzen!" shouted the Professor angrily. "What the deuce is the matter with you, then? You sit there like a set of stuck pigs staring at me. What is it, then?"

"It is the unexpected honour," stammered Spiegel, who was in the chair.

"Honour--rubbish!" said the Professor testily. "Do you think that just because I happen to have been exhibiting mesmerism to a parcel of old fossils, I am therefore too proud to associate with dear old friends like you? Come out of that chair, Spiegel my boy, for I shall preside now. Beer, or wine, or shnapps, my lads--call for what you like, and put it all down to me."

Never was there such an afternoon in the Gruner Mann. The foaming flagons of lager and the green-necked bottles of Rhenish circulated merrily. By degrees the students lost their shyness in the presence of their Professor. As for him, he shouted, he sang, he roared, he balanced a long tobacco-pipe upon his nose, and offered to run a hundred yards against any member of the company. The Kellner and the barmaid whispered to each other outside the door their astonishment at such proceedings on the part of a Regius Professor of the ancient university of Kleinplatz. They had still more to whisper about afterwards, for the learned man cracked the Kellner's crown, and kissed the barmaid behind the kitchen door.

"Gentlemen," said the Professor, standing up, albeit somewhat totteringly, at the end of the table, and balancing his high old-fashioned wine glass in his bony hand, "I must now explain to you what is the cause of this festivity."

"Hear! hear! " roared the students, hammering their beer glasses against the table; "a speech, a speech!--silence for a speech!"

"The fact is, my friends," said the Professor, beaming through his spectacles, "I hope very soon to be married."

"Married!" cried a student, bolder than the others "Is Madame dead, then?"

"Madame who?"

"Why, Madame von Baumgarten, of course."

"Ha, ha!" laughed the Professor; "I can see, then, that you know all about my former difficulties. No, she is not dead, but I have reason to believe that she will not oppose my marriage."

"That is very accommodating of her," remarked one of the company.

"In fact," said the Professor, "I hope that she will now be induced to aid me in getting a wife. She and I never took to each other very much; but now I hope all that may be ended, and when I marry she will come and stay with me."

"What a happy family!" exclaimed some wag.

"Yes, indeed; and I hope you will come to my wedding, all of you. I won't mention names, but here is to my little bride!" and the Professor waved his glass in the air.

"Here's to his little bride!" roared the roysterers, with shouts of laughter. "Here's her health. Sie soll leben--Hoch!" And so the fun waxed still more fast and furious, while each young fellow followed the Professor's example, and drank a toast to the girl of his heart.

While all this festivity had been going on at the Graner Mann, a very different scene had been enacted elsewhere. Young Fritz von Hartmann, with a solemn face and a reserved manner, had, after the experiment, consulted and adjusted some mathematical instruments; after which, with a few peremptory words to the janitors, he had walked out into the street and wended his way slowly in the direction of the house of the Professor. As he walked he saw Von Althaus, the professor of anatomy, in front of him, and quickening his pace he overtook him.

"I say, Von Althaus," he exclaimed, tapping him on the sleeve, "you were asking me for some information the other day concerning the middle coat of the cerebral arteries. Now I find----"

"Donnerwetter!" shouted Von Althaus, who was a peppery old fellow. "What the deuce do you mean by your impertinence! I'll have you up before the Academical Senate for this, sir;" with which threat he turned on his heel and hurried away. Von Hartmann was much surprised at this reception. "It's on account of this failure of my experiment," he said to himself, and continued moodily on his way.

Fresh surprises were in store for him, however. He was hurrying along when he was overtaken by two students. These youths, instead of raising their caps or showing any other sign of respect, gave a wild whoop of deligilt the instant that they saw him, and rushing at him, seized him by each arm and commenced dragging him along with them.

"Gott in himmel!" roared Von Hartmann. "What is the meaning of this unparalleled insult? Where are you taking me?"

"To crack a bottle of wine with us," said the two students. "Come along! That is an invitation which you have never refused."

"I never heard of such insolence in my life!" cried Von Hartmann. "Let go my arms! I shall certainly have you rusticated for this. Let me go, I say!" and he kicked furiously at his captors.

"Oh, if you choose to turn ill-tempered, you may go where you like," the students said, releasing him. "We can do very well without you."

"I know you. I'll pay you out," said Von Hartmann furiously, and continued in the direction which he imagined to be his own home, much incensed at the two episodes which had occurred to him on the way.

Now, Madame von Baumgarten, who was looking out of the window and wondering why her husband was late for dinner, was considerably astonished to see the young student come stalking down the road. As already remarked, she had a great antipathy to him, and if ever he ventured into the house it was on sufferance, and under the protection of the Professor. Still more astonished was she, therefore, when she beheld him undo the wicket-gate and stride up the garden path with the air of one who is master of the situation.

She could hardly believe her eyes, and hastened to the door with all her maternal instincts up in arms. From the upper windows the fair Elise had also observed this daring move upon the part of her lover, and her heart beat quick with mingled pride and consternation.

"Good day, sir," Madame Baumgarten remarked to the intruder, as she stood in gloomy majesty in the open doorway.

"A very fine day indeed, Martha," returned the other. "Now, don't stand there like a statue of Juno, but bustle about and get the dinner ready, for I am well-nigh starved."

"Martha! Dinner!" ejaculated the lady, falling back in astonishment.

"Yes, dinner, Martha, dinner!" howled Von Hartmann, who was becoming irritable. "Is there anything wonderful in that request when a man has been out all day? I'll wait in the dining-room. Anything will do. Schinken, and sausage, and prunes--any little thing that happens to be about. There you are, standing staring again. Woman, will you or will you not stir your legs?"

This last address, delivered with a perfect shriek of rage, had the effect of sending good Madame Baumgarten flying along the passage and through the kitchen, where she locked herself up in the scullery and went into violent hysterics. In the meantime Von Hartmann strode into the room and threw himself down upon the sofa in the worst of tempers.

"Elise!" he shouted. "Confound the girl! Elise!"

Thus roughly summoned, the young lady came timidly downstairs and into the presence of her lover. "Dearest!" she cried, throwing her arms round him, "I know this is all done for my sake! It is a RUSE in order to see me."

Von Hartmann's indignation at this fresh attack upon him was so great that he became speechless for a minute from rage, and could only glare and shake his fists, while he struggled in her embrace. When he at last regained his utterance, he indulged in such a bellow of passion that the young lady dropped back, petrified with fear, into an armchair.

"Never have I passed such a day in my life," Von Hartmann cried, stamping upon the floor. "My experiment has failed. Von Althaus has insulted me. Two students have dragged me along the public road. My wife nearly faints when I ask her for dinner, and my daughter flies at me and hugs me like a grizzly bear."

"You are ill, dear," the young lady cried. "Your mind is wandering. You have not even kissed me once."

"No, and I don't intend to either," Von Hartmann said with decision. "You ought to be ashamed of yourself. Why don't you go and fetch my slippers, and help your mother to dish the dinner?"

"And is it for this," Elise cried, burying her face in her handkerchief--"is it for this that I have loved you passionately for upwards of ten months? Is it for this that I have braved my mother's wrath? Oh, you have broken my heart; I am sure you have!" and she sobbed hysterically.

"I can't stand much more of this," roared Von Hartmann furiously. "What the deuce does the girl mean? What did I do ten months ago which inspired you with such a particular affection for me? If you are really so very fond, you would do better to run away down and find the schinken and some bread, instead of talking all this nonsense"

"Oh, my darling!" cried the unhappy maiden, throwing herself into the arms of what she imagined to be her lover, "you do but joke in order to frighten your little Elise."

Now it chanced that at the moment of this unexpected embrace Von Hartmann was still leaning back against the end of the sofa, which, like much German furniture, was in a somewhat rickety condition. It also chanced that beneath this end of the sofa there stood a tank full of water in which the physiologist was conducting certain experiments upon the ova of fish, and which he kept in his drawing-room in order to insure an equable temperature. The additional weight of the maiden, combined with the impetus with which she hurled herself upon him, caused the precarious piece of furniture to give way, and the body of the unfortunate student was hurled backwards into the tank, in which his head and shoulders were firmly wedged, while his lower extremities flapped helplessly about in the air. This was the last straw. Extricating himself with some difficulty from his unpleasant position, Von Hartmann gave an inarticulate yell of fury, and dashing out of the room, in spite of the entreaties of Elise, he seized his hat and rushed off into the town, all dripping and dishevelled, with the intention of seeking in some inn the food and comfort which he could not find at home.

As the spirit of Von Baumgarten encased in the body of Von Hartmann strode down the winding pathway which led down to the little town, brooding angrily over his many wrongs, he became aware that an elderly man was approaching him who appeared to be in an advanced state of intoxication. Von Hartmann waited by the side of the road and watched this individual, who came stumbling along, reeling from one side of the road to the other, and singing a student song in a very husky and drunken voice. At first his interest was merely excited by the fact of seeing a man of so venerable an appearance in such a disgraceful condition, but as he approached nearer, he became convinced that he knew the other well, though he could not recall when or where he had met him. This impression became so strong with him, that when the stranger came abreast of him he stepped in front of him and took a good look at his features.

"Well, sonny," said the drunken man, surveying Von Hartmann and swaying about in front of him, "where the Henker have I seen you before? I know you as well as I know myself. Who the deuce are you?"

"I am Professor von Baumgarten," said the student. "May I ask who you are? I am strangely familiar with your features."

"You should never tell lies, young man," said the other. "You're certainly not the Professor, for he is an ugly snuffy old chap, and you are a big broad-shouldered young fellow. As to myself, I am Fritz von Hartmann at your service."

"That you certainly are not," exclaimed the body of Von Hartmann. "You might very well be his father. But hullo, sir, are you aware that you are wearing my studs and my watch-chain?"

"Donnerwetter!" hiccoughed the other. " If those are not the trousers for which my tailor is about to sue me, may I never taste beer again."

Now as Von Hartmann, overwhelmed by the many strange things which had occurred to him that day, passed his hand over his forehead and cast his eyes downwards, he chanced to catch the reflection of his own face in a pool which the rain had left upon the road. To his utter astonishment he perceived that his face was that of a youth, that his dress was that of a fashionable young student, and that in every way he was the antithesis of the grave and scholarly figure in which his mind was wont to dwell. In an instant his active brain ran over the series of events which had occurred and sprang to the conclusion. He fairly reeled under the blow.

"Himmel!" he cried, "I see it all. Our souls are in the wrong bodies. I am you and you are I. My theory is proved--but at what an expense! Is the most scholarly mind in Europe to go about with this frivolous exterior? Oh the labours of a lifetime are ruined!" and he smote his breast in his despair.

"I say," remarked the real Von Hartmann from the body of the Professor, "I quite see the force of your remarks, but don't go knocking my body about like that. You received it in excellent condition, but I perceive that you have wet it and bruised it, and spilled snuff over my ruffled shirt-front."

"It matters little," the other said moodily. "Such as we are so must we stay. My theory is triumphantly proved, but the cost is terrible."

"If I thought so," said the spirit of the student, "it would be hard indeed. What could I do with these stiff old limbs, and how could I woo Elise and persuade her that I was not her father? No, thank Heaven, in spite of the beer which has upset me more than ever it could upset my real self, I can see a way out of it."

"How?" gasped the Professor.

"Why, by repeating the experiment. Liberate our souls once more, and the chances are that they will find their way back into their respective bodies."

No drowning man could clutch more eagerly at a straw than did

Von Baumgarten's spirit at this suggestion. In feverish haste he dragged his own frame to the side of the road and threw it into a mesmeric trance; he then extracted the crystal ball from the pocket, and managed to bring himself into the same condition.

Some students and peasants who chanced to pass during the next hour were much astonished to see the worthy Professor of Physiology and his favourite student both sitting upon a very muddy bank and both completely insensible. Before the hour was up quite a crowd had assembled, and they were discussing the advisability of sending for an ambulance to convey the pair to hospital, when the learned savant opened his eyes and gazed vacantly around him. For an instant he seemed to forget how he had come there, but next moment he astonished his audience by waving his skinny arms above his head and crying out in a voice of rapture, "Gott sei gedanket! I am myself again. I feel I am!" Nor was the amazement lessened when the student, springing to his feet, burst into the same cry, and the two performed a sort of pas de joie in the middle of the road.

For some time after that people had some suspicion of the sanity of both the actors in this strange episode. When the Professor published his experiences in the Medicalschrift as he had promised, he was met by an intimation, even from his colleagues, that he would do well to have his mind cared for, and that another such publication would certainly consign him to a madhouse. The student also found by experience that it was wisest to be silent about the matter.

When the worthy lecturer returned home that night he did not receive the cordial welcome which he might have looked for after his strange adventures. On the contrary, he was roundly upbraided by both his female relatives for smelling of drink and tobacco, and also for being absent while a young scapegrace invaded the house and insulted its occupants. It was long before the domestic atmosphere of the lecturer's house resumed its normal quiet, and longer still before the genial face of Von Hartmann was seen beneath its roof. Perseverance, however, conquers every obstacle, and the student eventually succeeded in pacifying the enraged ladies and in establishing himself upon the old footing. He has now no longer any cause to fear the enmity of Madame, for he is Hauptmann von Hartmann of the Emperor's own Uhlans, and his loving wife Elise has already presented him with two little Uhlans as a visible sign and token of her affection.

THE MAN FROM ARCHANGEL

On the fourth day of March, in the year 1867, being at that time in my five-and-twentieth year, I wrote down the following words in my note-book--the result of much mental perturbation and conflict:--
"The solar system, amidst a countless number of other systems as large as itself, rolls ever silently through space in the direction of the constellation of Hercules. The great spheres of which it is composed spin and spin through the eternal void ceaselessly and noiselessly. Of these one of the smallest and most insignificant is that conglomeration of solid and of liquid particles which we have named the earth. It whirls onwards now as it has done before my birth, and will do after my death--a revolving mystery, coming none know whence, and going none know whither. Upon the outer crust of this moving mass crawl many mites, of whom I, John M`Vittie, am one, helpless, impotent, being dragged aimlessly through space. Yet such is the state of things amongst us that the little energy and glimmering of reason which I possess is entirely taken up with the labours which are necessary in order to procure certain metallic disks, wherewith I may purchase the chemical elements necessary to build up my ever-wasting tissues, and keep a roof over me to shelter me from the inclemency of the weather. I thus have no thought to expend upon the vital questions which surround me on every side. Yet, miserable entity as I am, I can still at times feel some degree of happiness, and am even--save the mark!--puffed up occasionally with a sense of my own importance."
These words, as I have said, I wrote down in my note-book, and they reflected accurately the thoughts which I found rooted far down in my soul, ever present and unaffected by the passing emotions of the hour. At last, however, came a time when my uncle, M`Vittie of Glencairn, died--the same who was at one time chairman of committees of the House of Commons. He divided his great wealth among his many nephews, and I found myself with sufficient to provide amply for my wants during the remainder of my life, and became at the same time owner of a bleak tract of land upon the coast of Caithness, which I think the old man must have bestowed upon me in derision, for it was sandy and valueless, and he had ever a grim

sense of humour. Up to this time I had been an attorney in a midland town in England. Now I saw that I could put my thoughts into effect, and, leaving all petty and sordid aims, could elevate my mind by the study of the secrets of nature. My departure from my English home was somewhat accelerated by the fact that I had nearly slain a man in a quarrel, for my temper was fiery, and I was apt to forget my own strength when enraged. There was no legal action taken in the matter, but the papers yelped at me, and folk looked askance when I met them. It ended by my cursing them and their vile, smoke-polluted town, and hurrying to my northern possession, where I might at last find peace and an opportunity for solitary study and contemplation. I borrowed from my capital before I went, and so was able to take with me a choice collection of the most modern philosophical instruments and books, together with chemicals and such other things as I might need in my retirement.

The land which I had inherited was a narrow strip, consisting mostly of sand, and extending for rather over two miles round the coast of Mansie Bay, in Caithness. Upon this strip there had been a rambling, grey-stone building--when erected or wherefore none could tell me--and this I had repaired, so that it made a dwelling quite good enough for one of my simple tastes. One room was my laboratory, another my sitting-room, and in a third, just under the sloping roof, I slung the hammock in which I always slept. There were three other rooms, but I left them vacant, except one which was given over to the old crone who kept house for me. Save the Youngs and the M'Leods, who were fisher-folk living round at the other side of Fergus Ness, there were no other people for many miles in each direction. In front of the house was the great bay, behind it were two long barren hills, capped by other loftier ones beyond. There was a glen between the hills, and when the wind was from the land it used to sweep down this with a melancholy sough and whisper among the branches of the fir-trees beneath my attic window.

I dislike my fellow-mortals. Justice compels me to add that they appear for the most part to dislike me. I hate their little crawling ways, their conventionalities, their deceits, their narrow rights and wrongs. They take offence at my brusque outspokenness, my disregard for their social laws, my impatience of all constraint. Among my books and my drugs in my lonely den at Mansie I could let the great drove of the human race pass onwards with their politics and inventions and tittle-tattle, and I remained behind stagnant and happy. Not stagnant either, for I was working in my own little groove, and making progress. I have reason to believe that Dalton's atomic theory is founded upon error, and I know that mercury is not an element.

During the day I was busy with my distillations and analyses. Often I forgot my meals, and when old Madge summoned me to my tea I found my dinner lying untouched upon the table. At night I read Bacon, Descartes, Spinoza, Kant--all those who have pried into what is unknowable. They are all fruitless and empty, barren of result, but prodigal of polysyllables, reminding me of men who, while digging for gold, have turned up many worms, and then exhibit them exultantly as being what they sought. At times a restless spirit would come upon me, and I would walk thirty and forty miles without rest or breaking fast. On these occasions, when I used to stalk through the country villages, gaunt, unshaven, and dishevelled, the mothers would rush into the road and drag their children indoors, and the rustics would swarm out of their pot- houses to gaze at me. I believe that I was known far and wide as the "mad laird o' Mansie." It was rarely, however, that I made these raids into the country, for I usually took my exercise upon my own beach, where I soothed my spirit with strong black tobacco, and made the ocean my friend and my confidant.

What companion is there like the great restless, throbbing sea? What human mood is there which it does not match and sympathise with? There are none so gay but that they may feel gayer when they listen to its merry turmoil, and see the long green surges racing in, with the glint of the sunbeams in their sparkling crests. But when the grey waves toss their heads in anger, and the wind screams above them, goading them on to madder and more tumultuous efforts, then the darkest-minded of men feels that there is a melancholy principle in Nature which is as gloomy as his own thoughts. When it was calm in the Bay of Mansie the surface would be as clear and bright as a sheet of silver, broken only at one spot some little way from the shore, where a long black line projected out of the water looking like the jagged back of some sleeping monster. This was the top of the dangerous ridge of rocks known to the fishermen as the "ragged reef o' Mansie." When the wind blew from the east the waves would break upon it like thunder, and the spray would be tossed far over my house and up to the hills behind. The bay itself was a bold and noble one, but too much exposed to the northern and eastern gales, and too much dreaded for its reef, to be much used by mariners. There was something of romance about this lonely spot. I have lain in my boat upon a calm day, and peering over the edge I have seen far down the flickering, ghostly forms of great fish--fish, as it seemed to me, such as naturalist never knew, and which my imagination transformed into the genii of that desolate bay. Once, as I stood by the brink of the waters upon a quiet night, a great cry, as of a woman in hopeless grief, rose from the bosom of the deep, and swelled out upon the still air, now sinking and now rising, for a space of thirty seconds. This I heard with my own ears.

In this strange spot, with the eternal hills behind me and the eternal sea in front, I worked and brooded for more than two years unpestered by my fellow men. By degrees I had trained my old servant into habits of silence, so that she now rarely opened her lips, though I doubt not that when twice a year she visited her relations in Wick, her tongue during those few days made up for its enforced rest. I had come almost to forget that I was a member of the human family, and to live entirely with the dead whose books I pored over, when a sudden incident occurred which threw all my thoughts into a new channel.

Three rough days in June had been succeeded by one calm and peaceful one. There was not a breath of air that evening. The sun sank down in the west behind a line of purple clouds, and the smooth surface of the bay was gashed with scarlet streaks. Along the beach the pools left by the tide showed up like gouts of blood against the yellow sand, as if some wounded giant had toilfully passed that way, and had left these red traces of his grievous hurt behind him. As the darkness closed in, certain ragged clouds which had lain low on the eastern horizon coalesced and formed a great irregular cumulus. The glass was still low, and I knew that there was mischief brewing. About nine o'clock a dull moaning sound came up from the sea, as from a creature who, much harassed, learns that the hour of suffering has come round again. At ten a sharp breeze sprang up from the eastward. At eleven it had increased to a gale, and by midnight the most furious storm was raging which I ever remember upon that weather-beaten coast.

As I went to bed the shingle and seaweed were pattering up against my attic window, and the wind was screaming as though every gust were a lost soul. By that time the sounds of the tempest had become a lullaby to me. I knew that the grey walls of the old house would buffet it out, and for what occurred in the world outside I had small concern. Old Madge was usually as callous to such things as I was myself. It was a surprise to me when, about three in the morning, I was awoke by the sound of a great knocking at my door and excited cries in the wheezy voice of my house-keeper. I sprang out of my hammock, and roughly demanded of her what was the matter.

"Eh, maister, maister!" she screamed in her hateful dialect. "Come doun, mun; come doun! There's a muckle ship gaun ashore on the reef, and the puir folks are a' yammerin' and ca'in' for help--and I doobt they'll a' be drooned. Oh, Maister M`Vittie, come doun!"

"Hold your tongue, you hag!" I shouted back in a passion. "What is it to you whether they are drowned or not? Get back to your bed and leave me alone." I turned in again and drew the blankets over me. "Those men out there," I said to myself, "have already gone through half the horrors of death. If they be saved they will but have to go through the same once more in the space of a few brief years. It is best therefore that they should pass away now, since they have suffered that anticipation which is more than the pain of dissolution." With this thought in my mind I endeavoured to compose myself to sleep once more, for that philosophy which had taught me to consider death as a small and trivial incident in man's eternal and everchanging career, had also broken me of much curiosity concerning worldly matters. On this occasion I found, however, that the old leaven still fermented strongly in my soul. I tossed from side to side for some minutes endeavouring to beat down the impulses of the moment by the rules of conduct which I had framed during months of thought. Then I heard a dull roar amid the wild shriek of the gale, and I knew that it was the sound of a signal-gun. Driven by an uncontrollable impulse, I rose, dressed, and having lit my pipe, walked out on to the beach.

It was pitch dark when I came outside, and the wind blew with such violence that I had to put my shoulder against it and push my way along the shingle. My face pringled and smarted with the sting of the gravel which was blown against it, and the red ashes of my pipe streamed away behind me, dancing fantastically through the darkness. I went down to where the great waves were thundering in, and shading my eyes with my hands to keep off the salt spray, I peered out to sea. I could distinguish nothing, and yet it seemed to me that shouts and great inarticulate cries were borne to me by the blasts. Suddenly as I gazed I made out the glint of a light, and then the whole bay and the beach were lit up in a moment by a vivid blue glare. They were burning a coloured signal-light on board of the vessel. There she lay on her beam ends right in the centre of the jagged reef, hurled over to such an angle that I could see all the planking of her deck. She was a large two-masted schooner, of foreign rig, and lay perhaps a hundred and eighty or two hundred yards from the shore. Every spar and rope and writhing piece of cordage showed up hard and clear under the livid light which sputtered and flickered from the highest portion of the forecastle. Beyond the doomed ship out of the great darkness came the long rolling lines of black waves, never ending, never tiring, with a petulant tuft of foam here and there upon their crests. Each as it reached the broad circle of unnatural light appeared to gather strength and volume, and to hurry on more impetuously until, with a roar and a jarring crash, it sprang upon its victim. Clinging to the weather shrouds I could distinctly see some ten or twelve frightened seamen, who, when their light revealed my presence, turned their white faces towards me and waved their hands imploringly. I felt my gorge rise against these poor cowering worms. Why should they presume to shirk the narrow pathway along which all that is great and noble among mankind has travelled? There was one there who interested me more than they. He was a tall man, who stood apart from the others, balancing himself upon the swaying wreck as though he disdained to cling to rope or bulwark. His hands were clasped behind his back and his head was sunk upon his breast, but even in that despondent attitude there was a litheness and decision in his pose and in every motion which marked him as a man little likely to yield to despair. Indeed, I could see by his occasional rapid glances up and down and all around him that he was weighing every chance of safety, but though he often gazed across the raging surf to where he could see my dark figure upon the beach, his self-respect or some other reason forbade him from imploring my help in any way. He stood, dark, silent, and inscrutable, looking down on the black sea, and waiting for whatever fortune Fate might send him.

It seemed to me that that problem would very soon be settled. As I looked, an enormous billow, topping all the others, and coming after them, like a driver following a flock, swept over the vessel. Her foremast snapped short off, and the men who clung to the shrouds were brushed away like a swarm of flies. With a rending, riving sound the ship began to split in two, where the sharp back of the Mansie reef was sawing into her keel. The solitary man upon the forecastle ran rapidly across the deck and seized hold of a white bundle which I had already observed but failed to make out. As he lifted it up the light fell upon it, and I saw that the object was a woman, with a spar lashed across her body and under her arms in such a way that her head should always rise above water. He bore her tenderly to the side and seemed to speak for a minute or so to her, as though explaining the impossibility of remaining upon the ship. Her answer was a singular one. I saw her deliberately raise her hand and strike him across the face with it. He appeared to be silenced for a moment or so by this, but he addressed her again, directing her, as far as I could gather from his motions, how she should behave when in the water. She shrank away from him, but he caught her in his arms. He stooped over her for a moment and seemed to press his lips against her forehead. Then a great wave came welling up against the side of the breaking vessel, and leaning over he placed her upon the summit of it as gently as a child might be committed to its cradle. I saw her white dress flickering among the foam on the crest of the dark billow, and then the light sank gradually lower, and the riven ship and its lonely occupant were hidden from my eyes.

As I watched those things my manhood overcame my philosophy, and I felt a frantic impulse to be up and doing. I threw my cynicism to one side as a garment which I might don again at leisure, and I rushed wildly to my boat and my sculls. She was a leaky tub, but what then? Was I, who had cast many a wistful, doubtful glance at my opium bottle, to begin now to weigh chances and to cavil at danger. I dragged her down to the sea with the strength of a maniac and sprang in. For a moment or two it was a question whether she could live among the boiling surge, but a dozen frantic strokes took me through it, half full of water but still afloat. I was out on the unbroken waves now, at one time climbing, climbing up the broad black breast of one, then sinking down, down on the other side, until looking up I could see the gleam of the foam all around me against the dark heavens. Far behind me I could hear the wild wailings of old Madge, who, seeing me start, thought no doubt that my madness had come to a climax. As I rowed I peered over my shoulder, until at last on the belly of a great wave which was sweeping towards me I distinguished the vague white outline of the woman. Stooping over, I seized her as she swept by me, and with an effort lifted her, all sodden with water, into the boat. There was no need to row back, for the next billow carried us in and threw us upon the beach. I dragged the boat out of danger, and then lifting up the woman I carried her to the house, followed by my housekeeper, loud with congratulation and praise.

Now that I had done this thing a reaction set in upon me. I felt that my burden lived, for I heard the faint beat of her heart as I pressed my ear against her side in carrying her. Knowing this, I threw her down beside the fire which Madge had lit, with as little sympathy as though she had been a bundle of fagots. I never glanced at her to see if she were fair or no. For many years I had cared little for the face of a woman. As I lay in my hammock upstairs, however, I heard the old woman as she chafed the warmth back into her, crooning a chorus of, "Eh, the puir lassie! Eh, the bonnie lassie!" from which I gathered that this piece of jetsam was both young and comely.

The morning after the gale was peaceful and sunny. As I walked along the long sweep of sand I could hear the panting of the sea. It was heaving and swirling about the reef, but along the shore it rippled in gently enough. There was no sign of the schooner, nor was there any wreckage upon the beach, which did not surprise me, as I knew there was a great undertow in those waters. A couple of broad-winged gulls were hovering and skimming over the scene of the shipwreck, as though many strange things were visible to them beneath the waves. At times I could hear their raucous voices as they spoke to one another of what they saw.

When I came back from my walk the woman was waiting at the door for me. I began to wish when I saw her that I had never saved her, for here was an end of my privacy. She was very young--at the most nineteen, with a pale somewhat refined face, yellow hair, merry blue eyes, and shining teeth. Her beauty was of an ethereal type. She looked so white and light and fragile that she might have been the spirit of that storm-foam from out of which I plucked her. She had wreathed some of Madge's garments round her in a way which was quaint and not unbecoming. As I strode heavily up the pathway, she put out her hands with a pretty child-like gesture, and ran down towards me, meaning, as I surmise, to thank me for having saved her, but I put her aside with a wave of my hand and passed her. At this she seemed somewhat hurt, and the tears sprang into her eyes, but she followed me into the sitting-room and watched me wistfully. "What country do you come from?" I asked her suddenly.

She smiled when I spoke, but shook her head.

"Francais?" I asked. "Deutsch?" "Espagnol?"--each time she shook her head, and then she rippled off into a long statement in some tongue of which I could not understand one word.

After breakfast was over, however, I got a clue to her nationality.

Passing along the beach once more, I saw that in a cleft of the ridge a piece of wood had been jammed. I rowed out to it in my boat, and brought it ashore. It was part of the sternpost of a boat, and on it, or rather on the piece of wood attached to it, was the word "Archangel," painted in strange, quaint lettering.

"So," I thought, as I paddled slowly back, "this pale damsel is a Russian. A fit subject for the White Czar and a proper dweller on the shores of the White Sea!" It seemed to me strange that one of her apparent refinement should perform so long a journey in so frail a craft. When I came back into the house, I pronounced the word "Archangel" several times in different intonations, but she did not appear to recognise it.

I shut myself up in the laboratory all the morning, continuing a research which I was making upon the nature of the allotropic forms of carbon and of sulphur. When I came out at mid-day for some food she was sitting by the table with a needle and thread, mending some rents in her clothes, which were now dry. I resented her continued presence, but I could not turn her out on the beach to shift for herself. Presently she presented a new phase of her character. Pointing to herself and then to the scene of the shipwreck, she held up one finger, by which I understood her to be asking whether she was the only one saved. I nodded my head to indicate that she was. On this she sprang out of the chair with a cry of great joy, and holding the garment which she was mending over her head, and swaying it from side to side with the motion of her body, she danced as lightly as a feather all round the room, and then out through the open door into the sunshine. As she whirled round she sang in a plaintive shrill voice some uncouth barbarous chant, expressive of exultation. I called out to her, "Come in, you young fiend, come in and be silent!" but she went on with her dance. Then she suddenly ran towards me, and catching my hand before I could pluck it away, she kissed it. While we were at dinner she spied one of my pencils, and taking it up she wrote the two words "Sophie Ramusine" upon a piece of paper, and then pointed to herself as a sign that that was her name. She handed the pencil to me, evidently expecting that I would be equally communicative, but I put it in my pocket as a sign that I wished to hold no intercourse with her.

Every moment of my life now I regretted the unguarded precipitancy with which I had saved this woman. What was it to me whether she had lived or died? I was no young, hot-headed youth to do such things. It was bad enough to be compelled to have Madge in the house, but she was old and ugly, and could be ignored. This one was young and lively, and so fashioned as to divert attention from graver things. Where could I send her, and what could I do with her? If I sent information to Wick it would mean that officials and others would come to me and pry, and peep, and chatter--a hateful thought. It was better to endure her presence than that.

I soon found that there were fresh troubles in store for me. There is no place safe from the swarming, restless race of which I am a member. In the evening, when the sun was dipping down behind the hills, casting them into dark shadow, but gilding the sands and casting a great glory over the sea, I went, as is my custom, for a stroll along the beach. Sometimes on these occasions I took my book with me. I did so on this night, and stretching myself upon a sand-dune I composed myself to read. As I lay there I suddenly became aware of a shadow which interposed itself between the sun and myself. Looking round, I saw to my great surprise a very tall, powerful man, who was standing a few yards off, and who, instead of looking at me, was ignoring my existence completely, and was gazing over my head with a stern set face at the bay and the black line of the Mansie reef. His complexion was dark, with black hair, and short, curling beard, a hawk-like nose, and golden earrings in his ears--the general effect being wild and somewhat noble. He wore a faded velveteen jacket, a red-flannel shirt, and high sea boots, coming half-way up his thighs. I recognised him at a glance as being the same man who had been left on the wreck the night before.

"Hullo!" I said, in an aggrieved voice. "You got ashore all right, then?"

"Yes," he answered, in good English. "It was no doing of mine. The waves threw me up. I wish to God I had been allowed to drown!"

There was a slight foreign lisp in his accent which was rather pleasing. "Two good fishermen, who live round yonder point, pulled me out and cared for me; yet I could not honestly thank them for it."

"Ho! ho!" thought I, "here is a man of my own kidney. Why do you wish to be drowned?" I asked.

"Because," he cried, throwing out his long arms with a passionate, despairing gesture, "there--there in that blue smiling bay, lies my soul, my treasure--everything that I loved and lived for."

"Well, well," I said. "People are ruined every day, but there's no use making a fuss about it. Let me inform you that this ground on which you walk is my ground, and that the sooner you take yourself off it the better pleased I shall be. One of you is quite trouble enough."

"One of us?" he gasped.

"Yes--if you could take her off with you I should be still more grateful."

He gazed at me for a moment as if hardly able to realise what I said, and then with a wild cry he ran away from me with prodigious speed and raced along the sands towards my house. Never before or since have I seen a human being run so fast. I followed as rapidly as I could, furious at this threatened invasion, but long before I reached the house he had disappeared through the open door. I heard a great scream from the inside, and as I came nearer the sound of a man's bass voice speaking rapidly and loudly. When I looked in the girl, Sophie Ramusine, was crouching in a corner, cowering away, with fear and loathing expressed on her averted face and in every line of her shrinking form. The other, with his dark eyes flashing, and his outstretched hands quivering with emotion, was pouring forth a torrent of passionate pleading words. He made a step forward to her as I entered, but she writhed still further away, and uttered a sharp cry like that of a rabbit when the weasel has him by the throat.

"Here!" I said, pulling him back from her. "This is a pretty to- do! What do you mean? Do you think this is a wayside inn or place of public accommodation?"

"Oh, sir," he said, "excuse me. This woman is my wife, and I feared that she was drowned. You have brought me back to life."

"Who are you?" I asked roughly.

"I am a man from Archangel," he said simply; "a Russian man."

"What is your name?"

"Ourganeff."

"Ourganeff!--and hers is Sophie Ramusine. She is no wife of yours. She has no ring."

"We are man and wife in the sight of Heaven," he said solemnly, looking upwards. "We are bound by higher laws than those of earth." As he spoke the girl slipped behind me and caught me by the other hand, pressing it as though beseeching my protection. "Give me up my wife, sir," he went on. "Let me take her away from here."

"Look here, you--whatever your name is," I said sternly; "I don't want this wench here. I wish I had never seen her. If she died it would be no grief to me. But as to handing her over to you, when it is clear she fears and hates you, I won't do it. So now just clear your great body out of this, and leave me to my books. I hope I may never look upon your face again."

"You won't give her up to me?" he said hoarsely.

"I'll see you damned first!" I answered.

"Suppose I take her," he cried, his dark face growing darker.

All my tigerish blood flushed up in a moment. I picked up a billet of wood from beside the fireplace. "Go," I said, in a low voice; "go quick, or I may do you an injury." He looked at me irresolutely for a moment, and then he left the house. He came back again in a moment, however, and stood in the doorway looking in at us.

"Have a heed what you do," he said. "The woman is mine, and I shall have her. When it comes to blows, a Russian is as good a man as a Scotchman."

"We shall see that," I cried, springing forward, but he was already gone, and I could see his tall form moving away through the gathering darkness.

For a month or more after this things went smoothly with us. I never spoke to the Russian girl, nor did she ever address me. Sometimes when I was at work in my laboratory she would slip inside the door and sit silently there watching me with her great eyes. At first this intrusion annoyed me, but by degrees, finding that she made no attempt to distract my attention, I suffered her to remain. Encouraged by this concession, she gradually came to move the stool on which she sat nearer and nearer to my table, until after gaining a little every day during some weeks, she at last worked her way right up to me, and used to perch herself beside me whenever I worked. In this position she used, still without ever obtruding her presence in any way, to make herself very useful by holding my pens, test-tubes, or bottles, and handing me whatever I wanted, with never-failing sagacity. By ignoring the fact of her being a human being, and looking upon her as a useful automatic machine, I accustomed myself to her presence so far as to miss her on the few occasions when she was not at her post. I have a habit of talking aloud to myself at times when I work, so as to fix my results better in my mind. The girl must have had a surprising memory for sounds, for she could always repeat the words which I let fall in this way, without, of course, understanding in the least what they meant. I have often been amused at hearing her discharge a volley of chemical equations and algebraic symbols at old Madge, and then burst into a ringing laugh when the crone would shake her head, under the impression, no doubt, that she was being addressed in Russian.

She never went more than a few yards from the house, and indeed never put her foot over the threshold without looking carefully out of each window in order to be sure that there was nobody about. By this I knew that she suspected that her fellow-countryman was still in the neighbourhood, and feared that he might attempt to carry her off. She did something else which was significant. I had an old revolver with some cartridges, which had been thrown away among the rubbish. She found this one day, and at once proceeded to clean it and oil it. She hung it up near the door, with the cartridges in a little bag beside it, and whenever I went for a walk, she would take it down and insist upon my carrying it with me. In my absence she would always bolt the door. Apart from her apprehensions she seemed fairly happy, busying herself in helping Madge when she was not attending upon me. She was wonderfully nimble-fingered and natty in all domestic duties.

It was not long before I discovered that her suspicions were well founded, and that this man from Archangel was still lurking in the vicinity. Being restless one night I rose and peered out of the window. The weather was somewhat cloudy, and I could barely make out the line of the sea, and the loom of my boat upon the beach. As I gazed, however, and my eyes became accustomed to the obscurity, I became aware that there was some other dark blur upon the sands, and that in front of my very door, where certainly there had been nothing of the sort the preceding night. As I stood at my diamond-paned lattice still peering and peeping to make out what this might be, a great bank of clouds rolled slowly away from the face of the moon, and a flood of cold, clear light was poured down upon the silent bay and the long sweep of its desolate shores. Then I saw what this was which haunted my doorstep. It was he, the Russian. He squatted there like a gigantic toad, with his legs doubled under him in strange Mongolian fashion, and his eyes fixed apparently upon the window of the room in which the young girl and the housekeeper slept. The light fell upon his upturned face, and I saw once more the hawk-like grace of his countenance, with the single deeply-indented line of care upon his brow, and the protruding beard which marks the passionate nature. My first impulse was to shoot him as a trespasser, but, as I gazed, my resentment changed into pity and contempt. "Poor fool," I said to myself, "is it then possible that you, whom I have seen looking open-eyed at present death, should have your whole thoughts and ambition centred upon this wretched slip of a girl--a girl, too, who flies from you and hates you. Most women would love you--were it but for that dark face and great handsome body of yours--and yet you must needs hanker after the one in a thousand who will have no traffic with you." As I returned to my bed I chuckled much to myself over this thought. I knew that my bars were strong and my bolts thick. It mattered little to me whether this strange man spent his night at my door or a hundred leagues off, so long as he was gone by the morning. As I expected, when I rose and went out there was no sign of him, nor had he left any trace of his midnight vigil.

It was not long, however, before I saw him again. I had been out for a row one morning, for my head was aching, partly from prolonged stooping, and partly from the effects of a noxious drug which I had inhaled the night before. I pulled along the coast some miles, and then, feeling thirsty, I landed at a place where I knew that a fresh water stream trickled down into the sea. This rivulet passed through my land, but the mouth of it, where I found myself that day, was beyond my boundary line. I felt somewhat taken aback when rising from the stream at which I had slaked my thirst I found myself face to face with the Russian. I was as much a trespasser now as he was, and I could see at a glance that he knew it.

"I wish to speak a few words to you," he said gravely.

"Hurry up, then!" I answered, glancing at my watch. "I have no time to listen to chatter."

"Chatter!" he repeated angrily. "Ah, but there. You Scotch people are strange men. Your face is hard and your words rough, but so are those of the good fishermen with whom I stay, yet I find that beneath it all there lie kind honest natures. No doubt you are kind and good, too, in spite of your roughness."

"In the name of the devil," I said, "say your say, and go your way. I am weary of the sight of you."

"Can I not soften you in any way?" he cried. " Ah, see--see here"--he produced a small Grecian cross from inside his velvet jacket. "Look at this. Our religions may differ in form, but at least we have some common thoughts and feelings when we see this emblem."

"I am not so sure of that," I answered.

He looked at me thoughtfully.

"You are a very strange man," he said at last. "I cannot understand you. You still stand between me and Sophie. It is a dangerous position to take, sir. Oh, believe me, before it is too late. If you did but know what I have done to gain that woman--how I have risked my body, how I have lost my soul! You are a small obstacle to some which I have surmounted--you, whom a rip with a knife, or a blow from a stone, would put out of my way for ever. But God preserve me from that," he cried wildly. "I am deep--too deep--already. Anything rather than that."

"You would do better to go back to your country," I said, "than to skulk about these sand-hills and disturb my leisure. When I have proof that you have gone away I shall hand this woman over to the protection of the Russian Consul at Edinburgh. Until then, I shall guard her myself, and not you, nor any Muscovite that ever breathed, shall take her from me."

"And what is your object in keeping me from Sophie?" he asked.

"Do you imagine that I would injure her? Why, man, I would give my life freely to save her from the slightest harm. Why do you do this thing?"

"I do it because it is my good pleasure to act so," I answered. "I give no man reasons for my conduct."

"Look here!" he cried, suddenly blazing into fury, and advancing towards me with his shaggy mane bristling and his brown hands clenched. "If I thought you had one dishonest thought towards this girl--if for a moment I had reason to believe that you had any base motive for detaining her--as sure as there is a God in Heaven I should drag the heart out of your bosom with my hands." The very idea seemed to have put the man in a frenzy, for his face was all distorted and his hands opened and shut convulsively. I thought that he was about to spring at my throat.

"Stand off," I said, putting my hand on my pistol. "If you lay a finger on me I shall kill you."

He put his hand into his pocket, and for a moment I thought he was about to produce a weapon too, but instead of that he whipped out a cigarette and lit it, breathing the smoke rapidly into his lungs.

No doubt he had found by experience that this was the most effectual way of curbing his passions.

"I told you," he said in a quieter voice, "that my name is Ourganeff--Alexis Ourganeff. I am a Finn by birth, but I have spent my life in every part of the world. I was one who could never be still, nor settle down to a quiet existence. After I came to own my own ship there is hardly a port from Archangel to Australia which I have not entered. I was rough and wild and free, but there was one at home, sir, who was prim and white-handed and soft-tongued, skilful in little fancies and conceits which women love. This youth by his wiles and tricks stole from me the love of the girl whom I had ever marked as my own, and who up to that time had seemed in some sort inclined to return my passion. I had been on a voyage to Hammerfest for ivory, and coming back unexpectedly I learned that my pride and treasure was to be married to this soft-skinned boy, and that the party had actually gone to the church. In such moments, sir, something gives way in my head, and I hardly know what I do. I landed with a boat's crew--all men who had sailed with me for years, and who were as true as steel. We went up to the church. They were standing, she and he, before the priest, but the thing had not been done. I dashed between them and caught her round the waist. My men beat back the frightened bridegroom and the lookers on. We bore her down to the boat and aboard our vessel, and then getting up anchor we sailed away across the White Sea until the spires of Archangel sank down behind the horizon. She had my cabin, my room, every comfort. I slept among the men in the forecastle. I hoped that in time her aversion to me would wear away, and that she would consent to marry me in England or in France. For days and days we sailed. We saw the North Cape die away behind us, and we skirted the grey Norwegian coast, but still, in spite of every attention, she would not forgive me for tearing her from that pale-faced lover of hers. Then came this cursed storm which shattered both my ship and my hopes, and has deprived me even of the sight of the woman for whom I have risked so much. Perhaps she may learn to love me yet. You, sir," he said wistfully, "look like one who has seen much of the world. Do you not think that she may come to forget this man and to love me?"

"I am tired of your story," I said, turning away. "For my part, I think you are a great fool. If you imagine that this love of yours will pass away you had best amuse yourself as best you can until it does. If, on the other hand, it is a fixed thing, you cannot do better than cut your throat, for that is the shortest way out of it. I have no more time to waste on the matter." With this I hurried away and walked down to the boat. I never looked round, but I heard the dull sound of his feet upon the sands as he followed me.

"I have told you the beginning of my story," he said, "and you shall know the end some day. You would do well to let the girl go."

I never answered him, but pushed the boat off. When I had rowed some distance out I looked back and saw his tall figure upon the yellow sand as he stood gazing thoughtfully after me. When I looked again some minutes later he had disappeared.

For a long time after this my life was as regular and as monotonous as it had been before the shipwreck. At times I hoped that the man from Archangel had gone away altogether, but certain footsteps which I saw upon the sand, and more particularly a little pile of cigarette ash which I found one day behind a hillock from which a view of the house might be obtained, warned me that, though invisible, he was still in the vicinity. My relations with the Russian girl remained the same as before. Old Madge had been somewhat jealous of her presence at first, and seemed to fear that what little authority she had would be taken away from her. By degrees, however, as she came to realise my utter indifference, she became reconciled to the situation, and, as I have said before, profited by it, as our visitor performed much of the domestic work.

And now I am coming near the end of this narrative of mine, which I have written a great deal more for my own amusement than for that of any one else. The termination of the strange episode in which these two Russians had played a part was as wild and as sudden as the commencement. The events of one single night freed me from all my troubles, and left me once more alone with my books and my studies, as I had been before their intrusion. Let me endeavour to describe how this came about.

I had had a long day of heavy and wearying work, so that in the evening I determined upon taking a long walk. When I emerged from the house my attention was attracted by the appearance of the sea. It lay like a sheet of glass, so that never a ripple disturbed its surface. Yet the air was filled with that indescribable moaning sound which I have alluded to before--a sound as though the spirits of all those who lay beneath those treacherous waters were sending a sad warning of coming troubles to their brethren in the flesh. The fishermen's wives along that coast know the eerie sound, and look anxiously across the waters for the brown sails making for the land. When I heard it I stepped back into the house and looked at the glass. It was down below 29 degrees. Then I knew that a wild night was coming upon us.

Underneath the hills where I walked that evening it was dull and chill, but their summits were rosy-red, and the sea was brightened by the sinking sun. There were no clouds of importance in the sky, yet the dull groaning of the sea grew louder and stronger. I saw, far to the eastward, a brig beating up for Wick, with a reef in her topsails. It was evident that her captain had read the signs of nature as I had done. Behind her a long, lurid haze lay low upon the water, concealing the horizon. "I had better push on," I thought to myself, "or the wind may rise before I can get back."

I suppose I must have been at least half a mile from the house when I suddenly stopped and listened breathlessly. My ears were so accustomed to the noises of nature, the sighing of the breeze and the sob of the waves, that any other sound made itself heard at a great distance. I waited, listening with all my ears. Yes, there it was again--a long-drawn, shrill cry of despair, ringing over the sands and echoed back from the hills behind me--a piteous appeal for aid. It came from the direction of my house. I turned and ran back homewards at the top of my speed, ploughing through the sand, racing over the shingle. In my mind there was a great dim perception of what had occurred.

About a quarter of a mile from the house there is a high sand-hill, from which the whole country round is visible. When I reached the top of this I paused for a moment. There was the old grey building--there the boat. Everything seemed to be as I had left it. Even as I gazed, however, the shrill scream was repeated, louder than before, and the next moment a tall figure emerged from my door, the figure of the Russian sailor. Over his shoulder was the white form of the young girl, and even in his haste he seemed to bear her tenderly and with gentle reverence. I could hear her wild cries and see her desperate struggles to break away from him. Behind the couple came my old housekeeper, staunch and true, as the aged dog, who can no longer bite, still snarls with toothless gums at the intruder. She staggered feebly along at the heels of the ravisher, waving her long, thin arms, and hurling, no doubt, volleys of Scotch curses and imprecations at his head. I saw at a glance that he was making for the boat. A sudden hope sprang up in my soul that I might be in time to intercept him. I ran for the beach at the top of my speed. As I ran I slipped a cartridge into my revolver. This I determined should be the last of these invasions.

 I was too late. By the time I reached the water's edge he was a hundred yards away, making the boat spring with every stroke of his powerful arms. I uttered a wild cry of impotent anger, and stamped up and down the sands like a maniac. He turned and saw me. Rising from his seat he made me a graceful bow, and waved his hand to me. It was not a triumphant or a derisive gesture. Even my furious and distempered mind recognised it as being a solemn and courteous leave-taking. Then he settled down to his oars once more, and the little skiff shot away out over the bay. The sun had gone down now, leaving a single dull, red streak upon the water, which stretched away until it blended with the purple haze on the horizon. Gradually the skiff grew smaller and smaller as it sped across this lurid band, until the shades of night gathered round it and it became a mere blur upon the lonely sea. Then this vague loom died away also and darkness settled over it--a darkness which should never more be raised.

 And why did I pace the solitary shore, hot and wrathful as a wolf whose whelp has been torn from it? Was it that I loved this Muscovite girl? No--a thousand times no. I am not one who, for the sake of a white skin or a blue eye, would belie my own life, and change the whole tenor of my thoughts and existence. My heart was untouched. But my pride--ah, there I had been cruelly wounded.

 To think that I had been unable to afford protection to the helpless one who craved it of me, and who relied on me! It was that which made my heart sick and sent the blood buzzing through my ears.

That night a great wind rose up from the sea, and the wild waves shrieked upon the shore as though they would tear it back with them into the ocean. The turmoil and the uproar were congenial to my vexed spirit. All night I wandered up and down, wet with spray and rain, watching the gleam of the white breakers and listening to the outcry of the storm. My heart was bitter against the Russian. I joined my feeble pipe to the screaming of the gale. "If he would but come back again!" I cried with clenched hands; "if he would but come back!"

He came back. When the grey light of morning spread over the eastern sky, and lit up the great waste of yellow, tossing waters, with the brown clouds drifting swiftly over them, then I saw him once again. A few hundred yards off along the sand there lay a long dark object, cast up by the fury of the waves. It was my boat, much shattered and splintered. A little further on, a vague, shapeless something was washing to and fro in the shallow water, all mixed with shingle and with seaweed. I saw at a glance that it was the Russian, face downwards and dead. I rushed into the water and dragged him up on to the beach. It was only when I turned him over that I discovered that she was beneath him, his dead arms encircling her, his mangled body still intervening between her and the fury of the storm. It seemed that the fierce German Sea might beat the life from him, but with all its strength it was unable to tear this one-idea'd man from the woman whom he loved. There were signs which led me to believe that during that awful night the woman's fickle mind had come at last to learn the worth of the true heart and strong arm which struggled for her and guarded her so tenderly. Why else should her little head be nestling so lovingly on his broad breast, while her yellow hair entwined itself with his flowing beard? Why too should there be that bright smile of ineffable happiness and triumph, which death itself had not had power to banish from his dusky face? I fancy that death had been brighter to him than life had ever been.

Madge and I buried them there on the shores of the desolate northern sea. They lie in one grave deep down beneath the yellow sand. Strange things may happen in the world around them. Empires may rise and may fall, dynasties may perish, great wars may come and go, but, heedless of it all, those two shall embrace each other for ever and aye, in their lonely shrine by the side of the sounding ocean. I sometimes have thought that their spirits flit like shadowy sea-mews over the wild waters of the bay. No cross or symbol marks their resting-place, but old Madge puts wild flowers upon it at times, and when I pass on my daily walk and see the fresh blossoms scattered over the sand, I think of the strange couple who came from afar, and broke for a little space the dull tenor of my sombre life.

THE RING OF THOTH

Mr. John Vansittart Smith, F.R.S., of 147-A Gower Street, was a man whose energy of purpose and clearness of thought might have placed him in the very first rank of scientific observers. He was the victim, however, of a universal ambition which prompted him to aim at distinction in many subjects rather than preeminence in one.

In his early days he had shown an aptitude for zoology and for botany which caused his friends to look upon him as a second Darwin, but when a professorship was almost within his reach he had suddenly discontinued his studies and turned his whole attention to chemistry. Here his researches upon the spectra of the metals had won him his fellowship in the Royal Society; but again he played the coquette with his subject, and after a year's absence from the laboratory he joined the Oriental Society, and delivered a paper on the Hieroglyphic and Demotic inscriptions of El Kab, thus giving a crowning example both of the versatility and of the inconstancy of his talents.

The most fickle of wooers, however, is apt to be caught at last, and so it was with John Vansittart Smith. The more he burrowed his way into Egyptology the more impressed he became by the vast field which it opened to the inquirer, and by the extreme importance of a subject which promised to throw a light upon the first germs of human civilisation and the origin of the greater part of our arts and sciences. So struck was Mr. Smith that he straightway married an Egyptological young lady who had written upon the sixth dynasty, and having thus secured a sound base of operations he set himself to collect materials for a work which should unite the research of Lepsius and the ingenuity of Champollion. The preparation of this magnum opus entailed many hurried visits to the magnificent Egyptian collections of the Louvre, upon the last of which, no longer ago than the middle of last October, he became involved in a most strange and noteworthy adventure.

The trains had been slow and the Channel had been rough, so that the student arrived in Paris in a somewhat befogged and feverish condition. On reaching the Hotel de France, in the Rue Laffitte, he had thrown himself upon a sofa for a couple of hours, but finding that he was unable to sleep, he determined, in spite of his fatigue, to make his way to the Louvre, settle the point which he had come to decide, and take the evening train back to Dieppe. Having come to this conclusion, he donned his greatcoat, for it was a raw rainy day, and made his way across the Boulevard des Italiens and down the Avenue de l'Opera. Once in the Louvre he was on familiar ground, and he speedily made his way to the collection of papyri which it was his intention to consult.

The warmest admirers of John Vansittart Smith could hardly claim for him that he was a handsome man. His high-beaked nose and prominent chin had something of the same acute and incisive character which distinguished his intellect. He held his head in a birdlike fashion, and birdlike, too, was the pecking motion with which, in conversation, he threw out his objections and retorts. As he stood, with the high collar of his greatcoat raised to his ears, he might have seen from the reflection in the glass-case before him that his appearance was a singular one. Yet it came upon him as a sudden jar when an English voice behind him exclaimed in very audible tones, "What a queer-looking mortal!"

The student had a large amount of petty vanity in his composition which manifested itself by an ostentatious and overdone disregard of all personal considerations. He straightened his lips and looked rigidly at the roll of papyrus, while his heart filled with bitterness against the whole race of travelling Britons.

"Yes," said another voice, "he really is an extraordinary fellow."

"Do you know," said the first speaker, "one could almost believe that by the continual contemplation of mummies the chap has become half a mummy himself?"

"He has certainly an Egyptian cast of countenance," said the other.

John Vansittart Smith spun round upon his heel with the intention of shaming his countrymen by a corrosive remark or two. To his surprise and relief, the two young fellows who had been conversing had their shoulders turned towards him, and were gazing at one of the Louvre attendants who was polishing some brass-work at the other side of the room.

"Carter will be waiting for us at the Palais Royal," said one tourist to the other, glancing at his watch, and they clattered away, leaving the student to his labours.

"I wonder what these chatterers call an Egyptian cast of countenance," thought John Vansittart Smith, and he moved his position slightly in order to catch a glimpse of the man's face. He started as his eyes fell upon it. It was indeed the very face with which his studies had made him familiar. The regular statuesque features, broad brow, well-rounded chin, and dusky complexion were the exact counterpart of the innumerable statues, mummy-cases, and pictures which adorned the walls of the apartment.

The thing was beyond all coincidence. The man must be an Egyptian.

The national angularity of the shoulders and narrowness of the hips were alone sufficient to identify him.

John Vansittart Smith shuffled towards the attendant with some intention of addressing him. He was not light of touch in conversation, and found it difficult to strike the happy mean between the brusqueness of the superior and the geniality of the equal. As he came nearer, the man presented his side face to him, but kept his gaze still bent upon his work. Vansittart Smith, fixing his eyes upon the fellow's skin, was conscious of a sudden impression that there was something inhuman and preternatural about its appearance. Over the temple and cheek-bone it was as glazed and as shiny as varnished parchment. There was no suggestion of pores. One could not fancy a drop of moisture upon that arid surface. From brow to chin, however, it was cross- hatched by a million delicate wrinkles, which shot and interlaced as though Nature in some Maori mood had tried how wild and intricate a pattern she could devise.

"Ou est la collection de Memphis?" asked the student, with the awkward air of a man who is devising a question merely for the purpose of opening a conversation.

"C'est la," replied the man brusquely, nodding his head at the other side of the room.

"Vous etes un Egyptien, n'est-ce pas?" asked the Englishman.

The attendant looked up and turned his strange dark eyes upon his questioner. They were vitreous, with a misty dry shininess, such as Smith had never seen in a human head before. As he gazed into them he saw some strong emotion gather in their depths, which rose and deepened until it broke into a look of something akin both to horror and to hatred.

"Non, monsieur; je suis Fransais." The man turned abruptly and bent low over his polishing. The student gazed at him for a moment in astonishment, and then turning to a chair in a retired corner behind one of the doors he proceeded to make notes of his researches among the papyri. His thoughts, however refused to return into their natural groove. They would run upon the enigmatical attendant with the sphinx-like face and the parchment skin.

"Where have I seen such eyes?" said Vansittart Smith to himself. "There is something saurian about them, something reptilian. There's the membrana nictitans of the snakes," he mused, bethinking himself of his zoological studies. "It gives a shiny effect. But there was something more here. There was a sense of power, of wisdom--so I read them--and of weariness, utter weariness, and ineffable despair. It may be all imagination, but I never had so strong an impression. By Jove, I must have another look at them!" He rose and paced round the Egyptian rooms, but the man who had excited his curiosity had disappeared.

The student sat down again in his quiet corner, and continued to work at his notes. He had gained the information which he required from the papyri, and it only remained to write it down while it was still fresh in his memory. For a time his pencil travelled rapidiy over the paper, but soon the lines became less level, the words more blurred, and finally the pencil tinkled down upon the floor, and the head of the student dropped heavily forward upon his chest.

Tired out by his journey, he slept so soundly in his lonely post behind the door that neither the clanking civil guard, nor the footsteps of sightseers, nor even the loud hoarse bell which gives the signal for closing, were sufficient to arouse him.

Twilight deepened into darkness, the bustle from the Rue de Rivoli waxed and then waned, distant Notre Dame clanged out the hour of midnight, and still the dark and lonely figure sat silently in the shadow. It was not until close upon one in the morning that, with a sudden gasp and an intaking of the breath, Vansittart Smith returned to consciousness. For a moment it flashed upon him that he had dropped asleep in his study-chair at home. The moon was shining fitfully through the unshuttered window, however, and, as his eye ran along the lines of mummies and the endless array of polished cases, he remembered clearly where he was and how he came there. The student was not a nervous man. He possessed that love of a novel situation which is peculiar to his race. Stretching out his cramped limbs, he looked at his watch, and burst into a chuckle as he observed the hour. The episode would make an admirable anecdote to be introduced into his next paper as a relief to the graver and heavier speculations. He was a little cold, but wide awake and much refreshed. It was no wonder that the guardians had overlooked him, for the door threw its heavy black shadow right across him.

The complete silence was impressive. Neither outside nor inside was there a creak or a murmur. He was alone with the dead men of a dead civilisation. What though the outer city reeked of the garish nineteenth century! In all this chamber there was scarce an article, from the shrivelled ear of wheat to the pigment-box of the painter, which had not held its own against four thousand years. Here was the flotsam and jetsam washed up by the great ocean of time from that far-off empire. From stately Thebes, from lordly Luxor, from the great temples of Heliopolis, from a hundred rifled tombs, these relics had been brought. The student glanced round at the long silent figures who flickered vaguely up through the gloom, at the busy toilers who were now so restful, and he fell into a reverent and thoughtful mood. An unwonted sense of his own youth and insignificance came over him. Leaning back in his chair, he gazed dreamily down the long vista of rooms, all silvery with the moonshine, which extend through the whole wing of the widespread building. His eyes fell upon the yellow glare of a distant lamp.

John Vansittart Smith sat up on his chair with his nerves all on edge. The light was advancing slowly towards him, pausing from time to time, and then coming jerkily onwards. The bearer moved noiselessly. In the utter silence there was no suspicion of the pat of a footfall. An idea of robbers entered the Englishman's head. He snuggled up further into the corner. The light was two rooms off. Now it was in the next chamber, and still there was no sound. With something approaching to a thrill of fear the student observed a face, floating in the air as it were, behind the flare of the lamp. The figure was wrapped in shadow, but the light fell full upon the strange eager face. There was no mistaking the metallic glistening eyes and the cadaverous skin. It was the attendant with whom he had conversed.

Vansittart Smith's first impulse was to come forward and address him. A few words of explanation would set the matter clear, and lead doubtless to his being conducted to some side door from which he might make his way to his hotel. As the man entered the chamber, however, there was something so stealthy in his movements, and so furtive in his expression, that the Englishman altered his intention. This was clearly no ordinary official walking the rounds. The fellow wore felt-soled slippers, stepped with a rising chest, and glanced quickly from left to right, while his hurried gasping breathing thrilled the flame of his lamp. Vansittart Smith crouched silently back into the corner and watched him keenly, convinced that his errand was one of secret and probably sinister import.

There was no hesitation in the other's movements. He stepped lightly and swiftly across to one of the great cases, and, drawing a key from his pocket, he unlocked it. From the upper shelf he pulled down a mummy, which he bore away with him, and laid it with much care and solicitude upon the ground. By it he placed his lamp, and then squatting down beside it in Eastern fashion he began with long quivering fingers to undo the cerecloths and bandages which girt it round. As the crackling rolls of linen peeled off one after the other, a strong aromatic odour filled the chamber, and fragments of scented wood and of spices pattered down upon the marble floor.

It was clear to John Vansittart Smith that this mummy had never been unswathed before. The operation interested him keenly. He thrilled all over with curiosity, and his birdlike head protruded further and further from behind the door. When, however, the last roll had been removed from the four-thousand-year-old head, it was all that he could do to stifle an outcry of amazement. First, a cascade of long, black, glossy tresses poured over the workman's hands and arms. A second turn of the bandage revealed a low, white forehead, with a pair of delicately arched eyebrows. A third uncovered a pair of bright, deeply fringed eyes, and a straight, well-cut nose, while a fourth and last showed a sweet, full, sensitive mouth, and a beautifully curved chin. The whole face was one of extraordinary loveliness, save for the one blemish that in the centre of the forehead there was a single irregular, coffee- coloured splotch. It was a triumph of the embalmer's art. Vansittart Smith's eyes grew larger and larger as he gazed upon it, and he chirruped in his throat with satisfaction.

Its effect upon the Egyptologist was as nothing, however, compared with that which it produced upon the strange attendant. He threw his hands up into the air, burst into a harsh clatter of words, and then, hurling himself down upon the ground beside the mummy, he threw his arms round her, and kissed her repeatedly upon the lips and brow. "Ma petite!" he groaned in French. "Ma pauvre petite!" His voice broke with emotion, and his innumerable wrinkles quivered and writhed, but the student observed in the lamplight that his shining eyes were still as dry and tearless as two beads of steel. For some minutes he lay, with a twitching face, crooning and moaning over the beautiful head. Then he broke into a sudden smile, said some words in an unknown tongue, and sprang to his feet with the vigorous air of one who has braced himself for an effort.

In the centre of the room there was a large circular case which contained, as the student had frequently remarked, a magnificent collection of early Egyptian rings and precious stones. To this the attendant strode, and, unlocking it, he threw it open. On the ledge at the side he placed his lamp, and beside it a small earthenware jar which he had drawn from his pocket. He then took a handful of rings from the case, and with a most serious and anxious face he proceeded to smear each in turn with some liquid substance from the earthen pot, holding them to the light as he did so. He was clearly disappointed with the first lot, for he threw them petulantly back into the case, and drew out some more. One of these, a massive ring with a large crystal set in it, he seized and eagerly tested with the contents of the jar. Instantly he uttered a cry of joy, and threw out his arms in a wild gesture which upset the pot and sent the liquid streaming across the floor to the very feet of the Englishman. The attendant drew a red handkerchief from his bosom, and, mopping up the mess, he followed it into the corner, where in a moment he found himself face to face with his observer.

"Excuse me," said John Vansittart Smith, with all imaginable politeness; "I have been unfortunate enough to fall asleep behind this door."

"And you have been watching me?" the other asked in English, with a most venomous look on his corpse-like face.

The student was a man of veracity. "I confess," said he, "that I have noticed your movements, and that they have aroused my curiosity and interest in the highest degree."

The man drew a long flamboyant-bladed knife from his bosom. "You have had a very narrow escape," he said; "had I seen you ten minutes ago, I should have driven this through your heart. As it is, if you touch me or interfere with me in any way you are a dead man."

"I have no wish to interfere with you," the student answered. "My presence here is entirely accidental. All I ask is that you will have the extreme kindness to show me out through some side door." He spoke with great suavity, for the man was still pressing the tip of his dagger against the palm of his left hand, as though to assure himself of its sharpness, while his face preserved its malignant expression.

"If I thought----" said he. "But no, perhaps it is as well. What is your name?"

The Englishman gave it.

"Vansittart Smith," the other repeated. "Are you the same Vansittart Smith who gave a paper in London upon El Kab? I saw a report of it. Your knowledge of the subject is contemptible."

"Sir!" cried the Egyptologist.

"Yet it is superior to that of many who make even greater

pretensions. The whole keystone of our old life in Egypt was not the inscriptions or monuments of which you make so much, but was our hermetic philosophy and mystic knowledge, of which you say little or nothing."

"Our old life!" repeated the scholar, wide-eyed; and then suddenly, "Good God, look at the mummy's face!"

The strange man turned and flashed his light upon the dead woman, uttering a long doleful cry as he did so. The action of the air had already undone all the art of the embalmer. The skin had fallen away, the eyes had sunk inwards, the discoloured lips had writhed away from the yellow teeth, and the brown mark upon the forehead alone showed that it was indeed the same face which had shown such youth and beauty a few short minutes before.

The man flapped his hands together in grief and horror. Then mastering himself by a strong effort he turned his hard eyes once more upon the Englishman.

"It does not matter," he said, in a shaking voice. "It does not really matter. I came here to-night with the fixed determination to do something. It is now done. All else is as nothing. I have found my quest. The old curse is broken. I can rejoin her. What matter about her inanimate shell so long as her spirit is awaiting me at the other side of the veil!"

"These are wild words," said Vansittart Smith. He was becoming more and more convinced that he had to do with a madman.

"Time presses, and I must go," continued the other. "The moment is at hand for which I have waited this weary time. But I must show you out first. Come with me."

Taking up the lamp, he turned from the disordered chamber, and led the student swiftly through the long series of the Egyptian, Assyrian, and Persian apartments. At the end of the latter he pushed open a small door let into the wall and descended a winding stone stair. The Englishman felt the cold fresh air of the night upon his brow. There was a door opposite him which appeared to communicate with the street. To the right of this another door stood ajar, throwing a spurt of yellow light across the passage. "Come in here!" said the attendant shortly.

Vansittart Smith hesitated. He had hoped that he had come to the end of his adventure. Yet his curiosity was strong within him. He could not leave the matter unsolved, so he followed his strange companion into the lighted chamber.

It was a small room, such as is devoted to a concierge. A wood fire sparkled in the grate. At one side stood a truckle bed, and at the other a coarse wooden chair, with a round table in the centre, which bore the remains of a meal. As the visitor's eye glanced round he could not but remark with an ever-recurring thrill that all the small details of the room were of the most quaint design and antique workmanship. The candlesticks, the vases upon the chimney-piece, the fire-irons, the ornaments upon the walls, were all such as he had been wont to associate with the remote past. The gnarled heavy-eyed man sat himself down upon the edge of the bed, and motioned his guest into the chair.

"There may be design in this," he said, still speaking excellent English. "It may be decreed that I should leave some account behind as a warning to all rash mortals who would set their wits up against workings of Nature. I leave it with you. Make such use as you will of it. I speak to you now with my feet upon the threshold of the other world.

"I am, as you surmised, an Egyptian--not one of the down-trodden race of slaves who now inhabit the Delta of the Nile, but a survivor of that fiercer and harder people who tamed the Hebrew, drove the Ethiopian back into the southern deserts, and built those mighty works which have been the envy and the wonder of all after generations. It was in the reign of Tuthmosis, sixteen hundred years before the birth of Christ, that I first saw the light. You shrink away from me. Wait, and you will see that I am more to be pitied than to be feared.

"My name was Sosra. My father had been the chief priest of Osiris in the great temple of Abaris, which stood in those days upon the Bubastic branch of the Nile. I was brought up in the temple and was trained in all those mystic arts which are spoken of in your own Bible. I was an apt pupil. Before I was sixteen I had learned all which the wisest priest could teach me. From that time on I studied Nature's secrets for myself, and shared my knowledge with no man.

"Of all the questions which attracted me there were none over which I laboured so long as over those which concern themselves with the nature of life. I probed deeply into the vital principle. The aim of medicine had been to drive away disease when it appeared. It seemed to me that a method might be devised which should so fortify the body as to prevent weakness or death from ever taking hold of it. It is useless that I should recount my researches. You would scarce comprehend them if I did. They were carried out partly upon animals, partly upon slaves, and partly on myself. Suffice it that their result was to furnish me with a substance which, when injected into the blood, would endow the body with strength to resist the effects of time, of violence, or of disease. It would not indeed confer immortality, but its potency would endure for many thousands of years. I used it upon a cat, and afterwards drugged the creature with the most deadly poisons. That cat is alive in Lower Egypt at the present moment. There was nothing of mystery or magic in the matter. It was simply a chemical discovery, which may well be made again.

"Love of life runs high in the young. It seemed to me that I had broken away from all human care now that I had abolished pain and driven death to such a distance. With a light heart I poured the accursed stuff into my veins. Then I looked round for some one whom I could benefit. There was a young priest of Thoth, Parmes by name, who had won my goodwill by his earnest nature and his devotion to his studies. To him I whispered my secret, and at his request I injected him with my elixir. I should now, I reflected, never be without a companion of the same age as myself.

"After this grand discovery I relaxed my studies to some extent, but Parmes continued his with redoubled energy. Every day I could see him working with his flasks and his distiller in the Temple of Thoth, but he said little to me as to the result of his labours. For my own part, I used to walk through the city and look around me with exultation as I reflected that all this was destined to pass away, and that only I should remain. The people would bow to me as they passed me, for the fame of my knowledge had gone abroad.

"There was war at this time, and the Great King had sent down his soldiers to the eastern boundary to drive away the Hyksos. A Governor, too, was sent to Abaris, that he might hold it for the King. I had heard much of the beauty of the daughter of this Governor, but one day as I walked out with Parmes we met her, borne upon the shoulders of her slaves. I was struck with love as with lightning. My heart went out from me. I could have thrown myself beneath the feet of her bearers. This was my woman. Life without her was impossible. I swore by the head of Horus that she should be mine. I swore it to the Priest of Thoth. He turned away from me with a brow which was as black as midnight.

"There is no need to tell you of our wooing. She came to love me even as I loved her. I learned that Parmes had seen her before I did, and had shown her that he too loved her, but I could smile at his passion, for I knew that her heart was mine. The white plague had come upon the city and many were stricken, but I laid my hands upon the sick and nursed them without fear or scathe. She marvelled at my daring. Then I told her my secret, and begged her that she would let me use my art upon her.

"'Your flower shall then be unwithered, Atma,' I said. 'Other things may pass away, but you and I, and our great love for each other, shall outlive the tomb of King Chefru.'

"But she was full of timid, maidenly objections. 'Was it right?' she asked, 'was it not a thwarting of the will of the gods? If the great Osiris had wished that our years should be so long, would he not himself have brought it about?'

"With fond and loving words I overcame her doubts, and yet she hesitated. It was a great question, she said. She would think it over for this one night. In the morning I should know her resolution. Surely one night was not too much to ask. She wished to pray to Isis for help in her decision.

"With a sinking heart and a sad foreboding of evil I left her with her tirewomen. In the morning, when the early sacrifice was over, I hurried to her house. A frightened slave met me upon the steps. Her mistress was ill, she said, very ill. In a frenzy I broke my way through the attendants, and rushed through hall and corridor to my Atma's chamber. She lay upon her couch, her head high upon the pillow, with a pallid face and a glazed eye. On her forehead there blazed a single angry purple patch. I knew that hell-mark of old. It was the scar of the white plague, the sign- manual of death.

"Why should I speak of that terrible time? For months I was mad, fevered, delirious, and yet I could not die. Never did an Arab thirst after the sweet wells as I longed after death. Could poison or steel have shortened the thread of my existence, I should soon have rejoined my love in the land with the narrow portal. I tried, but it was of no avail. The accursed influence was too strong upon me. One night as I lay upon my couch, weak and weary, Parmes, the priest of Thoth, came to my chamber. He stood in the circle of the lamplight, and he looked down upon me with eyes which were bright with a mad joy.

"'Why did you let the maiden die?' he asked; 'why did you not strengthen her as you strengthened me?'

"'I was too late,' I answered. 'But I had forgot. You also loved her. You are my fellow in misfortune. Is it not terrible to think of the centuries which must pass ere we look upon her again? Fools, fools, that we were to take death to be our enemy!'

"'You may say that,' he cried with a wild laugh; 'the words come well from your lips. For me they have no meaning.'

"'What mean you?' I cried, raising myself upon my elbow. 'Surely, friend, this grief has turned your brain.' His face was aflame with joy, and he writhed and shook like one who hath a devil.

"'Do you know whither I go?' he asked.

"'Nay,' I answered, 'I cannot tell.'

"'I go to her,' said he. 'She lies embalmed in the further tomb by the double palm-tree beyond the city wall.'

"'Why do you go there?' I asked.

"'To die!' he shrieked, 'to die! I am not bound by earthen fetters.'

"'But the elixir is in your blood,' I cried.

"'I can defy it,' said he; 'I have found a stronger principle which will destroy it. It is working in my veins at this moment, and in an hour I shall be a dead man. I shall join her, and you shall remain behind.'

"As I looked upon him I could see that he spoke words of truth. The light in his eye told me that he was indeed beyond the power of the elixir.

"'You will teach me!' I cried.

"'Never!' he answered.

"'I implore you, by the wisdom of Thoth, by the majesty of Anubis!'

"'It is useless,' he said coldly.

"'Then I will find it out,' I cried.

"'You cannot,' he answered; 'it came to me by chance. There is one ingredient which you can never get. Save that which is in the ring of Thoth, none will ever more be made.

"'In the ring of Thoth!' I repeated; 'where then is the ring of Thoth?'

"'That also you shall never know,' he answered. 'You won her love.

Who has won in the end? I leave you to your sordid earth life. My chains are broken. I must go!' He turned upon his heel and fled from the chamber. In the morning came the news that the Priest of Thoth was dead.

"My days after that were spent in study. I must find this subtle poison which was strong enough to undo the elixir. From early dawn to midnight I bent over the test-tube and the furnace. Above all, I collected the papyri and the chemical flasks of the Priest of Thoth. Alas! they taught me little. Here and there some hint or stray expression would raise hope in my bosom, but no good ever came of it. Still, month after month, I struggled on. When my heart grew faint I would make my way to the tomb by the palm-trees.

There, standing by the dead casket from which the jewel had been rifled, I would feel her sweet presence, and would whisper to her that I would rejoin her if mortal wit could solve the riddle.

"Parmes had said that his discovery was connected with the ring of Thoth. I had some remembrance of the trinket. It was a large and weighty circlet, made, not of gold, but of a rarer and heavier metal brought from the mines of Mount Harbal. Platinum, you call it. The ring had, I remembered, a hollow crystal set in it, in which some few drops of liquid might be stored. Now, the secret of Parmes could not have to do with the metal alone, for there were many rings of that metal in the Temple. Was it not more likely that he had stored his precious poison within the cavity of the crystal? I had scarce come to this conclusion before, in hunting through his papers, I came upon one which told me that it was indeed so, and that there was still some of the liquid unused.

"But how to find the ring? It was not upon him when he was stripped for the embalmer. Of that I made sure. Neither was it among his private effects. In vain I searched every room that he had entered, every box, and vase, and chattel that he had owned. I sifted the very sand of the desert in the places where he had been wont to walk; but, do what I would, I could come upon no traces of the ring of Thoth. Yet it may be that my labours would have overcome all obstacles had it not been for a new and unlooked- for misfortune.

"A great war had been waged against the Hyksos, and the Captains of the Great King had been cut off in the desert, with all their bowmen and horsemen. The shepherd tribes were upon us like the locusts in a dry year. From the wilderness of Shur to the great bitter lake there was blood by day and fire by night. Abaris was the bulwark of Egypt, but we could not keep the savages back. The city fell. The Governor and the soldiers were put to the sword, and I, with many more, was led away into captivity.

"For years and years I tended cattle in the great plains by the Euphrates. My master died, and his son grew old, but I was still as far from death as ever. At last I escaped upon a swift camel, and made my way back to Egypt. The Hyksos had settled in the land which they had conquered, and their own King ruled over the country Abaris had been torn down, the city had been burned, and of the great Temple there was nothing left save an unsightly mound. Everywhere the tombs had been rifled and the monuments destroyed. Of my Atma's grave no sign was left. It was buried in the sands of the desert, and the palm-trees which marked the spot had long disappeared. The papers of Parmes and the remains of the Temple of Thoth were either destroyed or scattered far and wide over the deserts of Syria. All search after them was vain.

"From that time I gave up all hope of ever finding the ring or discovering the subtle drug. I set myself to live as patiently as might be until the effect of the elixir should wear away. How can you understand how terrible a thing time is, you who have experience only of the narrow course which lies between the cradle and the grave! I know it to my cost, I who have floated down the whole stream of history. I was old when Ilium fell. I was very old when Herodotus came to Memphis. I was bowed down with years when the new gospel came upon earth. Yet you see me much as other men are, with the cursed elixir still sweetening my blood, and guarding me against that which I would court. Now at last, at last I have come to the end of it!

"I have travelled in all lands and I have dwelt with all nations. Every tongue is the same to me. I learned them all to help pass the weary time. I need not tell you how slowly they drifted by, the long dawn of modern civilisation, the dreary middle years, the dark times of barbarism. They are all behind me now, I have never looked with the eyes of love upon another woman. Atma knows that I have been constant to her.

"It was my custom to read all that the scholars had to say upon Ancient Egypt. I have been in many positions, sometimes affluent, sometimes poor, but I have always found enough to enable me to buy the journals which deal with such matters. Some nine months ago I was in San Francisco, when I read an account of some discoveries made in the neighbourhood of Abaris. My heart leapt into my mouth as I read it. It said that the excavator had busied himself in exploring some tombs recently unearthed. In one there had been found an unopened mummy with an inscription upon the outer case setting forth that it contained the body of the daughter of the Governor of the city in the days of Tuthmosis. It added that on removing the outer case there had been exposed a large platinum ring set with a crystal, which had been laid upon the breast of the embalmed woman. This, then was where Parmes had hid the ring of Thoth. He might well say that it was safe, for no Egyptian would ever stain his soul by moving even the outer case of a buried friend.

"That very night I set off from San Francisco, and in a few weeks I found myself once more at Abaris, if a few sand-heaps and crumbling walls may retain the name of the great city. I hurried to the Frenchmen who were digging there and asked them for the ring. They replied that both the ring and the mummy had been sent to the Boulak Museum at Cairo. To Boulak I went, but only to be told that Mariette Bey had claimed them and had shipped them to the Louvre. I followed them, and there at last, in the Egyptian chamber, I came, after close upon four thousand years, upon the remains of my Atma, and upon the ring for which I had sought so long.

"But how was I to lay hands upon them? How was I to have them for my very own? It chanced that the office of attendant was vacant. I went to the Director. I convinced him that I knew much about Egypt. In my eagerness I said too much. He remarked that a Professor's chair would suit me better than a seat in the Conciergerie. I knew more, he said, than he did. It was only by blundering, and letting him think that he had over-estimated my knowledge, that I prevailed upon him to let me move the few effects which I have retained into this chamber. It is my first and my last night here.

"Such is my story, Mr. Vansittart Smith. I need not say more to a man of your perception. By a strange chance you have this night looked upon the face of the woman whom I loved in those far-off days. There were many rings with crystals in the case, and I had to test for the platinum to be sure of the one which I wanted. A glance at the crystal has shown me that the liquid is indeed within it, and that I shall at last be able to shake off that accursed health which has been worse to me than the foulest disease. I have nothing more to say to you. I have unburdened myself. You may tell my story or you may withhold it at your pleasure. The choice rests with you. I owe you some amends, for you have had a narrow escape of your life this night. I was a desperate man, and not to be baulked in my purpose. Had I seen you before the thing was done, I might have put it beyond your power to oppose me or to raise an alarm. This is the door. It leads into the Rue de Rivoli. Good night!"

The Englishman glanced back. For a moment the lean figure of Sosra the Egyptian stood framed in the narrow doorway. The next the door had slammed, and the heavy rasping of a bolt broke on the silent night.

It was on the second day after his return to London that Mr. John Vansittart Smith saw the following concise narrative in the Paris correspondence of the Times:--

"Curious Occurrence in the Louvre.--Yesterday morning a strange discovery was made in the principal Egyptian Chamber. The ouvriers who are employed to clean out the rooms in the morning found one of the attendants lying dead upon the floor with his arms round one of the mummies. So close was his embrace that it was only with the utmost difficulty that they were separated. One of the cases containing valuable rings had been opened and rifled. The authorities are of opinion that the man was bearing away the mummy with some idea of selling it to a private collector, but that he was struck down in the very act by long-standing disease of the heart. It is said that he was a man of uncertain age and eccentric habits, without any living relations to mourn over his dramatic and untimely end."

LOT NO. 249

Of the dealings of Edward Bellingham with William Monkhouse Lee, and of the cause of the great terror of Abercrombie Smith, it may be that no absolute and final judgment will ever be delivered. It is true that we have the full and clear narrative of Smith himself, and such corroboration as he could look for from Thomas Styles the servant, from the Reverend Plumptree Peterson, Fellow of Old's, and from such other people as chanced to gain some passing glance at this or that incident in a singular chain of events. Yet, in the main, the story must rest upon Smith alone, and the most will think that it is more likely that one brain, however outwardly sane, has some subtle warp in its texture, some strange flaw in its workings, than that the path of Nature has been overstepped in open day in so famed a centre of learning and light as the University of Oxford. Yet when we think how narrow and how devious this path of Nature is, how dimly we can trace it, for all our lamps of science, and how from the darkness which girds it round great and terrible possibilities loom ever shadowly upwards, it is a bold and confident man who will put a limit to the strange by- paths into which the human spirit may wander.

In a certain wing of what we will call Old College in Oxford there is a corner turret of an exceeding great age. The heavy arch which spans the open door has bent downwards in the centre under the weight of its years, and the grey, lichen-blotched blocks of stone are, bound and knitted together with withes and strands of ivy, as though the old mother had set herself to brace them up against wind and weather. From the door a stone stair curves upward spirally, passing two landings, and terminating in a third one, its steps all shapeless and hollowed by the tread of so many generations of the seekers after knowledge. Life has flowed like water down this winding stair, and, waterlike, has left these smooth- worn grooves behind it. From the long-gowned, pedantic scholars of Plantagenet days down to the young bloods of a later age, how full and strong had been that tide of young English life. And what was left now of all those hopes, those strivings, those fiery energies, save here and there in some old-world churchyard a few scratches upon a stone, and perchance a handful of dust in a mouldering coffin? Yet here were the silent stair and the grey old wall, with bend and saltire and many another heraldic device still to be read upon its surface, like grotesque shadows thrown back from the days that had passed.

In the month of May, in the year 1884, three young men occupied the sets of rooms which opened on to the separate landings of the old stair. Each set consisted simply of a sitting-room and of a bedroom, while the two corresponding rooms upon the ground- floor were used, the one as a coal-cellar, and the other as the living-room of the servant, or gyp, Thomas Styles, whose duty it was to wait upon the three men above him. To right and to left was a line of lecture-rooms and of offices, so that the dwellers in the old turret enjoyed a certain seclusion, which made the chambers popular among the more studious undergraduates. Such were the three who occupied them now--Abercrombie Smith above, Edward Bellingham beneath him, and William Monkhouse Lee upon the lowest storey.

It was ten o'clock on a bright spring night, and Abercrombie Smith lay back in his arm-chair, his feet upon the fender, and his briar-root pipe between his lips. In a similar chair, and equally at his ease, there lounged on the other side of the fireplace his old school friend Jephro Hastie. Both men were in flannels, for they had spent their evening upon the river, but apart from their dress no one could look at their hard-cut, alert faces without seeing that they were open-air men--men whose minds and tastes turned naturally to all that was manly and robust. Hastie, indeed, was stroke of his college boat, and Smith was an even better oar, but a coming examination had already cast its shadow over him and held him to his work, save for the few hours a week which health demanded. A litter of medical books upon the table, with scattered bones, models and anatomical plates, pointed to the extent as well as the nature of his studies, while a couple of single-sticks and a set of boxing-gloves above the mantelpiece hinted at the means by which, with Hastie's help, he might take his exercise in its most compressed and least distant form. They knew each other very well--so well that they could sit now in that soothing silence which is the very highest development of companionship.

"Have some whisky," said Abercrombie Smith at last between two cloudbursts. "Scotch in the jug and Irish in the bottle."

"No, thanks. I'm in for the sculls. I don't liquor when I'm training. How about you?"

"I'm reading hard. I think it best to leave it alone."

Hastie nodded, and they relapsed into a contented silence.

"By-the-way, Smith," asked Hastie, presently, have you made the acquaintance of either of the fellows on your stair yet?"

"Just a nod when we pass. Nothing more."

"Hum! I should be inclined to let it stand at that. I know something of them both. Not much, but as much as I want. I don't think I should take them to my bosom if I were you. Not that there's much amiss with Monkhouse Lee."

"Meaning the thin one?"

"Precisely. He is a gentlemanly little fellow. I don't think there is any vice in him. But then you can't know him without knowing Bellingham."

"Meaning the fat one?"

"Yes, the fat one. And he's a man whom I, for one, would rather not know."

Abercrombie Smith raised his eyebrows and glanced across at his companion.

"What's up, then?" he asked. "Drink? Cards? Cad? You used not to be censorious."

"Ah! you evidently don't know the man, or you wouldn't ask. There's something damnable about him-- something reptilian. My gorge always rises at him. I should put him down as a man with secret vices--an evil liver. He's no fool, though. They say that he is one of the best men in his line that they have ever had in the college."

"Medicine or classics?"

"Eastern languages. He's a demon at them. Chillingworth met him somewhere above the second cataract last long, and he told me that he just prattled to the Arabs as if he had been born and nursed and weaned among them. He talked Coptic to the Copts, and Hebrew to the Jews, and Arabic to the Bedouins, and they were all ready to kiss the hem of his frock-coat. There are some old hermit Johnnies up in those parts who sit on rocks and scowl and spit at the casual stranger. Well, when they saw this chap Bellingham, before he had said five words they just lay down on their bellies and wriggled. Chillingworth said that he never saw anything like it. Bellingham seemed to take it as his right, too, and strutted about among them and talked down to them like a Dutch uncle. Pretty good for an undergrad. of Old's, wasn't it?"

"Why do you say you can't know Lee without knowing Bellingham? "

"Because Bellingham is engaged to his sister Eveline. Such a bright little girl, Smith! I know the whole family well. It's disgusting to see that brute with her. A toad and a dove, that's what they always remind me of."

Abercrombie Smith grinned and knocked his ashes out against the side of the grate.

"You show every card in your hand, old chap," said he. "What a prejudiced, green-eyed, evil-thinking old man it is! You have really nothing against the fellow except that."

"Well, I've known her ever since she was as long as that cherry-wood pipe, and I don't like to see her taking risks. And it is a risk. He looks beastly. And he has a beastly temper, a venomous temper. You remember his row with Long Norton?"

"No; you always forget that I am a freshman."

"Ah, it was last winter. Of course. Well, you know the towpath along by the river. There were several fellows going along it, Bellingham in front, when they came on an old market-woman coming the other way. It had been raining—you know what those fields are like when it has rained—and the path ran between the river and a great puddle that was nearly as broad. Well, what does this swine do but keep the path, and push the old girl into the mud, where she and her marketings came to terrible grief. It was a blackguard thing to do, and Long Norton, who is as gentle a fellow as ever stepped, told him what he thought of it. One word led to another, and it ended in Norton laying his stick across the fellow's shoulders. There was the deuce of a fuss about it, and it's a treat to see the way in which Bellingham looks at Norton when they meet now. By Jove, Smith, it's nearly eleven o'clock!"

"No hurry. Light your pipe again."

"Not I. I'm supposed to be in training. Here I've been sitting gossiping when I ought to have been safely tucked up. I'll borrow your skull, if you can share it. Williams has had mine for a month. I'll take the little bones of your ear, too, if you are sure you won't need them. Thanks very much. Never mind a bag, I can carry them very well under my arm. Good-night, my son, and take my tip as to your neighbour."

When Hastie, bearing his anatomical plunder, had clattered off down the winding stair, Abercrombie Smith hurled his pipe into the wastepaper basket, and drawing his chair nearer to the lamp, plunged into a formidable green-covered volume, adorned with great colored maps of that strange internal kingdom of which we are the hapless and helpless monarchs. Though a freshman at Oxford, the student was not so in medicine, for he had worked for four years at Glasgow and at Berlin, and this coming examination would place him finally as a member of his profession. With his firm mouth, broad forehead, and clear-cut, somewhat hard-featured face, he was a man who, if he had no brilliant talent, was yet so dogged, so patient, and so strong that he might in the end overtop a more showy genius. A man who can hold his own among Scotchmen and North Germans is not a man to be easily set back. Smith had left a name at Glasgow and at Berlin, and he was bent now upon doing as much at Oxford, if hard work and devotion could accomplish it.

He had sat reading for about an hour, and the hands of the noisy carriage clock upon the side table were rapidly closing together upon the twelve, when a sudden sound fell upon the student's ear--a sharp, rather shrill sound, like the hissing intake of a man's breath who gasps under some strong emotion. Smith laid down his book and slanted his ear to listen. There was no one on either side or above him, so that the interruption came certainly from the neighbour beneath--the same neighbour of whom Hastie had given so unsavoury an account. Smith knew him only as a flabby, pale-faced man of silent and studious habits, a man, whose lamp threw a golden bar from the old turret even after he had extinguished his own. This community in lateness had formed a certain silent bond between them. It was soothing to Smith when the hours stole on towards dawning to feel that there was another so close who set as small a value upon his sleep as he did. Even now, as his thoughts turned towards him, Smith's feelings were kindly. Hastie was a good fellow, but he was rough, strong-fibred, with no imagination or sympathy. He could not tolerate departures from what he looked upon as the model type of manliness. If a man could not be measured by a public-school standard, then he was beyond the pale with Hastie. Like so many who are themselves robust, he was apt to confuse the constitution with the character, to ascribe to want of principle what was really a want of circulation. Smith, with his stronger mind, knew his friend's habit, and made allowance for it now as his thoughts turned towards the man beneath him.

There was no return of the singular sound, and Smith was about to turn to his work once more, when suddenly there broke out in the silence of the night a hoarse cry, a positive scream--the call of a man who is moved and shaken beyond all control. Smith sprang out of his chair and dropped his book. He was a man of fairly firm fibre, but there was something in this sudden, uncontrollable shriek of horror which chilled his blood and pringled in his skin. Coming in such a place and at such an hour, it brought a thousand fantastic possibilities into his head. Should he rush down, or was it better to wait? He had all the national hatred of making a scene, and he knew so little of his neighbour that he would not lightly intrude upon his affairs. For a moment he stood in doubt and even as he balanced the matter there was a quick rattle of footsteps upon the stairs, and young Monkhouse Lee, half dressed and as white as ashes, burst into his room.

"Come down!" he gasped. "Bellingham's ill."

Abercrombie Smith followed him closely down stairs into the sitting-room which was beneath his own, and intent as he was upon the matter in hand, he could not but take an amazed glance around him as he crossed the threshold. It was such a chamber as he had never seen before--a museum rather than a study. Walls and ceiling were thickly covered with a thousand strange relics from Egypt and the East. Tall, angular figures bearing burdens or weapons stalked in an uncouth frieze round the apartments. Above were bull-headed, stork-headed, cat-headed, owl-headed statues, with viper-crowned, almond-eyed monarchs, and strange, beetle-like deities cut out of the blue Egyptian lapis lazuli. Horus and Isis and Osiris peeped down from every niche and shelf, while across the ceiling a true son of Old Nile, a great, hanging-jawed crocodile, was slung in a double noose.

In the centre of this singular chamber was a large, square table, littered with papers, bottles, and the dried leaves of some graceful, palm-like plant. These varied objects had all been heaped together in order to make room for a mummy case, which had been conveyed from the wall, as was evident from the gap there, and laid across the front of the table. The mummy itself, a horrid, black, withered thing, like a charred head on a gnarled bush, was lying half out of the case, with its clawlike hand and bony forearm resting upon the table. Propped up against the sarcophagus was an old yellow scroll of papyrus, and in front of it, in a wooden armchair, sat the owner of the room, his head thrown back, his widely-opened eyes directed in a horrified stare to the crocodile above him, and his blue, thick lips puffing loudly with every expiration.

"My God! he's dying!" cried Monkhouse Lee distractedly.

He was a slim, handsome young fellow, olive-skinned and dark-eyed, of a Spanish rather than of an English type, with a Celtic intensity of manner which contrasted with the Saxon phlegm of Abercrombie Smith.

"Only a faint, I think," said the medical student. "Just give me a hand with him. You take his feet. Now on to the sofa. Can you kick all those little wooden devils off? What a litter it is! Now he will be all right if we undo his collar and give him some water. What has he been up to at all?"

"I don't know. I heard him cry out. I ran up. I know him pretty well, you know. It is very good of you to come down."

"His heart is going like a pair of castanets," said Smith, laying his hand on the breast of the unconscious man. "He seems to me to be frightened all to pieces. Chuck the water over him! What a face he has got on him!"

It was indeed a strange and most repellent face, for colour and outline were equally unnatural. It was white, not with the ordinary pallor of fear but with an absolutely bloodless white, like the under side of a sole. He was very fat, but gave the impression of having at some time been considerably fatter, for his skin hung loosely in creases and folds, and was shot with a meshwork of wrinkles. Short, stubbly brown hair bristled up from his scalp, with a pair of thick, wrinkled ears protruding on either side. His light grey eyes were still open, the pupils dilated and the balls projecting in a fixed and horrid stare. It seemed to Smith as he looked down upon him that he had never seen nature's danger signals flying so plainly upon a man's countenance, and his thoughts turned more seriously to the warning which Hastie had given him an hour before.

"What the deuce can have frightened him so?" he asked.

"It's the mummy."

"The mummy? How, then?"

"I don't know. It's beastly and morbid. I wish he would drop it. It's the second fright he has given me. It was the same last winter. I found him just like this, with that horrid thing in front of him."

"What does he want with the mummy, then?"

"Oh, he's a crank, you know. It's his hobby. He knows more about these things than any man in England. But I wish he wouldn't! Ah, he's beginning to come to."

A faint tinge of colour had begun to steal back into Bellingham's ghastly cheeks, and his eyelids shivered like a sail after a calm. He clasped and unclasped his hands, drew a long, thin breath between his teeth, and suddenly jerking up his head, threw a glance of recognition around him. As his eyes fell upon the mummy, he sprang off the sofa, seized the roll of papyrus, thrust it into a drawer, turned the key, and then staggered back on to the sofa.

"What's up?" he asked. "What do you chaps want?"

"You've been shrieking out and making no end of a fuss," said Monkhouse Lee. "If our neighbour here from above hadn't come down, I'm sure I don't know what I should have done with you."

"Ah, it's Abercrombie Smith," said Bellingham, glancing up at him.

"How very good of you to come in! What a fool I am! Oh, my God, what a fool I am!"

He sunk his head on to his hands, and burst into peal after peal of hysterical laughter.

"Look here! Drop it!" cried Smith, shaking him roughly by the shoulder.

"Your nerves are all in a jangle. You must drop these little midnight games with mummies, or you'll be going off your chump. You're all on wires now."

"I wonder," said Bellingham, "whether you would be as cool as I am if you had seen----"

"What then?"

"Oh, nothing. I meant that I wonder if you could sit up at night with a mummy without trying your nerves. I have no doubt that you are quite right. I dare say that I have been taking it out of myself too much lately. But I am all right now. Please don't go, though. Just wait for a few minutes until I am quite myself."

"The room is very close," remarked Lee, throwing open the window and letting in the cool night air.

"It's balsamic resin," said Bellingham. He lifted up one of the dried palmate leaves from the table and frizzled it over the chimney of the lamp. It broke away into heavy smoke wreaths, and a pungent, biting odour filled the chamber. "It's the sacred plant--the plant of the priests," he remarked. "Do you know anything of Eastern languages, Smith?"

"Nothing at all. Not a word."

The answer seemed to lift a weight from the Egyptologist's mind.

"By-the-way," he continued, "how long was it from the time that you ran down, until I came to my senses?"

"Not long. Some four or five minutes."

"I thought it could not be very long," said he, drawing a long breath. "But what a strange thing unconsciousness is! There is no measurement to it. I could not tell from my own sensations if it were seconds or weeks. Now that gentleman on the table was packed up in the days of the eleventh dynasty, some forty centuries ago, and yet if he could find his tongue he would tell us that this lapse of time has been but a closing of the eyes and a reopening of them. He is a singularly fine mummy, Smith."

Smith stepped over to the table and looked down with a professional eye at the black and twisted form in front of him. The features, though horribly discoloured, were perfect, and two little nutlike eyes still lurked in the depths of the black, hollow sockets. The blotched skin was drawn tightly from bone to bone, and a tangled wrap of black coarse hair fell over the ears. Two thin teeth, like those of a rat, overlay the shrivelled lower lip. In its crouching position, with bent joints and craned head, there was a suggestion of energy about the horrid thing which made Smith's gorge rise. The gaunt ribs, with their parchment-like covering, were exposed, and the sunken, leaden-hued abdomen, with the long slit where the embalmer had left his mark; but the lower limbs were wrapt round with coarse yellow bandages. A number of little clove-like pieces of myrrh and of cassia were sprinkled over the body, and lay scattered on the inside of the case.

"I don't know his name," said Bellingham, passing his hand over the shrivelled head. "You see the outer sarcophagus with the inscriptions is missing. Lot 249 is all the title he has now. You see it printed on his case. That was his number in the auction at which I picked him up."

"He has been a very pretty sort of fellow in his day," remarked Abercrombie Smith.

"He has been a giant. His mummy is six feet seven in length, and that would be a giant over there, for they were never a very robust race. Feel these great knotted bones, too. He would be a nasty fellow to tackle."

"Perhaps these very hands helped to build the stones into the pyramids," suggested Monkhouse Lee, looking down with disgust in his eyes at the crooked, unclean talons.

"No fear. This fellow has been pickled in natron, and looked after in the most approved style. They did not serve hodsmen in that fashion. Salt or bitumen was enough for them. It has been calculated that this sort of thing cost about seven hundred and thirty pounds in our money. Our friend was a noble at the least. What do you make of that small inscription near his feet, Smith?"

"I told you that I know no Eastern tongue."

"Ah, so you did. It is the name of the embalmer, I take it. A very conscientious worker he must have been. I wonder how many modern works will survive four thousand years?"

He kept on speaking lightly and rapidly, but it was evident to Abercrombie Smith that he was still palpitating with fear. His hands shook, his lower lip trembled, and look where he would, his eye always came sliding round to his gruesome companion. Through all his fear, however, there was a suspicion of triumph in his tone and manner. His eye shone, and his footstep, as he paced the room, was brisk and jaunty. He gave the impression of a man who has gone through an ordeal, the marks of which he still bears upon him, but which has helped him to his end.

"You're not going yet?" he cried, as Smith rose from the sofa. At the prospect of solitude, his fears seemed to crowd back upon him, and he stretched out a hand to detain him.

"Yes, I must go. I have my work to do. You are all right now. I think that with your nervous system you should take up some less morbid study."

"Oh, I am not nervous as a rule; and I have unwrapped mummies before."

"You fainted last time," observed Monkhouse Lee.

"Ah, yes, so I did. Well, I must have a nerve tonic or a course of electricity. You are not going, Lee?"

"I'll do whatever you wish, Ned."

"Then I'll come down with you and have a shake- down on your sofa. Good-night, Smith. I am so sorry to have disturbed you with my foolishness."

They shook hands, and as the medical student stumbled up the spiral and irregular stair he heard a key turn in a door, and the steps of his two new acquaintances as they descended to the lower floor.

In this strange way began the acquaintance between Edward Bellingham and Abercrombie Smith, an acquaintance which the latter, at least, had no desire to push further. Bellingham, however, appeared to have taken a fancy to his rough-spoken neighbour, and made his advances in such a way that he could hardly be repulsed without absolute brutality. Twice he called to thank Smith for his assistance, and many times afterwards he looked in with books, papers, and such other civilities as two bachelor neighbours can offer each other. He was, as Smith soon found, a man of wide reading, with catholic tastes and an extraordinary memory. His manner, too, was so pleasing and suave that one came, after a time, to overlook his repellent appearance. For a jaded and wearied man he was no unpleasant companion, and Smith found himself, after a time, looking forward to his visits, and even returning them.

Clever as he undoubtedly was, however, the medical student seemed to detect a dash of insanity in the man. He broke out at times into a high, inflated style of talk which was in contrast with the simplicity of his life.

"It is a wonderful thing," he cried, "to feel that one can command powers of good and of evil--a ministering angel or a demon of vengeance." And again, of Monkhouse Lee, he said,--"Lee is a good fellow, an honest fellow, but he is without strength or ambition. He would not make a fit partner for a man with a great enterprise. He would not make a fit partner for me."

At such hints and innuendoes stolid Smith, puffing solemnly at his pipe, would simply raise his eyebrows and shake his head, with little interjections of medical wisdom as to earlier hours and fresher air.

One habit Bellingham had developed of late which Smith knew to be a frequent herald of a weakening mind. He appeared to be forever talking to himself. At late hours of the night, when there could be no visitor with him, Smith could still hear his voice beneath him in a low, muffled monologue, sunk almost to a whisper, and yet very audible in the silence. This solitary babbling annoyed and distracted the student, so that he spoke more than once to his neighbour about it. Bellingham, however, flushed up at the charge, and denied curtly that he had uttered a sound; indeed, he showed more annoyance over the matter than the occasion seemed to demand.

Had Abercrombie Smith had any doubt as to his own ears he had not to go far to find corroboration. Tom Styles, the little wrinkled man-servant who had attended to the wants of the lodgers in the turret for a longer time than any man's memory could carry him, was sorely put to it over the same matter.

"If you please, sir," said he, as he tidied down the top chamber one morning, "do you think Mr. Bellingham is all right, sir?"

"All right, Styles?"

"Yes sir. Right in his head, sir."

"Why should he not be, then?"

"Well, I don't know, sir. His habits has changed of late. He's not the same man he used to be, though I make free to say that he was never quite one of my gentlemen, like Mr. Hastie or yourself, sir. He's took to talkin' to himself something awful. I wonder it don't disturb you. I don't know what to make of him, sir."

"I don't know what business it is of yours, Styles."

"Well, I takes an interest, Mr. Smith. It may be forward of me, but I can't help it. I feel sometimes as if I was mother and father to my young gentlemen. It all falls on me when things go wrong and the relations come. But Mr. Bellingham, sir. I want to know what it is that walks about his room sometimes when he's out and when the door's locked on the outside."

"Eh! you're talking nonsense, Styles."

"Maybe so, sir; but I heard it more'n once with my own ears."

"Rubbish, Styles."

"Very good, sir. You'll ring the bell if you want me."

Abercrombie Smith gave little heed to the gossip of the old man-servant, but a small incident occurred a few days later which left an unpleasant effect upon his mind, and brought the words of Styles forcibly to his memory.

Bellingham had come up to see him late one night, and was entertaining him with an interesting account of the rock tombs of Beni Hassan in Upper Egypt, when Smith, whose hearing was remarkably acute, distinctly heard the sound of a door opening on the landing below.

"There's some fellow gone in or out of your room," he remarked.

Bellingham sprang up and stood helpless for a moment, with the expression of a man who is half incredulous and half afraid.

"I surely locked it. I am almost positive that I locked it," he stammered. "No one could have opened it."

"Why, I hear someone coming up the steps now," said Smith.

Bellingham rushed out through the door, slammed it loudly behind him, and hurried down the stairs. About half-way down Smith heard him stop, and thought he caught the sound of whispering. A moment later the door beneath him shut, a key creaked in a lock, and Bellingham, with beads of moisture upon his pale face, ascended the stairs once more, and re-entered the room.

"It's all right," he said, throwing himself down in a chair. "It was that fool of a dog. He had pushed the door open. I don't know how I came to forget to lock it."

"I didn't know you kept a dog," said Smith, looking very thoughtfully at the disturbed face of his companion.

"Yes, I haven't had him long. I must get rid of him. He's a great nuisance."

"He must be, if you find it so hard to shut him up. I should have thought that shutting the door would have been enough, without locking it."

"I want to prevent old Styles from letting him out. He's of some value, you know, and it would be awkward to lose him."

"I am a bit of a dog-fancier myself," said Smith, still gazing hard at his companion from the corner of his eyes. "Perhaps you'll let me have a look at it."

"Certainly. But I am afraid it cannot be to- night; I have an appointment. Is that clock right? Then I am a quarter of an hour late already. You'll excuse me, I am sure."

He picked up his cap and hurried from the room. In spite of his appointment, Smith heard him re-enter his own chamber and lock his door upon the inside.

This interview left a disagreeable impression upon the medical student's mind. Bellingham had lied to him, and lied so clumsily that it looked as if he had desperate reasons for concealing the truth. Smith knew that his neighbour had no dog. He knew, also, that the step which he had heard upon the stairs was not the step of an animal. But if it were not, then what could it be? There was old Styles's statement about the something which used to pace the room at times when the owner was absent. Could it be a woman? Smith rather inclined to the view. If so, it would mean disgrace and expulsion to Bellingham if it were discovered by the authorities, so that his anxiety and falsehoods might be accounted for. And yet it was inconceivable that an undergraduate could keep a woman in his rooms without being instantly detected. Be the explanation what it might, there was something ugly about it, and Smith determined, as he turned to his books, to discourage all further attempts at intimacy on the part of his soft-spoken and ill-favoured neighbour.

But his work was destined to interruption that night. He had hardly caught tip the broken threads when a firm, heavy footfall came three steps at a time from below, and Hastie, in blazer and flannels, burst into the room.

"Still at it!" said he, plumping down into his wonted arm-chair. "What a chap you are to stew! I believe an earthquake might come and knock Oxford into a cocked hat, and you would sit perfectly placid with your books among the rains. However, I won't bore you long. Three whiffs of baccy, and I am off."

"What's the news, then?" asked Smith, cramming a plug of bird's-eye into his briar with his forefinger.

"Nothing very much. Wilson made 70 for the freshmen against the eleven. They say that they will play him instead of Buddicomb, for Buddicomb is clean off colour. He used to be able to bowl a little, but it's nothing but half-vollies and long hops now."

"Medium right," suggested Smith, with the intense gravity which comes upon a 'varsity man when he speaks of athletics.

"Inclining to fast, with a work from leg. Comes with the arm about three inches or so. He used to be nasty on a wet wicket. Oh, by-the-way, have you heard about Long Norton?"

"What's that?"

117

"He's been attacked."

"Attacked?"

"Yes, just as he was turning out of the High Street, and within a hundred yards of the gate of Old's."

"But who----"

"Ah, that's the rub! If you said 'what,' you would be more grammatical. Norton swears that it was not human, and, indeed, from the scratches on his throat, I should be inclined to agree with him."

"What, then? Have we come down to spooks?"

Abercrombie Smith puffed his scientific contempt.

"Well, no; I don't think that is quite the idea, either. I am inclined to think that if any showman has lost a great ape lately, and the brute is in these parts, a jury would find a true bill against it. Norton passes that way every night, you know, about the same hour. There's a tree that hangs low over the path--the big elm from Rainy's garden. Norton thinks the thing dropped on him out of the tree. Anyhow, he was nearly strangled by two arms, which, he says, were as strong and as thin as steel bands. He saw nothing; only those beastly arms that tightened and tightened on him. He yelled his head nearly off, and a couple of chaps came running, and the thing went over the wall like a cat. He never got a fair sight of it the whole time. It gave Norton a shake up, I can tell you. I tell him it has been as good as a change at the sea-side for him."

"A garrotter, most likely," said Smith.

"Very possibly. Norton says not; but we don't mind what he says. The garrotter had long nails, and was pretty smart at swinging himself over walls. By-the-way, your beautiful neighbour would be pleased if he heard about it. He had a grudge against Norton, and he's not a man, from what I know of him, to forget his little debts. But hallo, old chap, what have you got in your noddle?"

"Nothing," Smith answered curtly.

He had started in his chair, and the look had flashed over his face which comes upon a man who is struck suddenly by some unpleasant idea.

"You looked as if something I had said had taken you on the raw. By-the-way, you have made the acquaintance of Master B. since I looked in last, have you not? Young Monkhouse Lee told me something to that effect."

"Yes; I know him slightly. He has been up here once or twice."

"Well, you're big enough and ugly enough to take care of yourself. He's not what I should call exactly a healthy sort of Johnny, though, no doubt, he's very clever, and all that. But you'll soon find out for yourself. Lee is all right; he's a very decent little fellow. Well, so long, old chap! I row Mullins for the Vice-Chancellor's pot on Wednesday week, so mind you come down, in case I don't see you before."

Bovine Smith laid down his pipe and turned stolidly to his books once more. But with all the will in the world, he found it very hard to keep his mind upon his work. It would slip away to brood upon the man beneath him, and upon the little mystery which hung round his chambers. Then his thoughts turned to this singular attack of which Hastie had spoken, and to the grudge which Bellingham was said to owe the object of it. The two ideas would persist in rising together in his mind, as though there were some close and intimate connection between them. And yet the suspicion was so dim and vague that it could not be put down in words.

"Confound the chap!" cried Smith, as he shied his book on pathology across the room. "He has spoiled my night's reading, and that's reason enough, if there were no other, why I should steer clear of him in the future."

For ten days the medical student confined himself so closely to his studies that he neither saw nor heard anything of either of the men beneath him. At the hours when Bellingham had been accustomed to visit him, he took care to sport his oak, and though he more than once heard a knocking at his outer door, he resolutely refused to answer it. One afternoon, however, he was descending the stairs when, just as he was passing it, Bellingham's door flew open, and young Monkhouse Lee came out with his eyes sparkling and a dark flush of anger upon his olive cheeks. Close at his heels followed Bellingham, his fat, unhealthy face all quivering with malignant passion.

"You fool!" he hissed. "You'll be sorry."

"Very likely," cried the other. "Mind what I say. It's off! I won't hear of it!"

"You've promised, anyhow."

"Oh, I'll keep that! I won't speak. But I'd rather little Eva was in her grave. Once for all, it's off. She'll do what I say. We don't want to see you again."

So much Smith could not avoid hearing, but he hurried on, for he had no wish to be involved in their dispute. There had been a serious breach between them, that was clear enough, and Lee was going to cause the engagement with his sister to be broken off. Smith thought of Hastie's comparison of the toad and the dove, and was glad to think that the matter was at an end. Bellingham's face when he was in a passion was not pleasant to look upon. He was not a man to whom an innocent girl could be trusted for life. As he walked, Smith wondered languidly what could have caused the quarrel, and what the promise might be which Bellingham had been so anxious that Monkhouse Lee should keep.

It was the day of the sculling match between Hastie and Mullins, and a stream of men were making their way down to the banks of the Isis. A May sun was shining brightly, and the yellow path was barred with the black shadows of the tall elm- trees. On either side the grey colleges lay back from the road, the hoary old mothers of minds looking out from their high, mullioned windows at the tide of young life which swept so merrily past them. Black- clad tutors, prim officials, pale reading men, brown- faced, straw-hatted young athletes in white sweaters or many-coloured blazers, all were hurrying towards the blue winding river which curves through the Oxford meadows.

Abercrombie Smith, with the intuition of an old oarsman, chose his position at the point where he knew that the struggle, if there were a struggle, would come. Far off he heard the hum which announced the start, the gathering roar of the approach, the thunder of running feet, and the shouts of the men in the boats beneath him. A spray of half- clad, deep- breathing runners shot past him, and craning over their shoulders, he saw Hastie pulling a steady thirty-six, while his opponent, with a jerky forty, was a good boat's length behind him. Smith gave a cheer for his friend, and pulling out his watch, was starting off again for his chambers, when he felt a touch upon his shoulder, and found that young Monkhouse Lee was beside him.

"I saw you there," he said, in a timid, deprecating way. "I wanted to speak to you, if you could spare me a half-hour. This cottage is mine. I share it with Harrington of King's. Come in and have a cup of tea."

"I must be back presently," said Smith. "I am hard on the grind at present. But I'll come in for a few minutes with pleasure. I wouldn't have come out only Hastie is a friend of mine."

"So he is of mine. Hasn't he a beautiful style? Mullins wasn't in it. But come into the cottage. It's a little den of a place, but it is pleasant to work in during the summer months."

It was a small, square, white building, with green doors and shutters, and a rustic trellis-work porch, standing back some fifty yards from the river's bank. Inside, the main room was roughly fitted up as a study--deal table, unpainted shelves with books, and a few cheap oleographs upon the wall. A kettle sang upon a spirit-stove, and there were tea things upon a tray on the table.

"Try that chair and have a cigarette," said Lee. "Let me pour you out a cup of tea. It's so good of you to come in, for I know that your time is a good deal taken up. I wanted to say to you that, if I were you, I should change my rooms at once."

"Eh?"

Smith sat staring with a lighted match in one hand and his unlit cigarette in the other.

"Yes; it must seem very extraordinary, and the worst of it is that I cannot give my reasons, for I am under a solemn promise--a very solemn promise. But I may go so far as to say that I don't think Bellingham is a very safe man to live near. I intend to camp out here as much as I can for a time."

"Not safe! What do you mean?"

"Ah, that's what I mustn't say. But do take my advice, and move your rooms. We had a grand row to-day. You must have heard us, for you came down the stairs."

"I saw that you had fallen out."

"He's a horrible chap, Smith. That is the only word for him. I have had doubts about him ever since that night when he fainted--you remember, when you came down. I taxed him to-day, and he told me things that made my hair rise, and wanted me to stand in with him. I'm not strait-laced, but I am a clergyman's son, you know, and I think there are some things which are quite beyond the pale. I only thank God that I found him out before it was too late, for he was to have married into my family."

"This is all very fine, Lee," said Abercrombie Smith curtly. "But either you are saying a great deal too much or a great deal too little."

"I give you a warning."

"If there is real reason for warning, no promise can bind you. If I see a rascal about to blow a place up with dynamite no pledge will stand in my way of preventing him."

"Ah, but I cannot prevent him, and I can do nothing but warn you."

"Without saying what you warn me against."

"Against Bellingham."

"But that is childish. Why should I fear him, or any man?"

"I can't tell you. I can only entreat you to change your rooms. You are in danger where you are. I don't even say that Bellingham would wish to injure you. But it might happen, for he is a dangerous neighbour just now."

"Perhaps I know more than you think," said Smith, looking keenly at the young man's boyish, earnest face. "Suppose I tell you that some one else shares Bellingham's rooms."

Monkhouse Lee sprang from his chair in uncontrollable excitement.

"You know, then?" he gasped.

"A woman."

Lee dropped back again with a groan.

"My lips are sealed," he said. "I must not speak."

"Well, anyhow," said Smith, rising, "it is not likely that I should allow myself to be frightened out of rooms which suit me very nicely. It would be a little too feeble for me to move out all my goods and chattels because you say that Bellingham might in some unexplained way do me an injury. I think that I'll just take my chance, and stay where I am, and as I see that it's nearly five o'clock, I must ask you to excuse me."

He bade the young student adieu in a few curt words, and made his way homeward through the sweet spring evening feeling half-ruffled, half-amused, as any other strong, unimaginative man might who has been menaced by a vague and shadowy danger.

There was one little indulgence which Abercrombie Smith always allowed himself, however closely his work might press upon him. Twice a week, on the Tuesday and the Friday, it was his invariable custom to walk over to Farlingford, the residence of Dr. Plumptree Peterson, situated about a mile and a half out of Oxford. Peterson had been a close friend of Smith's elder brother Francis, and as he was a bachelor, fairly well-to-do, with a good cellar and a better library, his house was a pleasant goal for a man who was in need of a brisk walk. Twice a week, then, the medical student would swing out there along the dark country roads, and spend a pleasant hour in Peterson's comfortable study, discussing, over a glass of old port, the gossip of the 'varsity or the latest developments of medicine or of surgery.

On the day which followed his interview with Monkhouse Lee, Smith shut up his books at a quarter past eight, the hour when he usually started for his friend's house. As he was leaving his room, however, his eyes chanced to fall upon one of the books which Bellingham had lent him, and his conscience pricked him for not having returned it. However repellent the man might be, he should not be treated with discourtesy. Taking the book, he walked downstairs and knocked at his neighbour's door. There was no answer; but on turning the handle he found that it was unlocked.

Pleased at the thought of avoiding an interview, he stepped inside, and placed the book with his card upon the table.

The lamp was turned half down, but Smith could see the details of the room plainly enough. It was all much as he had seen it before--the frieze, the animal-headed gods, the banging crocodile, and the table littered over with papers and dried leaves. The mummy case stood upright against the wall, but the mummy itself was missing. There was no sign of any second occupant of the room, and he felt as he withdrew that he had probably done Bellingham an injustice. Had he a guilty secret to preserve, he would hardly leave his door open so that all the world might enter.

The spiral stair was as black as pitch, and Smith was slowly making his way down its irregular steps, when he was suddenly conscious that something had passed him in the darkness. There was a faint sound, a whiff of air, a light brushing past his elbow, but so slight that he could scarcely be certain of it. He stopped and listened, but the wind was rustling among the ivy outside, and he could hear nothing else.

"Is that you, Styles?" he shouted.

There was no answer, and all was still behind him. It must have been a sudden gust of air, for there were crannies and cracks in the old turret. And yet he could almost have sworn that be heard a footfall by his very side. He had emerged into the quadrangle, still turning the matter over in his head, when a man came running swiftly across the smooth-cropped lawn.

"Is that you, Smith?"

"Hullo, Hastie!"

"For God's sake come at once! Young Lee is drowned! Here's Harrington of King's with the news. The doctor is out. You'll do, but come along at once. There may be life in him."

"Have you brandy?"

"No. "

"I'll bring some. There's a flask on my table."

Smith bounded up the stairs, taking three at a time, seized the flask, and was rushing down with it, when, as he passed Bellingham's room, his eyes fell upon something which left him gasping and staring upon the landing.

The door, which he had closed behind him, was now open, and right in front of him, with the lamp-light shining upon it, was the mummy case. Three minutes ago it had been empty. He could swear to that. Now it framed the lank body of its horrible occupant, who stood, grim and stark, with his black shrivelled face towards the door.

The form was lifeless and inert, but it seemed to Smith as he gazed that there still lingered a lurid spark of vitality, some faint sign of consciousness in the little eyes which lurked in the depths of the hollow sockets. So astounded and shaken was he that he had forgotten his errand, and was still staring at the lean, sunken figure when the voice of his friend below recalled him to himself.

"Come on, Smith!" he shouted. "It's life and death, you know. Hurry up! Now, then," he added, as the medical student reappeared, "let us do a sprint. It is well under a mile, and we should do it in five minutes. A human life is better worth running for than a pot."

Neck and neck they dashed through the darkness, and did not pull up until, panting and spent, they had reached the little cottage by the river. Young Lee, limp and dripping like a broken water-plant, was stretched upon the sofa, the green scum of the river upon his black hair, and a fringe of white foam upon his leaden-hued lips. Beside him knelt his fellow-student Harrington, endeavouring to chafe some warmth back into his rigid limbs.

"I think there's life in him," said Smith, with his hand to the lad's side. "Put your watch glass to his lips. Yes, there's dimming on it. You take one arm, Hastie. Now work it as I do, and we'll soon pull him round."

For ten minutes they worked in silence, inflating and depressing the chest of the unconscious man. At the end of that time a shiver ran through his body, his lips trembled, and he opened his eyes. The three students burst out into an irrepressible cheer.

"Wake up, old chap. You've frightened us quite enough."

"Have some brandy. Take a sip from the flask."

"He's all right now," said his companion Harrington. "Heavens, what a fright I got! I was reading here, and he had gone for a stroll as far as the river, when I heard a scream and a splash. Out I ran, and by the time that I could find him and fish him out, all life seemed to have gone. Then Simpson couldn't get a doctor, for he has a game-leg, and I had to run, and I don't know what I'd have done without you fellows. That's right, old chap. Sit up."

Monkhouse Lee had raised himself on his hands, and looked wildly about him.

"What's up?" he asked. "I've been in the water. Ah, yes; I remember."

A look of fear came into his eyes, and he sank his face into his hands.

"How did you fall in?"

"I didn't fall in."

"How, then?"

"I was thrown in. I was standing by the bank, and something from behind picked me up like a feather and hurled me in. I heard nothing, and I saw nothing. But I know what it was, for all that."

"And so do I, " whispered Smith.

Lee looked up with a quick glance of surprise. "You've learned, then!" he said. "You remember the advice I gave you?"

"Yes, and I begin to think that I shall take it."

"I don't know what the deuce you fellows are talking about," said Hastie, "but I think, if I were you, Harrington, I should get Lee to bed at once. It will be time enough to discuss the why and the wherefore when he is a little stronger. I think, Smith, you and I can leave him alone now. I am walking back to college; if you are coming in that direction, we can have a chat."

But it was little chat that they had upon their homeward path. Smith's mind was too full of the incidents of the evening, the absence of the mummy from his neighbour's rooms, the step that passed him on the stair, the reappearance--the extraordinary, inexplicable reappearance of the grisly thing--and then this attack upon Lee, corresponding so closely to the previous outrage upon another man against whom Bellingham bore a grudge. All this settled in his thoughts, together with the many little incidents which had previously turned him against his neighbour, and the singular circumstances under which he was first called in to him. What had been a dim suspicion, a vague, fantastic conjecture, had suddenly taken form, and stood out in his mind as a grim fact, a thing not to be denied. And yet, how monstrous it was! how unheard of! how entirely beyond all bounds of human experience. An impartial judge, or even the friend who walked by his side, would simply tell him that his eyes had deceived him, that the mummy had been there all the time, that young Lee had tumbled into the river as any other man tumbles into a river, and that a blue pill was the best thing for a disordered liver. He felt that he would have said as much if the positions had been reversed. And yet he could swear that Bellingham was a murderer at heart, and that he wielded a weapon such as no man had ever used in all the grim history of crime.

Hastie had branched off to his rooms with a few crisp and emphatic comments upon his friend's unsociability, and Abercrombie Smith crossed the quadrangle to his corner turret with a strong feeling of repulsion for his chambers and their associations. He would take

Lee's advice, and move his quarters as soon as possible, for how could a man study when his ear was ever straining for every murmur or footstep in the room below? He observed, as he crossed over the lawn, that the light was still shining in Bellingham's window, and as he passed up the staircase the door opened, and the man himself looked out at him. With his fat, evil face he was like some bloated spider fresh from the weaving of his poisonous web.

"Good-evening," said he. "Won't you come in?"

"No," cried Smith, fiercely.

"No? You are busy as ever? I wanted to ask you about Lee. I was sorry to hear that there was a rumour that something was amiss with him."

His features were grave, but there was the gleam of a hidden laugh in his eyes as he spoke. Smith saw it, and he could have knocked him down for it.

"You'll be sorrier still to hear that Monkhouse Lee is doing very well, and is out of all danger," he answered. "Your hellish tricks have not come off this time. Oh, you needn't try to brazen it out. I know all about it."

Bellingham took a step back from the angry student, and half-closed the door as if to protect himself.

"You are mad," he said. "What do you mean? Do you assert that I had anything to do with Lee's accident?"

"Yes," thundered Smith. "You and that bag of bones behind you; you worked it between you. I tell you what it is, Master B., they have given up burning folk like you, but we still keep a hangman, and, by George! if any man in this college meets his death while you are here, I'll have you up, and if you don't swing for it, it won't be my fault. You'll find that your filthy Egyptian tricks won't answer in England."

"You're a raving lunatic," said Bellingham.

"All right. You just remember what I say, for you'll find that I'll be better than my word."

The door slammed, and Smith went fuming up to his chamber, where he locked the door upon the inside, and spent half the night in smoking his old briar and brooding over the strange events of the evening.

Next morning Abercrombie Smith heard nothing of his neighbour, but Harrington called upon him in the afternoon to say that Lee was almost himself again. All day Smith stuck fast to his work, but in the evening he determined to pay the visit to his friend Dr. Peterson upon which he had started upon the night before. A good walk and a friendly chat would be welcome to his jangled nerves.

Bellingham's door was shut as he passed, but glancing back when he was some distance from the turret, he saw his neighbour's head at the window outlined against the lamp-light, his face pressed apparently against the glass as he gazed out into the darkness. It was a blessing to be away from all contact with him, but if for a few hours, and Smith stepped out briskly, and breathed the soft spring air into his lungs. The half-moon lay in the west between two Gothic pinnacles, and threw upon the silvered street a dark tracery from the stone-work above. There was a brisk breeze, and light, fleecy clouds drifted swiftly across the sky. Old's was on the very border of the town, and in five minutes Smith found himself beyond the houses and between the hedges of a May-scented Oxfordshire lane.

It was a lonely and little frequented road which led to his friend's house. Early as it was, Smith did not meet a single soul upon his way. He walked briskly along until he came to the avenue gate, which opened into the long gravel drive leading up to Farlingford. In front of him he could see the cosy red light of the windows glimmering through the foliage. He stood with his hand upon the iron latch of the swinging gate, and he glanced back at the road along which he had come. Something was coming swiftly down it.

It moved in the shadow of the hedge, silently and furtively, a dark, crouching figure, dimly visible against the black background. Even as he gazed back at it, it had lessened its distance by twenty paces, and was fast closing upon him. Out of the darkness he had a glimpse of a scraggy neck, and of two eyes that will ever haunt him in his dreams. He turned, and with a cry of terror he ran for his life up the avenue. There were the red lights, the signals of safety, almost within a stone's throw of him. He was a famous runner, but never had he run as he ran that night.

The heavy gate had swung into place behind him, but he heard it dash open again before his pursuer. As he rushed madly and wildly through the night, he could hear a swift, dry patter behind him, and could see, as he threw back a glance, that this horror was bounding like a tiger at his heels, with blazing eyes and one stringy arm outthrown. Thank God, the door was ajar. He could see the thin bar of light which shot from the lamp in the hall. Nearer yet sounded the clatter from behind. He heard a hoarse gurgling at his very shoulder. With a shriek he flung himself against the door, slammed and bolted it behind him, and sank half-fainting on to the hall chair.

"My goodness, Smith, what's the matter?" asked Peterson,

appearing at the door of his study.

"Give me some brandy!"

Peterson disappeared, and came rushing out again with a glass and a decanter.

"You need it," he said, as his visitor drank off what he poured out for him. "Why, man, you are as white as a cheese."

Smith laid down his glass, rose up, and took a deep breath.

"I am my own man again now," said he. "I was never so unmanned before. But, with your leave, Peterson, I will sleep here to-night, for I don't think I could face that road again except by daylight. It's weak, I know, but I can't help it."

Peterson looked at his visitor with a very questioning eye.

"Of course you shall sleep here if you wish. I'll tell Mrs. Burney to make up the spare bed. Where are you off to now?"

"Come up with me to the window that overlooks the door. I want you to see what I have seen."

They went up to the window of the upper hall whence they could look down upon the approach to the house. The drive and the fields on either side lay quiet and still, bathed in the peaceful moonlight.

"Well, really, Smith," remarked Peterson, "it is well that I know you to be an abstemious man. What in the world can have frightened you?"

"I'll tell you presently. But where can it have gone? Ah, now look, look! See the curve of the road just beyond your gate."

"Yes, I see; you needn't pinch my arm off. I saw someone pass. I should say a man, rather thin, apparently, and tall, very tall. But what of him? And what of yourself? You are still shaking like an aspen leaf."

"I have been within hand-grip of the devil, that's all. But come down to your study, and I shall tell you the whole story."

He did so. Under the cheery lamplight, with a glass of wine on the table beside him, and the portly form and florid face of his friend in front, he narrated, in their order, all the events, great and small, which had formed so singular a chain, from the night on which he had found Bellingham fainting in front of the mummy case until his horrid experience of an hour ago.

"There now," he said as he concluded, "that's the whole black business. It is monstrous and incredible, but it is true."

Dr. Plumptree Peterson sat for some time in silence with a very puzzled expression upon his face.

"I never heard of such a thing in my life, never!" he said at last. "You have told me the facts. Now tell me your inferences."

"You can draw your own."

"But I should like to hear yours. You have thought over the matter, and I have not."

"Well, it must be a little vague in detail, but the main points seem to me to be clear enough. This fellow Bellingham, in his Eastern studies, has got hold of some infernal secret by which a mummy--or possibly only this particular mummy--can be temporarily brought to life. He was trying this disgusting business on the night when he fainted. No doubt the sight of the creature moving had shaken his nerve, even though he had expected it. You remember that almost the first words he said were to call out upon himself as a fool. Well, he got more hardened afterwards, and carried the matter through without fainting. The vitality which he could put into it was evidently only a passing thing, for I have seen it continually in its case as dead as this table. He has some elaborate process, I fancy, by which he brings the thing to pass. Having done it, he naturally bethought him that he might use the creature as an agent. It has intelligence and it has strength. For some purpose he took Lee into his confidence; but Lee, like a decent Christian, would have nothing to do with such a business. Then they had a row, and Lee vowed that he would tell his sister of Bellingham's true character. Bellingham's game was to prevent him, and he nearly managed it, by setting this creature of his on his track. He had already tried its powers upon another man-- Norton-- towards whom he had a grudge. It is the merest chance that he has not two murders upon his soul. Then, when I taxed him with the matter, he had the strongest reasons for wishing to get me out of the way before I could convey my knowledge to anyone else. He got his chance when I went out, for he knew my habits, and where I was bound for. I have had a narrow shave, Peterson, and it is mere luck you didn't find me on your doorstep in the morning. I'm not a nervous man as a rule, and I never thought to have the fear of death put upon me as it was to- night."

"My dear boy, you take the matter too seriously," said his companion. "Your nerves are out of order with your work, and you make too much of it. How could such a thing as this stride about the streets of Oxford, even at night, without being seen?"

"It has been seen. There is quite a scare in the town about an escaped ape, as they imagine the creature to be. It is the talk of the place."

"Well, it's a striking chain of events. And yet, my dear fellow, you must allow that each incident in itself is capable of a more natural explanation."

"What! even my adventure of to-night?"

"Certainly. You come out with your nerves all unstrung, and your head full of this theory of yours. Some gaunt, half-famished tramp steals after you, and seeing you run, is emboldened to pursue you. Your fears and imagination do the rest."

"It won't do, Peterson; it won't do."

"And again, in the instance of your finding the mummy case empty, and then a few moments later with an occupant, you know that it was lamplight, that the lamp was half turned down, and that you had no special reason to look hard at the case. It is quite possible that you may have overlooked the creature in the first instance."

"No, no; it is out of the question."

"And then Lee may have fallen into the river, and Norton been garrotted. It is certainly a formidable indictment that you have against Bellingham; but if you were to place it before a police magistrate, he would simply laugh in your face."

"I know he would. That is why I mean to take the matter into my own hands."

"Eh?"

"Yes; I feel that a public duty rests upon me, and, besides, I must do it for my own safety, unless I choose to allow myself to be hunted by this beast out of the college, and that would be a little too feeble. I have quite made up my mind what I shall do. And first of all, may I use your paper and pens for an hour?"

"Most certainly. You will find all that you want upon that side table."

Abercrombie Smith sat down before a sheet of foolscap, and for an hour, and then for a second hour his pen travelled swiftly over it. Page after page was finished and tossed aside while his friend leaned back in his arm-chair, looking across at him with patient curiosity. At last, with an exclamation of satisfaction, Smith sprang to his feet, gathered his papers up into order, and laid the last one upon Peterson's desk.

"Kindly sign this as a witness," he said.

"A witness? Of what?"

"Of my signature, and of the date. The date is the most important. Why, Peterson, my life might hang upon it."

"My dear Smith, you are talking wildly. Let me beg you to go to bed."

"On the contrary, I never spoke so deliberately in my life. And I will promise to go to bed the moment you have signed it."

"But what is it?"

"It is a statement of all that I have been telling you to-night. I wish you to witness it."

"Certainly," said Peterson, signing his name under that of his companion. "There you are! But what is the idea?"

"You will kindly retain it, and produce it in case I am arrested."

"Arrested? For what?"

"For murder. It is quite on the cards. I wish to be ready for every event. There is only one course open to me, and I am determined to take it."

"For Heaven's sake, don't do anything rash!"

"Believe me, it would be far more rash to adopt any other course. I hope that we won't need to bother you, but it will ease my mind to know that you have this statement of my motives. And now I am ready to take your advice and to go to roost, for I want to be at my best in the morning."

Abercrombie Smith was not an entirely pleasant man to have as an enemy. Slow and easytempered, he was formidable when driven to action. He brought to every purpose in life the same deliberate resoluteness which had distinguished him as a scientific student. He had laid his studies aside for a day, but he intended that the day should not be wasted. Not a word did he say to his host as to his plans, but by nine o'clock he was well on his way to Oxford.

In the High Street he stopped at Clifford's, the gun-maker's, and bought a heavy revolver, with a box of central-fire cartridges. Six of them he slipped into the chambers, and half-cocking the weapon, placed it in the pocket of his coat. He then made his way to Hastie's rooms, where the big oarsman was lounging over his breakfast, with the Sporting Times propped up against the coffeepot.

"Hullo! What's up?" he asked. "Have some coffee?"

"No, thank you. I want you to come with me, Hastie, and do what I ask you."

"Certainly, my boy."

"And bring a heavy stick with you."

"Hullo!" Hastie stared. "Here's a hunting-crop that would fell an ox."

"One other thing. You have a box of amputating knives. Give me the longest of them."

"There you are. You seem to be fairly on the war trail. Anything else?"

"No; that will do." Smith placed the knife inside his coat, and led the way to the quadrangle. "We are neither of us chickens, Hastie," said he. "I think I can do this job alone, but I take you as a precaution. I am going to have a little talk with Bellingham. If I have only him to deal with, I won't, of course, need you. If I shout, however, up you come, and lam out with your whip as hard as you can lick. Do you understand?"

"All right. I'll come if I hear you bellow."

"Stay here, then. It may be a little time, but don't budge until I come down."

"I'm a fixture."

Smith ascended the stairs, opened Bellingham's door and stepped in. Bellingham was seated behind his table, writing. Beside him, among his litter of strange possessions, towered the mummy case, with its sale number 249 still stuck upon its front, and its hideous occupant stiff and stark within it. Smith looked very deliberately round him, closed the door, locked it, took the key from the inside, and then stepping across to the fireplace, struck a match and set the fire alight. Bellingham sat staring, with amazement and rage upon his bloated face.

"Well, really now, you make yourself at home," he gasped.

Smith sat himself deliberately down, placing his watch upon the table, drew out his pistol, cocked it, and laid it in his lap. Then he took the long amputating knife from his bosom, and threw it down in front of Bellingham.

"Now, then," said he, "just get to work and cut up that mummy."

"Oh, is that it?" said Bellingham with a sneer.

"Yes, that is it. They tell me that the law can't touch you. But I have a law that will set matters straight. If in five minutes you have not set to work, I swear by the God who made me that I will put a bullet through your brain!"

"You would murder me?"

Bellingham had half risen, and his face was the colour of putty.

"Yes."

"And for what?"

"To stop your mischief. One minute has gone."

"But what have I done?"

"I know and you know."

"This is mere bullying."

"Two minutes are gone."

"But you must give reasons. You are a madman--a dangerous madman. Why should I destroy my own property? It is a valuable mummy."

"You must cut it up, and you must burn it."

"I will do no such thing."

"Four minutes are gone."

Smith took up the pistol and he looked towards Bellingham with an inexorable face. As the second-hand stole round, he raised his hand, and the finger twitched upon the trigger.

"There! there! I'll do it!" screamed Bellingham.

In frantic haste he caught up the knife and hacked at the figure of the mummy, ever glancing round to see the eye and the weapon of his terrible visitor bent upon him. The creature crackled and snapped under every stab of the keen blade. A thick yellow dust rose up from it. Spices and dried essences rained down upon the floor. Suddenly, with a rending crack, its backbone snapped asunder, and it fell, a brown heap of sprawling limbs, upon the floor.

"Now into the fire!" said Smith.

The flames leaped and roared as the dried and tinderlike debris was piled upon it. The little room was like the stoke-hole of a steamer and the sweat ran down the faces of the two men; but still the one stooped and worked, while the other sat watching him with a set face. A thick, fat smoke oozed out from the fire, and a heavy smell of burned rosin and singed hair filled the air. In a quarter of an hour a few charred and brittle sticks were all that was left of Lot No. 249.

"Perhaps that will satisfy you," snarled Bellingham, with hate and fear in his little grey eyes as he glanced back at his tormenter.

"No; I must make a clean sweep of all your materials. We must have no more devil's tricks. In with all these leaves! They may have something to do with it."

"And what now?" asked Bellingham, when the leaves also had been added to the blaze.

"Now the roll of papyrus which you had on the table that night. It is in that drawer, I think."

"No, no," shouted Bellingham. "Don't burn that! Why, man, you don't know what you do. It is unique; it contains wisdom which is nowhere else to be found."

"Out with it!"

"But look here, Smith, you can't really mean it. I'll share the knowledge with you. I'll teach you all that is in it. Or, stay, let me only copy it before you burn it!"

Smith stepped forward and turned the key in the drawer. Taking out the yellow, curled roll of paper, he threw it into the fire, and pressed it down with his heel. Bellingham screamed, and grabbed at it; but Smith pushed him back, and stood over it until it was reduced to a formless grey ash.

"Now, Master B.," said he, "I think I have pretty well drawn your teeth. You'll hear from me again, if you return to your old tricks. And now good-morning, for I must go back to my studies."

And such is the narrative of Abercrombie Smith as to the singular events which occurred in Old College, Oxford, in the spring of '84. As Bellingham left the university immediately afterwards, and was last heard of in the Soudan, there is no one who can contradict his statement. But the wisdom of men is small, and the ways of nature are strange, and who shall put a bound to the dark things which may be found by those who seek for them?

THE CASE OF LADY SANNOX

The relations between Douglas Stone and the notorious Lady Sannox were very well known both among the fashionable circles of which she was a brilliant member, and the scientific bodies which numbered him among their most illustrious confreres. There was naturally, therefore, a very widespread interest when it was announced one morning that the lady had absolutely and for ever taken the veil, and that the world would see her no more. When, at the very tail of this rumour, there came the assurance that the celebrated operating surgeon, the man of steel nerves, had been found in the morning by his valet, seated on one side of his bed, smiling pleasantly upon the universe, with both legs jammed into one side of his breeches and his great brain about as valuable as a cap full of porridge, the matter was strong enough to give quite a little thrill of interest to folk who had never hoped that their jaded nerves were capable of such a sensation.

Douglas Stone in his prime was one of the most remarkable men in England. Indeed, he could hardly be said to have ever reached his prime, for he was but nine-and-thirty at the time of this little incident. Those who knew him best were aware that, famous as he was as a surgeon, he might have succeeded with even greater rapidity in any of a dozen lines of life. He could have cut his way to fame as a soldier, struggled to it as an explorer, bullied for it in the courts, or built it out of stone and iron as an engineer. He was born to be great, for he could plan what another man dare not do, and he could do what another man dare not plan. In surgery none could follow him. His nerve, his judgment, his intuition, were things apart. Again and again his knife cut away death, but grazed the very springs of life in doing it, until his assistants were as white as the patient. His energy, his audacity, his full-blooded self-confidence--does not the memory of them still linger to the south of Marylebone Road and the north of Oxford Street?

His vices were as magnificent as his virtues, and infinitely more picturesque. Large as was his income, and it was the third largest of all professional men in London, it was far beneath the luxury of his living. Deep in his complex nature lay a rich vein of sensualism, at the sport of which he placed all the prizes of his life. The eye, the ear, the touch, the palate--all were his masters. The bouquet of old vintages, the scent of rare exotics, the curves and tints of the daintiest potteries of Europe--it was to these that the quick- running stream of gold was transformed. And then there came his sudden mad passion for Lady Sannox, when a single interview with two challenging glances and a whispered word set him ablaze. She was the loveliest woman in London, and the only one to him. He was one of the handsomest men in London, but not the only one to her. She had a liking for new experiences, and was gracious to most men who wooed her. It may have been cause or it may have been effect that Lord Sannox looked fifty, though he was but six-and-thirty.

He was a quiet, silent, neutral-tinted man, this lord, with thin lips and heavy eyelids, much given to gardening, and full of home-like habits. He had at one time been fond of acting, had even rented a theatre in London, and on its boards had first seen Miss Marion Dawson, to whom he had offered his hand, his title, and the third of a county. Since his marriage this early hobby had become distasteful to him. Even in private theatricals it was no longer possible to persuade him to exercise the talent which he had often shown that he possessed. He was happier with a spud and a watering-can among his orchids and chrysanthemums.

It was quite an interesting problem whether he was absolutely devoid of sense, or miserably wanting in spirit. Did he know his lady's ways and condone them, or was he a mere blind, doting fool? It was a point to be discussed over the teacups in snug little drawing-rooms, or with the aid of a cigar in the bow windows of clubs. Bitter and plain were the comments among men upon his conduct. There was but one who had a good word to say for him, and he was the most silent member in the smoking-room. He had seen him break in a horse at the university, and it seemed to have left an impression upon his mind.

But when Douglas Stone became the favourite, all doubts as to Lord Sannox's knowledge or ignorance were set for ever at rest. There, was no subterfuge about Stone. In his high-handed, impetuous fashion, he set all caution and discretion at defiance. The scandal became notorious. A learned body intimated that his name had been struck from the list of its vice-presidents. Two friends implored him to consider his professional credit. He cursed them all three, and spent forty guineas on a bangle to take with him to the lady. He was at her house every evening, and she drove in his carriage in the afternoons. There was not an attempt on either side to conceal their relations; but there came at last a little incident to interrupt them.

It was a dismal winter's night, very cold and gusty, with the wind whooping in the chimneys and blustering against the window-panes. A thin spatter of rain tinkled on the glass with each fresh sough of the gale, drowning for the instant the dull gurgle and drip from the eves. Douglas Stone had finished his dinner, and sat by his fire in the study, a glass of rich port upon the malachite table at his elbow. As he raised it to his lips, he held it up against the lamplight, and watched with the eye of a connoisseur the tiny scales of beeswing which floated in its rich ruby depths. The fire, as it spurted up, threw fitful lights upon his bold, clear-cut face, with its widely-opened grey eyes, its thick and yet firm lips, and the deep, square jaw, which had something Roman in its strength and its animalism. He smiled from time to time as he nestled back in his luxurious chair. Indeed, he had a right to feel well pleased, for, against the advice of six colleagues, he had performed an operation that day of which only two cases were on record, and the result had been brilliant beyond all expectation. No other man in London would have had the daring to plan, or the skill to execute, such a heroic measure.

But he had promised Lady Sannox to see her that evening and it was already half-past eight. His hand was outstretched to the bell to order the carriage when he heard the dull thud of the knocker. An instant later there was the shuffling of feet in the hall, and the sharp closing of a door.

"A patient to see you, sir, in the consulting- room, said the butler.

"About himself?"

"No, sir; I think he wants you to go out."

"It is too late, cried Douglas Stone peevishly. "I won't go."

"This is his card, sir."

The butler presented it upon the gold salver which had been given to his master by the wife of a Prime Minister.

"'Hamil Ali, Smyrna.' Hum! The fellow is a Turk, I suppose."

"Yes, sir. He seems as if he came from abroad, sir. And he's in a terrible way."

"Tut, tut! I have an engagement. I must go somewhere else. But I'll see him. Show him in here, Pim."

A few moments later the butler swung open the door and ushered in a small and decrepit man, who walked with a bent back and with the forward push of the face and blink of the eyes which goes with extreme short sight. His face was swarthy, and his hair and beard of the deepest black. In one hand he held a turban of white muslin striped with red, in the other a small chamois leather bag.

"Good-evening," said Douglas Stone, when the butler had closed the door. "You speak English, I presume?"

"Yes, sir. I am from Asia Minor, but I speak English when I speak slow."

"You wanted me to go out, I understand?"

"Yes, sir. I wanted very much that you should see my wife."

"I could come in the morning, but I have an engagement which prevents me from seeing your wife to-night."

The Turk's answer was a singular one. He pulled the string which closed the mouth of the chamois leather bag, and poured a flood of gold on to the table.

"There are one hundred pounds there," said he, "and I promise you that it will not take you an hour. I have a cab ready at the door."

Douglas Stone glanced at his watch. An hour would not make it too late to visit Lady Sannox. He had been there later. And the fee was an extraordinarily high one. He had been pressed by his creditors lately, and he could not afford to let such a chance pass. He would go.

"What is the case?" he asked.

"Oh, it is so sad a one! So sad a one! You have not, perhaps, heard of the daggers of the Almohades?"

"Never."

"Ah, they are Eastern daggers of a great age and of a singular shape, with the hilt like what you call a stirrup. I am a curiosity dealer, you understand, and that is why I have come to England from Smyrna, but next week I go back once more. Many things I brought with me, and I have a few things left, but among them, to my sorrow, is one of these daggers."

"You will remember that I have an appointment, sir," said the surgeon, with some irritation. "Pray confine yourself to the necessary details."

"You will see that it is necessary. To-day my wife fell down in a faint in the room in which I keep my wares, and she cut her lower lip upon this cursed dagger of Almohades."

"I see," said Douglas Stone, rising. "And you wish me to dress the wound?"

"No, no, it is worse than that."

"What then?"

"These daggers are poisoned."

"Poisoned!"

"Yes, and there is no man, East or West, who can tell now what is the poison or what the cure. But all that is known I know, for my father was in this trade before me, and we have had much to do with these poisoned weapons."

"What are the symptoms?"

"Deep sleep, and death in thirty hours."

"And you say there is no cure. Why then should you pay me this considerable fee?"

"No drug can cure, but the knife may."

"And how?"

"The poison is slow of absorption. It remains for hours in the wound."

"Washing, then, might cleanse it?"

"No more than in a snake-bite. It is too subtle and too deadly."

"Excision of the wound, then?"

"That is it. If it be on the finger, take the finger off. So said my father always. But think of where this wound is, and that it is my wife. It is dreadful!"

But familiarity with such grim matters may take the finer edge from a man's sympathy. To Douglas Stone this was already an interesting case, and he brushed aside as irrelevant the feeble objections of the husband.

"It appears to be that or nothing," said he brusquely. It is better to lose a lip than a life."

"Ah, yes, I know that you are right. Well, well, it is kismet, and must be faced. I have the cab, and you will come with me and do this thing."

Douglas Stone took his case of bistouries from a drawer, and placed it with a roll of bandage and a compress of lint in his pocket. He must waste no more time if he were to see Lady Sannox.

"I am ready," said he, pulling on his overcoat. Will you take a glass of wine before you go out into this cold air?"

His visitor shrank away, with a protesting hand upraised.

"You forget that I am a Mussulman, and a true follower of the Prophet," said he. "But tell me what is the bottle of green glass which you have placed in your pocket?"

"It is chloroform."

"Ah, that also is forbidden to us. It is a spirit, and we make no use of such things."

"What! You would allow your wife to go through an operation

without an anaesthetic?"

"Ah! she will feel nothing, poor soul. The deep sleep has already come on, which is the first working of the poison. And then I have given her of our Smyrna opium. Come, sir, for already an hour has passed."

As they stepped out into the darkness, a sheet of rain was driven in upon their faces, and the hall lamp, which dangled from the arm of a marble caryatid, went out with a fluff. Pim, the butler, pushed the heavy door to, straining hard with his shoulder against the wind, while the two men groped their way towards the yellow glare which showed where the cab was waiting. An instant later they were rattling upon their journey.

"Is it far?" asked Douglas Stone.

"Oh, no. We have a very little quiet place off the Euston Road."

The surgeon pressed the spring of his repeater and listened to the little tings which told him the hour. It was a quarter past nine. He calculated the distances, and the short time which it would take him to perform so trivial an operation. He ought to reach Lady Sannox by ten o'clock. Through the fogged windows he saw the blurred gas-lamps dancing past, with occasionally the broader glare of a shop front. The rain was pelting and rattling upon the leathern top of the carriage and the wheels swashed as they rolled through puddle and mud. Opposite to him the white headgear of his companion gleamed faintly through the obscurity. The surgeon felt in his pockets and arranged his needles, his ligatures and his safety-pins, that no time might be wasted when they arrived. He chafed with impatience and drummed his foot upon the floor.

But the cab slowed down at last and pulled up. In an instant Douglas Stone was out, and the Smyrna merchant's toe was at his very heel.

"You can wait," said he to the driver.

It was a mean-looking house in a narrow and sordid street. The surgeon, who knew his London well, cast a swift glance into the shadows, but there was nothing distinctive--no shop, no movement, nothing but a double line of dull, flat-faced houses, a double stretch of wet flagstones which gleamed in the lamplight, and a double rush of water in the gutters which swirled and gurgled towards the sewer gratings. The door which faced them was blotched and discoloured, and a faint light in the fan pane above it served to show the dust and the grime which covered it. Above, in one of the bedroom windows, there was a dull yellow glimmer. The merchant knocked loudly, and, as he turned his dark face towards the light, Douglas Stone could see that it was contracted with anxiety. A bolt was drawn, and an elderly woman with a taper stood in the doorway, shielding the thin flame with her gnarled hand.

"Is all well?" gasped the merchant.

"She is as you left her, sir."

"She has not spoken?"

"No; she is in a deep sleep."

The merchant closed the door, and Douglas Stone walked down the narrow passage, glancing about him in some surprise as he did so. There was no oilcloth, no mat, no hat-rack. Deep grey dust and heavy festoons of cobwebs met his eyes everywhere. Following the old woman up the winding stair, his firm footfall echoed harshly through the silent house. There was no carpet.

The bedroom was on the second landing. Douglas Stone followed the old nurse into it, with the merchant at his heels. Here, at least, there was furniture and to spare. The floor was littered and the corners piled with Turkish cabinets, inlaid tables, coats of chain mail, strange pipes, and grotesque weapons. A single small lamp stood upon a bracket on the wall. Douglas Stone took it down, and picking his way among the lumber, walked over to a couch in the corner, on which lay a woman dressed in the Turkish fashion, with yashmak and veil. The lower part of the face was exposed, and the surgeon saw a jagged cut which zigzagged along the border of the under lip.

"You will forgive the yashmak," said the Turk. "You know our views about woman in the East."

But the surgeon was not thinking about the yashmak. This was no longer a woman to him. It was a case. He stooped and examined the wound carefully.

"There are no signs of irritation," said he. "We might delay the operation until local symptoms develop."

The husband wrung his hands in incontrollable agitation.

"Oh! sir, sir!" he cried. "Do not trifle. You do not know. It is deadly. I know, and I give you my assurance that an operation is absolutely necessary. Only the knife can save her."

"And yet I am inclined to wait," said Douglas Stone.

"That is enough!" the Turk cried, angrily. "Every minute is of importance, and I cannot stand here and see my wife allowed to sink. It only remains for me to give you my thanks for having come, and to call in some other surgeon before it is too late."

Douglas Stone hesitated. To refund that hundred pounds was no pleasant matter. But of course if he left the case he must return the money. And if the Turk were right and the woman died, his position before a coroner might be an embarrassing one.

"You have had personal experience of this poison?" he asked.

"I have."

"And you assure me that an operation is needful."

"I swear it by all that I hold sacred."

"The disfigurement will be frightful."

"I can understand that the mouth will not be a pretty one to kiss."

Douglas Stone turned fiercely upon the man. The speech was a brutal one. But the Turk has his own fashion of talk and of thought, and there was no time for wrangling. Douglas Stone drew a bistoury from his case, opened it and felt the keen straight edge with his forefinger. Then he held the lamp closer to the bed. Two dark eyes were gazing up at him through the slit in the yashmak. They were all iris, and the pupil was hardly to be seen.

"You have given her a very heavy dose of opium."

"Yes, she has had a good dose."

He glanced again at the dark eyes which looked straight at his own. They were dull and lustreless, but, even as he gazed, a little shifting sparkle came into them, and the lips quivered.

"She is not absolutely unconscious," said he.

"Would it not be well to use the knife while it would be painless?"

The same thought had crossed the surgeon's mind. He grasped the wounded lip with his forceps, and with two swift cuts he took out a broad V-shaped piece. The woman sprang up on the couch with a dreadful gurgling scream. Her covering was torn from her face. It was a face that he knew. In spite of that protruding upper lip and that slobber of blood, it was a face that he knew. She kept on putting her hand up to the gap and screaming. Douglas Stone sat down at the foot of the couch with his knife and his forceps. The room was whirling round, and he had felt something go like a ripping seam behind his ear. A bystander would have said that his face was the more ghastly of the two. As in a dream, or as if he had been looking at something at the play, he was conscious that the Turk's hair and beard lay upon the table, and that Lord Sannox was leaning against the wall with his hand to his side, laughing silently. The screams had died away now, and the dreadful head had dropped back again upon the pillow, but Douglas Stone still sat motionless, and Lord Sannox still chuckled quietly to himself.

"It was really very necessary for Marion, this operation," said he, "not physically, but morally, you know, morally."

Douglas Stone stooped forwards and began to play with the fringe of the coverlet. His knife tinkled down upon the ground, but he still held the forceps and something more.

"I had long intended to make a little example," said Lord Sannox, suavely. "Your note of Wednesday miscarried, and I have it here in my pocket-book. I took some pains in carrying out my idea. The wound, by the way, was from nothing more dangerous than my signet ring."

He glanced keenly at his silent companion, and cocked the small revolver which he held in his coat pocket. But Douglas Stone was still picking at the coverlet.

"You see you have kept your appointment after all," said Lord Sannox.

And at that Douglas Stone began to laugh. He laughed long and loudly. But Lord Sannox did not laugh now. Something like fear sharpened and hardened his features. He walked from the room, and he walked on tiptoe. The old woman was waiting outside.

"Attend to your mistress when she awakes," said Lord Sannox.

Then he went down to the street. The cab was at the door, and the driver raised his hand to his hat.

"John," said Lord Sannox, "you will take the doctor home first. He will want leading downstairs, I think. Tell his butler that he has been taken ill at a case."

"Very good, sir."

"Then you can take Lady Sannox home."

"And how about yourself, sir?"

"Oh, my address for the next few months will be Hotel di Roma, Venice. Just see that the letters are sent on. And tell Stevens to exhibit all the purple chrysanthemums next Monday and to wire me the result."

THE HORROR OF THE HEIGHTS

(WHICH INCLUDES THE MANUSCRIPT KNOWN AS THE JOYCE-ARMSTRONG FRAGMENT)

The idea that the extraordinary narrative which has been called the Joyce- Armstrong Fragment is an elaborate practical joke evolved by some unknown person, cursed by a perverted and sinister sense of humour, has now been abandoned by all who have examined the matter. The most macabre and imaginative of plotters would hesitate before linking his morbid fancies with the unquestioned and tragic facts which reinforce the statement. Though the assertions contained in it are amazing and even monstrous, it is none the less forcing itself upon the general intelligence that they are true, and that we must readjust our ideas to the new situation. This world of ours appears to be separated by a slight and precarious margin of safety from a most singular and unexpected danger. I will endeavour in this narrative, which reproduces the original document in its necessarily somewhat fragmentary form, to lay before the reader the whole of the facts up to date, prefacing my statement by saying that, if there be any who doubt the narrative of Joyce-Armstrong, there can be no question at all as to the facts concerning Lieutenant Myrtle, R.N., and Mr. Hay Connor, who undoubtedly met their end in the manner described.

The Joyce-Armstrong Fragment was found in the field which is called Lower Haycock, lying one mile to the westward of the village of Withyham, upon the Kent and Sussex border. It was on the fifteenth of September last that an agricultural labourer, James Flynn, in the employment of Mathew Dodd, farmer, of the Chauntry Farm, Withyham, perceived a briar pipe lying near the footpath which skirts the hedge in Lower Haycock. A few paces farther on he picked up a pair of broken binocular glasses. Finally, among some nettles in the ditch, he caught sight of a flat, canvas-backed book, which proved to be a note-book with detachable leaves, some of which had come loose and were fluttering along the base of the hedge. These he collected, but some, including the first, were never recovered, and leave a deplorable hiatus in this all-important statement. The notebook was taken by the labourer to his master, who in turn showed it to Dr. J. H. Atherton, of Hartfield. This gentleman at once recognised the need for an expert examination, and the manuscript was forwarded to the Aero Club in London, where it now lies.

The first two pages of the manuscript are missing. There is also one torn away at the end of the narrative, though none of these affect the general coherence of the story. It is conjectured that the missing opening is concerned with the record of Mr. Joyce-Armstrong's qualifications as an aeronaut, which can be gathered from other sources and are admitted to be unsurpassed among the air-pilots of England. For many years he has been looked upon as among the most daring and the most intellectual of flying men, a combination which has enabled him to both invent and test several new devices, including the common gyroscopic attachment which is known by his name. The main body of the manuscript is written neatly in ink, but the last few lines are in pencil and are so ragged as to be hardly legible--exactly, in fact, as they might be expected to appear if they were scribbled off hurriedly from the seat of a moving aeroplane. There are, it may be added, several stains, both on the last page and on the outside cover, which have been pronounced by the Home Office experts to be blood--probably human and certainly mammalian. The fact that something closely resembling the organism of malaria was discovered in this blood, and that Joyce-Armstrong is known to have suffered from intermittent fever, is a remarkable example of the new weapons which modern science has placed in the hands of our detectives.

And now a word as to the personality of the author of this epoch-making statement. Joyce-Armstrong, according to the few friends who really knew something of the man, was a poet and a dreamer, as well as a mechanic and an inventor. He was a man of considerable wealth, much of which he had spent in the pursuit of his aeronautical hobby. He had four private aeroplanes in his hangars near Devizes, and is said to have made no fewer than one hundred and seventy ascents in the course of last year. He was a retiring man with dark moods, in which he would avoid the society of his fellows. Captain Dangerfield, who knew him better than any one, says that there were times when his eccentricity threatened to develop into something more serious. His habit of carrying a shot-gun with him in his aeroplane was one manifestation of it.

Another was the morbid effect which the fall of Lieutenant Myrtle had upon his mind. Myrtle, who was attempting the height record, fell from an altitude of something over thirty thousand feet. Horrible to narrate, his head was entirely obliterated, though his body and limbs preserved their configuration. At every gathering of airmen, Joyce-

Armstrong, according to Dangerfield, would ask, with an enigmatic smile: "And where, pray, is Myrtle's head?"

On another occasion after dinner, at the mess of the Flying School on Salisbury Plain, he started a debate as to what will be the most permanent danger which airmen will have to encounter. Having listened to successive opinions as to air-pockets, faulty construction, and over-banking, he ended by shrugging his shoulders and refusing to put forward his own views, though he gave the impression that they differed from any advanced by his companions.

It is worth remarking that after his own complete disappearance it was found that his private affairs were arranged with a precision which may show that he had a strong premonition of disaster. With these essential explanations I will now give the narrative exactly as it stands, beginning at page three of the blood-soaked note-book:--

"Nevertheless, when I dined at Rheims with Coselli and Gustav Raymond I found that neither of them was aware of any particular danger in the higher layers of the atmosphere. I did not actually say what was in my thoughts, but I got so near to it that if they had any corresponding idea they could not have failed to express it. But then they are two empty, vainglorious fellows with no thought beyond seeing their silly names in the newspaper. It is interesting to note that neither of them had ever been much beyond the twenty-thousand-foot level. Of course, men have been higher than this both in balloons and in the ascent of mountains. It must be well above that point that the aeroplane enters the danger zone--always presuming that my premonitions are correct.

"Aeroplaning has been with us now for more than twenty years, and one might well ask: Why should this peril be only revealing itself in our day? The answer is obvious. In the old days of weak engines, when a hundred horse-power Gnome or Green was considered ample for every need, the flights were very restricted. Now that three hundred horse-power is the rule rather than the exception, visits to the upper layers have become easier and more common. Some of us can remember how, in our youth, Garros made a world-wide reputation by attaining nineteen thousand feet, and it was considered a remarkable achievement to fly over the Alps. Our standard now has been immeasurably raised, and there are twenty high flights for one in former years. Many of them have been undertaken with impunity. The thirty-thousand-foot level has been reached time after time with no discomfort beyond cold and asthma. What does this prove? A visitor might descend upon this planet a thousand times and never see a tiger. Yet tigers exist, and if he chanced to come down into a jungle he might be devoured. There are jungles of the upper air, and there are worse things than tigers which inhabit them. I believe in time they will map these jungles accurately out. Even at the present moment I could name two of them. One of them lies over the Pau- Biarritz district of France. Another is just over my head as I write here in my house in Wiltshire. I rather think there is a third in the Homburg-Wiesbaden district.

"It was the disappearance of the airmen that first set me thinking. Of course, every one said that they had fallen into the sea, but that did not satisfy me at all. First, there was Verrier in France; his machine was found near Bayonne, but they never got his body. There was the case of Baxter also, who vanished, though his engine and some of the iron fixings were found in a wood in Leicestershire. In that case, Dr. Middleton, of Amesbury, who was watching the flight with a telescope, declares that just before the clouds obscured the view he saw the machine, which was at an enormous height, suddenly rise perpendicularly upwards in a succession of jerks in a manner that he would have thought to be impossible. That was the last seen of Baxter. There was a correspondence in the papers, but it never led to anything. There were several other similar cases, and then there was the death of Hay Connor. What a cackle there was about an unsolved mystery of the air, and what columns in the halfpenny papers, and yet how little was ever done to get to the bottom of the business! He came down in a tremendous vol-plane from an unknown height. He never got off his machine and died in his pilot's seat. Died of what? 'Heart disease,' said the doctors. Rubbish! Hay Connor's heart was as sound as mine is. What did Venables say? Venables was the only man who was at his side when he died. He said that he was shivering and looked like a man who had been badly scared. 'Died of fright,' said Venables, but could not imagine what he was frightened about. Only said one word to Venables, which sounded like 'Monstrous.' They could make nothing of that at the inquest. But I could make something of it. Monsters! That was the last word of poor Harry Hay Connor. And he did die of fright, just as Venables thought.

"And then there was Myrtle's head. Do you really believe--does anybody really believe--that a man's head could be driven clean into his body by the force of a fall? Well, perhaps it may be possible, but I, for one, have never believed that it was so with Myrtle. And the grease upon his clothes--'all slimy with grease,' said somebody at the inquest. Queer that nobody got thinking after that! I did--but, then, I had been thinking for a good long time. I've made three ascents--how Dangerfield used to chaff me about my shot-gun!--but I've never been high enough. Now, with this new light Paul Veroner machine and its one hundred and seventy-five Robur, I should easily touch the thirty thousand to-morrow. I'll have a shot at the record. Maybe I shall have a shot at something else as well. Of course, it's dangerous. If a fellow wants to avoid danger he had best keep out of flying altogether and subside finally into flannel slippers and a dressing-gown. But I'll visit the air-jungle to- morrow--and if there's anything there I shall know it. If I return, I'll find myself a bit of a celebrity. If I don't, this note-book may explain what I am trying to do, and how I lost my life in doing it. But no drivel about accidents or mysteries, if you please.

"I chose my Paul Veroner monoplane for the job. There's nothing like a monoplane when real work is to be done. Beaumont found that out in very early days. For one thing, it doesn't mind damp, and the weather looks as if we should be in the clouds all the time. It's a bonny little model and answers my hand like a tender-mouthed horse. The engine is a ten- cylinder rotary Robur working up to one hundred and seventy-five. It has all the modern improvements--enclosed fuselage, high-curved landing skids, brakes, gyroscopic steadiers, and three speeds, worked by an alteration of the angle of the planes upon the Venetian-blind principle. I took a shot-gun with me and a dozen cartridges filled with buck-shot. You should have seen the face of Perkins, my old mechanic, when I directed him to put them in. I was dressed like an Arctic explorer, with two jerseys under my overalls, thick socks inside my padded boots, a storm-cap with flaps, and my talc goggles. It was stifling outside the hangars, but I was going for the summit of the Himalayas, and had to dress for the part. Perkins knew there was something on and implored me to take him with me. Perhaps I should if I were using the biplane, but a monoplane is a one-man show--if you want to get the last foot of lift out of it. Of course, I took an oxygen bag; the man who goes for the altitude record without one will either be frozen or smothered--or both.

"I had a good look at the planes, the rudder-bar, and the elevating lever before I got in. Everything was in order so far as I could see. Then I switched on my engine and found that she was running sweetly. When they let her go she rose almost at once upon the lowest speed. I circled my home field once or twice just to warm her up, and then, with a wave to Perkins and the others, I flattened out my planes and put her on her highest. She skimmed like a swallow down wind for eight or ten miles until I turned her nose up a little and she began to climb in a great spiral for the cloud-bank above me. It's all-important to rise slowly and adapt yourself to the pressure as you go.

"It was a close, warm day for an English September, and there was the hush and heaviness of impending rain. Now and then there came sudden puffs of wind from the south-west--one of them so gusty and unexpected that it caught me napping and turned me half-round for an instant. I remember the time when gusts and whirls and air-pockets used to be things of danger--before we learned to put an overmastering power into our engines. Just as I reached the cloud-banks, with the altimeter marking three thousand, down came the rain. My word, how it poured! It drummed upon my wings and lashed against my face, blurring my glasses so that I could hardly see. I got down on to a low speed, for it was painful to travel against it. As I got higher it became hail, and I had to turn tail to it. One of my cylinders was out of action--a dirty plug, I should imagine, but still I was rising steadily with plenty of power. After a bit the trouble passed, whatever it was, and I heard the full, deep-throated purr--the ten singing as one. That's where the beauty of our modern silencers comes in. We can at last control our engines by ear. How they squeal and squeak and sob when they are in trouble! All those cries for help were wasted in the old days, when every sound was swallowed up by the monstrous racket of the machine. If only the early aviators could come back to see the beauty and perfection of the mechanism which have been bought at the cost of their lives!

"About nine-thirty I was nearing the clouds. Down below me, all blurred and shadowed with rain, lay the vast expanse of Salisbury Plain. Half-a- dozen flying machines were doing hackwork at the thousand-foot level, looking like little black swallows against the green background. I dare say they were wondering what I was doing up in cloud-land. Suddenly a grey curtain drew across beneath me and the wet folds of vapour were swirling round my face. It was clammily cold and miserable. But I was above the hail-storm, and that was something gained. The cloud was as dark and thick as a London fog. In my anxiety to get clear, I cocked her nose up until the automatic alarm-bell rang, and I actually began to slide backwards. My sopped and dripping wings had made me heavier than I thought, but presently I was in lighter cloud, and soon had cleared the first layer. There was a second--opal-coloured and fleecy--at a great height above my head, a white unbroken ceiling above, and a dark unbroken floor below, with the monoplane labouring upwards upon a vast spiral between them. It is deadly lonely in these cloud-spaces. Once a great flight of some small water-birds went past me, flying very fast to the westwards. The quick whirr of their wings and their musical cry were cheery to my ear. I fancy that they were teal, but I am a wretched zoologist. Now that we humans have become birds we must really learn to know our brethren by sight.

"The wind down beneath me whirled and swayed the broad cloud-plain. Once a great eddy formed in it, a whirlpool of vapour, and through it, as down a funnel, I caught sight of the distant world. A large white biplane was passing at a vast depth beneath me. I fancy it was the morning mail service betwixt Bristol and London. Then the drift swirled inwards again and the great solitude was unbroken.

"Just after ten I touched the lower edge of the upper cloud-stratum. It consisted of fine diaphanous vapour drifting swiftly from the westward. The wind had been steadily rising all this time and it was now blowing a sharp breeze--twenty-eight an hour by my gauge. Already it was very cold, though my altimeter only marked nine thousand. The engines were working beautifully, and we went droning steadily upwards. The cloud- bank was thicker than I had expected, but at last it thinned out into a golden mist before me, and then in an instant I had shot out from it, and there was an unclouded sky and a brilliant sun above my head--all blue and gold above, all shining silver below, one vast glimmering plain as far as my eyes could reach. It was a quarter past ten o'clock, and the barograph needle pointed to twelve thousand eight hundred. Up I went and up, my ears concentrated upon the deep purring of my motor, my eyes busy always with the watch, the revolution indicator, the petrol lever, and the oil pump. No wonder aviators are said to be a fearless race. With so many things to think of there is no time to trouble about oneself. About this time I noted how unreliable is the compass when above a certain height from earth. At fifteen thousand feet mine was pointing east and a point south. The sun and the wind gave me my true bearings.

"I had hoped to reach an eternal stillness in these high altitudes, but with every thousand feet of ascent the gale grew stronger. My machine groaned and trembled in every joint and rivet as she faced it, and swept away like a sheet of paper when I banked her on the turn, skimming down wind at a greater pace, perhaps, than ever mortal man has moved. Yet I had always to turn again and tack up in the wind's eye, for it was not merely a height record that I was after. By all my calculations it was above little Wiltshire that my air-jungle lay, and all my labour might be lost if I struck the outer layers at some farther point.

"When I reached the nineteen-thousand-foot level, which was about midday, the wind was so severe that I looked with some anxiety to the stays of my wings, expecting momentarily to see them snap or slacken. I even cast loose the parachute behind me, and fastened its hook into the ring of my leathern belt, so as to be ready for the worst. Now was the time when a bit of scamped work by the mechanic is paid for by the life of the aeronaut. But she held together bravely. Every cord and strut was humming and vibrating like so many harp-strings, but it was glorious to see how, for all the beating and the buffeting, she was still the conqueror of Nature and the mistress of the sky. There is surely something divine in man himself that he should rise so superior to the limitations which Creation seemed to impose--rise, too, by such unselfish, heroic devotion as this air-conquest has shown. Talk of human degeneration! When has such a story as this been written in the annals of our race?

"These were the thoughts in my head as I climbed that monstrous inclined plane with the wind sometimes beating in my face and sometimes whistling behind my ears, while the cloud-land beneath me fell away to such a distance that the folds and hummocks of silver had all smoothed out into one flat, shining plain. But suddenly I had a horrible and unprecedented experience. I have known before what it is to be in what our neighbours have called a tourbillon, but never on such a scale as this. That huge, sweeping river of wind of which I have spoken had, as it appears, whirlpools within it which were as monstrous as itself. Without a moment's warning I was dragged suddenly into the heart of one. I spun round for a minute or two with such velocity that I almost lost my senses, and then fell suddenly, left wing foremost, down the vacuum funnel in the centre. I dropped like a stone, and lost nearly a thousand feet. It was only my belt that kept me in my seat, and the shock and breathlessness left me hanging half-insensible over the side of the fuselage. But I am always capable of a supreme effort--it is my one great merit as an aviator. I was conscious that the descent was slower. The whirlpool was a cone rather than a funnel, and I had come to the apex. With a terrific wrench, throwing my weight all to one side, I levelled my planes and brought her head away from the wind. In an instant I had shot out of the eddies and was skimming down the sky. Then, shaken but victorious, I turned her nose up and began once more my steady grind on the upward spiral. I took a large sweep to avoid the danger- spot of the whirlpool, and soon I was safely above it. Just after one o'clock I was twenty-one thousand feet above the sea-level. To my great joy I had topped the gale, and with every hundred feet of ascent the air grew stiller. On the other hand, it was very cold, and I was conscious of that peculiar nausea which goes with rarefaction of the air. For the first time I unscrewed the mouth of my oxygen bag and took an occasional whiff of the glorious gas. I could feel it running like a cordial through my veins, and I was exhilarated almost to the point of drunkenness. I shouted and sang as I soared upwards into the cold, still outer world.

"It is very clear to me that the insensibility which came upon Glaisher, and in a lesser degree upon Coxwell, when, in 1862, they ascended in a balloon to the height of thirty thousand feet, was due to the extreme speed with which a perpendicular ascent is made. Doing it at an easy gradient and accustoming oneself to the lessened barometric pressure by slow degrees, there are no such dreadful symptoms. At the same great height I found that even without my oxygen inhaler I could breathe without undue distress. It was bitterly cold, however, and my thermometer was at zero Fahrenheit. At one-thirty I was nearly seven miles above the surface of the earth, and still ascending steadily. I found, however, that the rarefied air was giving markedly less support to my planes, and that my angle of ascent had to be considerably lowered in consequence. It was already clear that even with my light weight and strong engine-power there was a point in front of me where I should be held. To make matters worse, one of my sparking-plugs was in trouble again and there was intermittent missfiring in the engine. My heart was heavy with the fear of failure.

"It was about that time that I had a most extraordinary experience. Something whizzed past me in a trail of smoke and exploded with a loud, hissing sound, sending forth a cloud of steam. For the instant I could not imagine what had happened. Then I remembered that the earth is for ever being bombarded by meteor stones, and would be hardly inhabitable were they not in nearly every case turned to vapour in the outer layers of the atmosphere. Here is a new danger for the high-altitude man, for two others passed me when I was nearing the forty-thousand-foot mark. I cannot doubt that at the edge of the earth's envelope the risk would be a very real one.

"My barograph needle marked forty-one thousand three hundred when I became aware that I could go no farther. Physically, the strain was not as yet greater than I could bear, but my machine had reached its limit. The attenuated air gave no firm support to the wings, and the least tilt developed into side-slip, while she seemed sluggish on her controls. Possibly, had the engine been at its best, another thousand feet might have been within our capacity, but it was still missfiring, and two out of the ten cylinders appeared to be out of action. If I had not already reached the zone for which I was searching then I should never see it upon this journey. But was it not possible that I had attained it? Soaring in circles like a monstrous hawk upon the forty-thousand-foot level I let the monoplane guide herself, and with my Mannheim glass I made a careful observation of my surroundings. The heavens were perfectly clear; there was no indication of those dangers which I had imagined.

"I have said that I was soaring in circles. It struck me suddenly that I would do well to take a wider sweep and open up a new air-tract. If the hunter entered an earth-jungle he would drive through it if he wished to find his game. My reasoning had led me to believe that the air-jungle which I had imagined lay somewhere over Wiltshire. This should be to the south and west of me. I took my bearings from the sun, for the compass was hopeless and no trace of earth was to be seen--nothing but the distant silver cloud-plain. However, I got my direction as best I might and kept her head straight to the mark. I reckoned that my petrol supply would not last for more than another hour or so, but I could afford to use it to the last drop, since a single magnificent vol-plane could at any time take me to the earth.

"Suddenly I was aware of something new. The air in front of me had lost its crystal clearness. It was full of long, ragged wisps of something which I can only compare to very fine cigarette-smoke. It hung about in wreaths and coils, turning and twisting slowly in the sunlight. As the monoplane shot through it, I was aware of a faint taste of oil upon my lips, and there was a greasy scum upon the woodwork of the machine. Some infinitely fine organic matter appeared to be suspended in the atmosphere. There was no life there. It was inchoate and diffuse, extending for many square acres and then fringing off into the void. No, it was not life. But might it not be the remains of life? Above all, might it not be the food of life, of monstrous life, even as the humble grease of the ocean is the food for the mighty whale? The thought was in my mind when my eyes looked upwards and I saw the most wonderful vision that ever man has seen. Can I hope to convey it to you even as I saw it myself last Thursday?

"Conceive a jelly-fish such as sails in our summer seas, bell-shaped and of enormous size--far larger, I should judge, than the dome of St. Paul's. It was of a light pink colour veined with a delicate green, but the whole huge fabric so tenuous that it was but a fairy outline against the dark blue sky. It pulsated with a delicate and regular rhythm.

From it there depended two long, drooping green tentacles, which swayed slowly backwards and forwards. This gorgeous vision passed gently with noiseless dignity over my head, as light and fragile as a soap-bubble, and drifted upon its stately way.

"I had half-turned my monoplane, that I might look after this beautiful creature, when, in a moment, I found myself amidst a perfect fleet of them, of all sizes, but none so large as the first. Some were quite small, but the majority about as big as an average balloon, and with much the same curvature at the top. There was in them a delicacy of texture and colouring which reminded me of the finest Venetian glass. Pale shades of pink and green were the prevailing tints, but all had a lovely iridescence where the sun shimmered through their dainty forms. Some hundreds of them drifted past me, a wonderful fairy squadron of strange, unknown argosies of the sky--creatures whose forms and substance were so attuned to these pure heights that one could not conceive anything so delicate within actual sight or sound of earth.

"But soon my attention was drawn to a new phenomenon--the serpents of the outer air. These were long, thin, fantastic coils of vapour-like material, which turned and twisted with great speed, flying round and round at such a pace that the eyes could hardly follow them. Some of these ghost-like creatures were twenty or thirty feet long, but it was difficult to tell their girth, for their outline was so hazy that it seemed to fade away into the air around them. These air-snakes were of a very light grey or smoke colour, with some darker lines within, which gave the impression of a definite organism. One of them whisked past my very face, and I was conscious of a cold, clammy contact, but their composition was so unsubstantial that I could not connect them with any thought of physical danger, any more than the beautiful bell-like creatures which had preceded them. There was no more solidity in their frames than in the floating spume from a broken wave.

"But a more terrible experience was in store for me. Floating downwards from a great height there came a purplish patch of vapour, small as I saw it first, but rapidly enlarging as it approached me, until it appeared to be hundreds of square feet in size. Though fashioned of some transparent, jelly-like substance, it was none the less of much more definite outline and solid consistence than anything which I had seen before. There were more traces, too, of a physical organization, especially two vast shadowy, circular plates upon either side, which may have been eyes, and a perfectly solid white projection between them which was as curved and cruel as the beak of a vulture.

"The whole aspect of this monster was formidable and threatening, and it kept changing its colour from a very light mauve to a dark, angry purple so thick that it cast a shadow as it drifted between my monoplane and the sun. On the upper curve of its huge body there were three great projections which I can only describe as enormous bubbles, and I was convinced as I looked at them that they were charged with some extremely light gas which served to buoy-up the misshapen and semi-solid mass in the rarefied air. The creature moved swiftly along, keeping pace easily with the monoplane, and for twenty miles or more it formed my horrible escort, hovering over me like a bird of prey which is waiting to pounce. Its method of progression--done so swiftly that it was not easy to follow--was to throw out a long, glutinous streamer in front of it, which in turn seemed to draw forward the rest of the writhing body. So elastic and gelatinous was it that never for two successive minutes was it the same shape, and yet each change made it more threatening and loathsome than the last.

"I knew that it meant mischief. Every purple flush of its hideous body told me so. The vague, goggling eyes which were turned always upon me were cold and merciless in their viscid hatred. I dipped the nose of my monoplane downwards to escape it. As I did so, as quick as a flash there shot out a long tentacle from this mass of floating blubber, and it fell as light and sinuous as a whip-lash across the front of my machine. There was a loud hiss as it lay for a moment across the hot engine, and it whisked itself into the air again, while the huge flat body drew itself together as if in sudden pain. I dipped to a volpique, but again a tentacle fell over the monoplane and was shorn off by the propeller as easily as it might have cut through a smoke wreath. A long, gliding, sticky, serpent-like coil came from behind and caught me round the waist, dragging me out of the fuselage. I tore at it, my fingers sinking into the smooth, glue-like surface, and for an instant I disengaged myself, but only to be caught round the boot by another coil, which gave me a jerk that tilted me almost on to my back.

"As I fell over I blazed off both barrels of my gun, though, indeed, it was like attacking an elephant with a pea-shooter to imagine that any human weapon could cripple that mighty bulk. And yet I aimed better than I knew, for, with a loud report, one of the great blisters upon the creature's back exploded with the puncture of the buck-shot. It was very clear that my conjecture was right, and that these vast clear bladders were distended with some lifting gas, for in an instant the huge cloud-like body turned sideways, writhing desperately to find its balance, while the white beak snapped and gaped in horrible fury. But already I had shot away on the steepest glide that I dared to attempt, my engine still full on, the flying propeller and the force of gravity shooting me downwards like an aerolite. Far behind me I saw a dull, purplish smudge growing swiftly smaller and merging into the blue sky behind it. I was safe out of the deadly jungle of the outer air.

"Once out of danger I throttled my engine, for nothing tears a machine to pieces quicker than running on full power from a height. It was a glorious spiral vol-plane from nearly eight miles of altitude--first, to the level of the silver cloud-bank, then to that of the storm-cloud beneath it, and finally, in beating rain, to the surface of the earth. I saw the Bristol Channel beneath me as I broke from the clouds, but, having still some petrol in my tank, I got twenty miles inland before I found myself stranded in a field half a mile from the village of Ashcombe. There I got three tins of petrol from a passing motor-car, and at ten minutes past six that evening I alighted gently in my own home meadow at Devizes, after such a journey as no mortal upon earth has ever yet taken and lived to tell the tale. I have seen the beauty and I have seen the horror of the heights--and greater beauty or greater horror than that is not within the ken of man.

"And now it is my plan to go once again before I give my results to the world. My reason for this is that I must surely have something to show by way of proof before I lay such a tale before my fellow-men. It is true that others will soon follow and will confirm what I have said, and yet I should wish to carry conviction from the first. Those lovely iridescent bubbles of the air should not be hard to capture. They drift slowly upon their way, and the swift monoplane could intercept their leisurely course. It is likely enough that they would dissolve in the heavier layers of the atmosphere, and that some small heap of amorphous jelly might be all that I should bring to earth with me. And yet something there would surely be by which I could substantiate my story. Yes, I will go, even if I run a risk by doing so. These purple horrors would not seem to be numerous. It is probable that I shall not see one. If I do I shall dive at once. At the worst there is always the shot-gun and my knowledge of . . ."

Here a page of the manuscript is unfortunately missing. On the next page is written, in large, straggling writing:--

"Forty-three thousand feet. I shall never see earth again. They are beneath me, three of them. God help me; it is a dreadful death to die!"

Such in its entirety is the Joyce-Armstrong Statement. Of the man nothing has since been seen. Pieces of his shattered monoplane have been picked up in the preserves of Mr. Budd-Lushington upon the borders of Kent and Sussex, within a few miles of the spot where the note-book was discovered. If the unfortunate aviator's theory is correct that this air- jungle, as he called it, existed only over the south-west of England, then it would seem that he had fled from it at the full speed of his monoplane, but had been overtaken and devoured by these horrible creatures at some spot in the outer atmosphere above the place where the grim relics were found. The picture of that monoplane skimming down the sky, with the nameless terrors flying as swiftly beneath it and cutting it off always from the earth while they gradually closed in upon their victim, is one upon which a man who valued his sanity would prefer not to dwell. There are many, as I am aware, who still jeer at the facts which I have here set down, but even they must admit that Joyce-Armstrong has disappeared, and I would commend to them his own words: "This note-book may explain what I am trying to do, and how I lost my life in doing it. But no drivel about accidents or mysteries, if you please."

THE SURGEON OF GASTER FELL

I--HOW THE WOMAN CAME TO KIRKBY-MALHOUSE

Bleak and wind-swept is the little town of Kirkby-Malhouse, harsh and forbidding are the fells upon which it stands. It stretches in a single line of grey-stone, slate-roofed houses, dotted down the furze-clad slope of the rolling moor.

In this lonely and secluded village, I, James Upperton, found myself in the summer of '85. Little as the hamlet had to offer, it contained that for which I yearned above all things--seclusion and freedom from all which might distract my mind from the high and weighty subjects which engaged it. But the inquisitiveness of my landlady made my lodgings undesirable and I determined to seek new quarters.

As it chanced, I had in one of my rambles come upon an isolated dwelling in the very heart of these lonely moors, which I at once determined should be my own. It was a two-roomed cottage, which had once belonged to some shepherd, but had long been deserted, and was crumbling rapidly to ruin. In the winter floods, the Gaster Beck, which runs down Gaster Fell, where the little dwelling stood, had overswept its banks and torn away a part of the wall. The roof was in ill case, and the scattered slates lay thick amongst the grass. Yet the main shell of the house stood firm and true; and it was no great task for me to have all that was amiss set right.

The two rooms I laid out in a widely different manner--my own tastes are of a Spartan turn, and the outer chamber was so planned as to accord with them. An oil-stove by Rippingille of Birmingham furnished me with the means of cooking; while two great bags, the one of flour, and the other of potatoes, made me independent of all supplies from without. In diet I had long been a Pythagorean, so that the scraggy, long-limbed sheep which browsed upon the wiry grass by the Gaster Beck had little to fear from their new companion. A nine-gallon cask of oil served me as a sideboard; while a square table, a deal chair and a truckle-bed completed the list of my domestic fittings. At the head of my couch hung two unpainted shelves--the lower for my dishes and cooking utensils, the upper for the few portraits which took me back to the little that was pleasant in the long, wearisome toiling for wealth and for pleasure which had marked the life I had left behind.

If this dwelling-room of mine were plain even to squalor, its poverty was more than atoned for by the luxury of the chamber which was destined to serve me as my study. I had ever held that it was best for my mind to be surrounded by such objects as would be in harmony with the studies which occupied it, and that the loftiest and most ethereal conditions of thought are only possible amid surroundings which please the eye and gratify the senses. The room which I had set apart for my mystic studies was set forth in a style as gloomy and majestic as the thoughts and aspirations with which it was to harmonise. Both walls and ceilings were covered with a paper of the richest and glossiest black, on which was traced a lurid and arabesque pattern of dead gold. A black velvet curtain covered the single diamond-paned window; while a thick, yielding carpet of the same material prevented the sound of my own footfalls, as I paced backward and forward, from breaking the current of my thought. Along the cornices ran gold rods, from which depended six pictures, all of the sombre and imaginative caste, which chimed best with my fancy.

And yet it was destined that ere ever I reached this quiet harbour I should learn that I was still one of humankind, and that it is an ill thing to strive to break the bond which binds us to our fellows. It was but two nights before the date I had fixed upon for my change of dwelling, when I was conscious of a bustle in the house beneath, with the bearing of heavy burdens up the creaking stair, and the harsh voice of my landlady, loud in welcome and protestations of joy. From time to time, amid the whirl of words, I could hear a gentle and softly modulated voice, which struck pleasantly upon my ear after the long weeks during which I had listened only to the rude dialect of the dalesmen. For an hour I could hear the dialogue beneath--the high voice and the low, with clatter of cup and clink of spoon, until at last a light, quick step passed my study door, and I knew that my new fellow lodger had sought her room.

On the morning after this incident I was up betimes, as is my wont; but I was surprised, on glancing from my window, to see that our new inmate was earlier still. She was walking down the narrow pathway, which zigzags over the fell--a tall woman, slender, her head sunk upon her breast, her arms filled with a bristle of wild flowers, which she had gathered in her morning rambles. The white and pink of her dress, and the touch of deep red ribbon in her broad drooping hat, formed a pleasant dash of colour against the dun-tinted landscape. She was some distance off when I first set eyes upon her, yet I knew that this wandering woman could be none other than our arrival of last night, for there was a grace and refinement in her bearing which marked her from the dwellers of the fells. Even as I watched, she passed swiftly and lightly down the pathway, and turning through the wicket gate, at the further end of our cottage garden, she seated herself upon the green bank which faced my window, and strewing her flowers in front of her, set herself to arrange them.

As she sat there, with the rising sun at her back, and the glow of the morning spreading like an aureole around her stately and well-poised head, I could see that she was a woman of extraordinary personal beauty. Her face was Spanish rather than English in its type--oval, olive, with black, sparkling eyes, and a sweetly sensitive mouth. From under the broad straw hat two thick coils of blue-black hair curved down on either side of her graceful, queenly neck. I was surprised, as I watched her, to see that her shoes and skirt bore witness to a journey rather than to a mere morning ramble. Her light dress was stained, wet and bedraggled; while her boots were thick with the yellow soil of the fells. Her face, too, wore a weary expression, and her young beauty seemed to be clouded over by the shadow of inward trouble. Even as I watched her, she burst suddenly into wild weeping, and throwing down her bundle of flowers ran swiftly into the house.

Distrait as I was and weary of the ways of the world, I was conscious of a sudden pang of sympathy and grief as I looked upon the spasm of despair which, seemed to convulse this strange and beautiful woman. I bent to my books, and yet my thoughts would ever turn to her proud clear-cut face, her weather-stained dress, her drooping head, and the sorrow which lay in each line and feature of her pensive face.

Mrs. Adams, my landlady, was wont to carry up my frugal breakfast; yet it was very rarely that I allowed her to break the current of my thoughts, or to draw my mind by her idle chatter from weightier things. This morning, however, for once, she found me in a listening mood, and with little prompting, proceeded to pour into my ears all that she knew of our beautiful visitor.

"Miss Eva Cameron be her name, sir," she said: "but who she be, or where she came fra, I know little more than yoursel'. Maybe it was the same reason that brought her to Kirkby-Malhouse as fetched you there yoursel', sir."

"Possibly," said I, ignoring the covert question; "but I should hardly have thought that Kirkby-Malhouse was a place which offered any great attractions to a young lady."

"Heh, sir!" she cried, "there's the wonder of it. The leddy has just come fra France; and how her folk come to learn of me is just a wonder. A week ago, up comes a man to my door--a fine man, sir, and a gentleman, as one could see with half an eye. 'You are Mrs. Adams,' says he. 'I engage your rooms for Miss Cameron,' says he. 'She will be here in a week,' says he; and then off without a word of terms. Last night there comes the young leddy hersel'--soft-spoken and downcast, with a touch of the French in her speech. But my sakes, sir! I must away and mak' her some tea, for she'll feel lonesome-like, poor lamb, when she wakes under a strange roof."

II--HOW I WENT FORTH TO GASTER FELL

I was still engaged upon my breakfast when I heard the clatter of dishes and the landlady's footfall as she passed toward her new lodger's room. An instant afterward she had rushed down the passage and burst in upon me with uplifted hand and startled eyes. "Lord 'a mercy, sir!" she cried, "and asking your pardon for troubling you, but I'm feared o' the young leddy, sir; she is not in her room."

"Why, there she is," said I, standing up and glancing through the casement. "She has gone back for the flowers she left upon the bank."

"Oh, sir, see her boots and her dress!" cried the landlady, wildly. "I wish her mother was here, sir--I do. Where she has been is more than I ken, but her bed has not been lain on this night."

"She has felt restless, doubtless, and went for a walk, though the hour was certainly a strange one."

Mrs. Adams pursed her lip and shook her head. But then as she stood at the casement, the girl beneath looked smilingly up at her and beckoned to her with a merry gesture to open the window.

"Have you my tea there?" she asked in a rich, clear voice, with a touch of the mincing French accent.

"It is in your room, miss."

"Look at my boots, Mrs. Adams!" she cried, thrusting them out from under her skirt. "These fells of yours are dreadful places--effroyable--one inch, two inch; never have I seen such mud! My dress, too--voila!"

"Eh, miss, but you are in a pickle," cried the landlady, as she gazed down at the bedraggled gown. "But you must be main weary and heavy for sleep."

"No, no," she answered, laughingly, "I care not for sleep. What is sleep? it is a little death--voila tout. But for me to walk, to run, to beathe the air--that is to live. I was not tired, and so all night I have explored these fells of Yorkshire."

"Lord 'a mercy, miss, and where did you go?" asked Mrs. Adams.

She waved her hand round in a sweeping gesture which included the whole western horizon. "There," she cried. "O comme elles sont tristes et sauvages, ces collines! But I have flowers here. You will give me water, will you not? They will wither else." She gathered her treasures in her lap, and a moment later we heard her light, springy footfall upon the stair.

So she had been out all night, this strange woman. What motive could have taken her from her snug room on to the bleak, wind-swept hills? Could it be merely the restlessness, the love of adventure of a young girl? Or was there, possibly, some deeper meaning in this nocturnal journey?

Deep as were the mysteries which my studies had taught me to solve, here was a human problem which for the moment at least was beyond my comprehension. I had walked out on the moor in the forenoon, and on my return, as I topped the brow that overlooks the little town, I saw my fellow-lodger some little distance off among the gorse. She had raised a light easel in front of her, and with papered board laid across it, was preparing to paint the magnificent landscape of rock and moor which stretched away in front of her. As I watched her I saw that she was looking anxiously to right and left. Close by me a pool of water had formed in a hollow. Dipping the cup of my pocket-flask into it, I carried it across to her.

"Miss Cameron, I believe," said I. "I am your fellow-lodger. Upperton is my name. We must introduce ourselves in these wilds if we are not to be for ever strangers."

"Oh, then, you live also with Mrs. Adams!" she cried. "I had thought that there were none but peasants in this strange place."

"I am a visitor, like yourself," I answered. "I am a student, and have come for quiet and repose, which my studies demand."

"Quiet, indeed!" said she, glancing round at the vast circle of silent moors, with the one tiny line of grey cottages which sloped down beneath us.

"And yet not quiet enough," I answered, laughing, "for I have been forced to move further into the fells for the absolute peace which I require."

"Have you, then, built a house upon the fells?" she asked, arching her eyebrows.

"I have, and hope within a few days to occupy it."

"Ah, but that is triste," she cried. "And where is it, then, this house which you have built?"

"It is over yonder," I answered. "See that stream which lies like a silver band upon the distant moor? It is the Gaster Beck, and it runs through Gaster Fell."

She started, and turned upon me her great dark, questioning eyes with a look in which surprise, incredulity, and something akin to horror seemed to be struggling for mastery.

"And you will live on the Gaster Fell?" she cried.

"So I have planned. But what do you know of Gaster Fell, Miss Cameron?" I asked. "I had thought that you were a stranger in these parts."

"Indeed, I have never been here before," she answered. "But I have heard my brother talk of these Yorkshire moors; and, if I mistake not, I have heard him name this very one as the wildest and most savage of them all."

"Very likely," said I, carelessly. "It is indeed a dreary place."

"Then why live there?" she cried, eagerly. "Consider the loneliness, the barrenness, the want of all comfort and of all aid, should aid be needed."

"Aid! What aid should be needed on Gaster Fell?"

She looked down and shrugged her shoulders. "Sickness may come in all places," said she. "If I were a man I do not think I would live alone on Gaster Fell."

"I have braved worse dangers than that," said I, laughing; "but I fear that your picture will be spoiled, for the clouds are banking up, and already I feel a few raindrops."

Indeed, it was high time we were on our way to shelter, for even as I spoke there came the sudden, steady swish of the shower. Laughing merrily, my companion threw her light shawl over her head, and, seizing picture and easel, ran with the lithe grace of a young fawn down the furze-clad slope, while I followed after with camp-stool and paint-box.

* * * * *

It was the eve of my departure from Kirkby-Malhouse that we sat upon the green bank in the garden, she with dark dreamy eyes looking sadly out over the sombre fells; while I, with a book upon my knee, glanced covertly at her lovely profile and marvelled to myself how twenty years of life could have stamped so sad and wistful an expression upon it.

"You have read much," I remarked at last. "Women have opportunities now such as their mothers never knew. Have you ever thought of going further--or seeking a course of college or even a learned profession?"

She smiled wearily at the thought.

"I have no aim, no ambition," she said. "My future is black--confused--a chaos. My life is like to one of these paths upon the fells. You have seen them, Monsieur Upperton. They are smooth and straight and clear where they begin; but soon they wind to left and wind to right, and so mid rocks and crags until they lose themselves in some quagmire. At Brussels my path was straight; but now, mon Dieu! who is there can tell me where it leads?"

"It might take no prophet to do that, Miss Cameron," quoth I, with the fatherly manner which twoscore years may show toward one. "If I may read your life, I would venture to say that you were destined to fulfil the lot of women--to make some good man happy, and to shed around, in some wider circle, the pleasure which your society has given me since first I knew you."

"I will never marry," said she, with a sharp decision, which surprised and somewhat amused me.

"Not marry--and why?"

A strange look passed over her sensitive features, and she plucked nervously at the grass on the bank beside her.

"I dare not," said she in a voice that quivered with emotion.

"Dare not?"

"It is not for me. I have other things to do. That path of which I spoke is one which I must tread alone."

"But this is morbid," said I. "Why should your lot, Miss Cameron, be separate from that of my own sisters, or the thousand other young ladies whom every season brings out into the world? But perhaps it is that you have a fear and distrust of mankind. Marriage brings a risk as well as a happiness."

"The risk would be with the man who married me," she cried. And then in an instant, as though she had said too much, she sprang to her feet and drew her mantle round her. "The night air is chill, Mr. Upperton," said she, and so swept swiftly away, leaving me to muse over the strange words which had fallen from her lips.

Clearly, it was time that I should go. I set my teeth and vowed that another day should not have passed before I should have snapped this newly formed tie and sought the lonely retreat which awaited me upon the moors. Breakfast was hardly over in the morning before a peasant dragged up to the door the rude hand-cart which was to convey my few personal belongings to my new dwelling. My fellow-lodger had kept her room; and, steeled as my mind was against her influence, I was yet conscious of a little throb of disappointment that she should allow me to depart without a word of farewell. My hand-cart with its load of books had already started, and I, having shaken hands with Mrs. Adams, was about to follow it, when there was a quick scurry of feet on the stair, and there she was beside me all panting with her own haste.

"Then you go--you really go?" said she.

"My studies call me."

"And to Gaster Fell?" she asked.

"Yes; to the cottage which I have built there."

"And you will live alone there?"

"With my hundred companions who lie in that cart."

"Ah, books!" she cried, with a pretty shrug of her graceful shoulders. "But you will make me a promise?"

"What is it?" I asked, in surprise.

"It is a small thing. You will not refuse me?"

"You have but to ask it."

She bent forward her beautiful face with an expression of the most intense earnestness. "You will bolt your door at night?" said she; and was gone ere I could say a word in answer to her extraordinary request.

It was a strange thing for me to find myself at last duly installed in my lonely dwelling. For me, now, the horizon was bounded by the barren circle of wiry, unprofitable grass, patched over with furze bushes and scarred by the profusion of Nature's gaunt and granite ribs. A duller, wearier waste I have never seen; but its dullness was its very charm.

And yet the very first night which I spent at Gaster Fell there came a strange incident to lead my thoughts back once more to the world which I had left behind me.

It had been a sullen and sultry evening, with great livid cloud-banks mustering in the west. As the night wore on, the air within my little cabin became closer and more oppressive. A weight seemed to rest upon my brow and my chest. From far away the low rumble of thunder came moaning over the moor. Unable to sleep, I dressed, and standing at my cottage door, looked on the black solitude which surrounded me.

Taking the narrow sheep path which ran by this stream, I strolled along it for some hundred yards, and had turned to retrace my steps, when the moon was finally buried beneath an ink-black cloud, and the darkness deepened so suddenly that I could see neither the path at my feet, the stream upon my right, nor the rocks upon my left. I was standing groping about in the thick gloom, when there came a crash of thunder with a flash of lightning which lighted up the whole vast fell, so that every bush and rock stood out clear and hard in the vivid light. It was but for an instant, and yet that momentary view struck a thrill of fear and astonishment through me, for in my very path, not twenty yards before me, there stood a woman, the livid light beating upon her face and showing up every detail of her dress and features.

There was no mistaking those dark eyes, that tall, graceful figure. It was she--Eva Cameron, the woman whom I thought I had for ever left. For an instant I stood petrified, marvelling whether this could indeed be she, or whether it was some figment conjured up by my excited brain. Then I ran swiftly forward in the direction where I had seen her, calling loudly upon her, but without reply. Again I called, and again no answer came back, save the melancholy wail of the owl. A second flash illuminated the landscape, and the moon burst out from behind its cloud. But I could not, though I climbed upon a knoll which overlooked the whole moor, see any sign of this strange midnight wanderer. For an hour or more I traversed the fell, and at last found myself back at my little cabin, still uncertain as to whether it had been a woman or a shadow upon which I gazed.

III--OF THE GREY COTTAGE IN THE GLEN

It was either on the fourth or the fifth day after I had taken possession of my cottage that I was astonished to hear footsteps upon the grass outside, quickly followed by a crack, as from a stick upon the door. The explosion of an infernal machine would hardly have surprised or discomfited me more. I had hoped to have shaken off all intrusion for ever, yet here was somebody beating at my door with as little ceremony as if it had been a village ale-house. Hot with anger, I flung down my book and withdrew the bolt just as my visitor had raised his stick to renew his rough application for admittance. He was a tall, powerful man, tawny- bearded and deep-chested, clad in a loose-fitting suit of tweed, cut for comfort rather than elegance. As he stood in the shimmering sunlight, I took in every feature of his face. The large, fleshy nose; the steady blue eyes, with their thick thatch of overhanging brows; the broad forehead, all knitted and lined with furrows, which were strangely at variance with his youthful bearing. In spite of his weather-stained felt hat, and the coloured handkerchief slung round his muscular brown neck, I could see at a glance he was a man of breeding and education. I had been prepared for some wandering shepherd or uncouth tramp, but this apparition fairly disconcerted me.

"You look astonished," said he, with a smile. "Did you think, then, that you were the only man in the world with a taste for solitude? You see that there are other hermits in the wilderness besides yourself."

"Do you mean to say that you live here?" I asked in no conciliatory voice.

"Up yonder," he answered, tossing his head backward. "I thought as we were neighbours, Mr. Upperton, that I could not do less than look in and see if I could assist you in any way."

"Thank you," I said coldly, standing with my hand upon the latch of the door. "I am a man of simple tastes, and you can do nothing for me. You have the advantage of me in knowing my name."

He appeared to be chilled by my ungracious manner.

"I learned it from the masons who were at work here," he said. "As for me, I am a surgeon, the surgeon of Gaster Fell. That is the name I have gone by in these parts, and it serves as well as another."

"Not much room for practice here?" I observed.

"Not a soul except yourself for miles on either side."

"You appear to have had need of some assistance yourself," I remarked, glancing at a broad white splash, as from the recent action of some powerful acid, upon his sunburnt cheek.

"That is nothing," he answered, curtly, turning his face half round to hide the mark. "I must get back, for I have a companion who is waiting for me. If I can ever do anything for you, pray let me know. You have only to follow the beck upward for a mile or so to find my place. Have you a bolt on the inside of your door?"

"Yes," I answered, rather startled at this question.

"Keep it bolted, then," he said. "The fell is a strange place. You never know who may be about. It is as well to be on the safe side.

Goodbye." He raised his hat, turned on his heel and lounged away along the bank of the little stream.

I was still standing with my hand upon the latch, gazing after my unexpected visitor, when I became aware of yet another dweller in the wilderness. Some distance along the path which the stranger was taking there lay a great grey boulder, and leaning against this was a small, wizened man, who stood erect as the other approached, and advanced to meet him. The two talked for a minute or more, the taller man nodding his head frequently in my direction, as though describing what had passed between us. Then they walked on together, and disappeared in a dip of the fell. Presently I saw them ascending once more some rising ground farther on. My acquaintance had thrown his arm round his elderly friend, either from affection or from a desire to aid him up the steep incline. The square burly figure and its shrivelled, meagre companion stood out against the sky-line, and turning their faces, they looked back at me. At the sight, I slammed the door, lest they should be encouraged to return. But when I peeped from the window some minutes afterward, I perceived that they were gone.

All day I bent over the Egyptian papyrus upon which I was engaged; but neither the subtle reasonings of the ancient philosopher of Memphis, nor the mystic meaning which lay in his pages, could raise my mind from the things of earth. Evening was drawing in before I threw my work aside in despair. My heart was bitter against this man for his intrusion. Standing by the beck which purled past the door of my cabin, I cooled my heated brow, and thought the matter over. Clearly it was the small mystery hanging over these neighbours of mine which had caused my mind to run so persistently on them. That cleared up, they would no longer cause an obstacle to my studies. What was to hinder me, then, from walking in the direction of their dwelling, and observing for myself, without permitting them to suspect my presence, what manner of men they might be? Doubtless, their mode of life would be found to admit of some simple and prosaic explanation. In any case, the evening was fine, and a walk would be bracing for mind and body. Lighting my pipe, I set off over the moors in the direction which they had taken.

About half-way down a wild glen there stood a small clump of gnarled and stunted oak trees. From behind these, a thin dark column of smoke rose into the still evening air. Clearly this marked the position of my neighbour's house. Trending away to the left, I was able to gain the shelter of a line of rocks, and so reach a spot from which I could command a view of the building without exposing myself to any risk of being observed. It was a small, slate-covered cottage, hardly larger than the boulders among which it lay. Like my own cabin, it showed signs of having been constructed for the use of some shepherd; but, unlike mine, no pains had been taken by the tenants to improve and enlarge it. Two little peeping windows, a cracked and weather-beaten door, and a discoloured barrel for catching the rain water, were the only external objects from which I might draw deductions as to the dwellers within. Yet even in these there was food for thought, for as I drew nearer, still concealing myself behind the ridge, I saw that thick bars of iron covered the windows, while the old door was slashed and plated with the same metal. These strange precautions, together with the wild surroundings and unbroken solitude, gave an indescribably ill omen and fearsome character to the solitary building. Thrusting my pipe into my pocket, I crawled upon my hands and knees through the gorse and ferns until I was within a hundred yards of my neighbour's door. There, finding that I could not approach nearer without fear of detection, I crouched down, and set myself to watch.

I had hardly settled into my hiding place, when the door of the cottage swung open, and the man who had introduced himself to me as the surgeon of Gaster Fell came out, bareheaded, with a spade in his hands. In front of the door there was a small cultivated patch containing potatoes, peas and other forms of green stuff, and here he proceeded to busy himself, trimming, weeding and arranging, singing the while in a powerful though not very musical voice. He was all engrossed in his work, with his back to the cottage, when there emerged from the half-open door the same attenuated creature whom I had seen in the morning. I could perceive now that he was a man of sixty, wrinkled, bent, and feeble, with sparse, grizzled hair, and long, colourless face. With a cringing, sidelong gait, he shuffled toward his companion, who was unconscious of his approach until he was close upon him. His light footfall or his breathing may have finally given notice of his proximity, for the worker sprang round and faced him. Each made a quick step toward the other, as though in greeting, and then--even now I feel the horror of the instant--the tall man rushed upon and knocked his companion to the earth, then whipping up his body, ran with great speed over the intervening ground and disappeared with his burden into the house.

Case hardened as I was by my varied life, the suddenness and violence of the thing made me shudder. The man's age, his feeble frame, his humble and deprecating manner, all cried shame against the deed. So hot was my anger, that I was on the point of striding up to the cabin, unarmed as I was, when the sound of voices from within showed me that the victim had recovered. The sun had sunk beneath the horizon, and all was grey, save a red feather in the cap of Pennigent. Secure in the failing light, I approached near and strained my ears to catch what was passing. I could hear the high, querulous voice of the elder man and the deep, rough monotone of his assailant, mixed with a strange metallic jangling and clanking. Presently the surgeon came out, locked the door behind him and stamped up and down in the twilight, pulling at his hair and brandishing his arms, like a man demented. Then he set off, walking rapidly up the valley, and I soon lost sight of him among the rocks.

When his footsteps had died away in the distance, I drew nearer to the cottage. The prisoner within was still pouring forth a stream of words, and moaning from time to time like a man in pain. These words resolved themselves, as I approached, into prayers--shrill, voluble prayers, pattered forth with the intense earnestness of one who sees impending an imminent danger. There was to me something inexpressibly awesome in this gush of solemn entreaty from the lonely sufferer, meant for no human ear, and jarring upon the silence of the night. I was still pondering whether I should mix myself in the affair or not, when I heard in the distance the sound of the surgeon's returning footfall. At that I drew myself up quickly by the iron bars and glanced in through the diamond-paned window. The interior of the cottage was lighted up by a lurid glow, coming from what I afterward discovered to be a chemical furnace. By its rich light I could distinguish a great litter of retorts, test tubes and condensers, which sparkled over the table, and threw strange, grotesque shadows on the wall. On the further side of the room was a wooden framework resembling a hencoop, and in this, still absorbed in prayer, knelt the man whose voice I heard. The red glow beating upon his upturned face made it stand out from the shadow like a painting from Rembrandt, showing up every wrinkle upon the parchment-like skin. I had but time for a fleeting glance; then, dropping from the window, I made off through the rocks and the heather, nor slackened my pace until I found myself back in my cabin once more. There I threw myself upon my couch, more disturbed and shaken than I had ever thought to feel again.

Such doubts as I might have had as to whether I had indeed seen my former fellow-lodger upon the night of the thunderstorm were resolved the next morning. Strolling along down the path which led to the fell, I saw in one spot where the ground was soft the impressions of a foot--the small, dainty foot of a well-booted woman. That tiny heel and high instep could have belonged to none other than my companion of Kirkby-Malhouse. I followed her trail for some distance, till it still pointed, as far as I could discern it, to the lonely and ill-omened cottage. What power could there be to draw this tender girl, through wind and rain and darkness, across the fearsome moors to that strange rendezvous?

I have said that a little beck flowed down the valley and past my very door. A week or so after the doings which I have described, I was seated by my window when I perceived something white drifting slowly down the stream. My first thought was that it was a drowning sheep; but picking up my stick, I strolled to the bank and hooked it ashore. On examination it proved to be a large sheet, torn and tattered, with the initials J. C. in the corner. What gave it its sinister significance, however, was that from hem to hem it was all dabbled and discoloured.

Shutting the door of my cabin, I set off up the glen in the direction of the surgeon's cabin. I had not gone far before I perceived the very man himself. He was walking rapidly along the hillside, beating the furze bushes with a cudgel and bellowing like a madman. Indeed, at the sight of him, the doubts as to his sanity which had arisen in my mind were strengthened and confirmed.

As he approached I noticed that his left arm was suspended in a sling. On perceiving me he stood irresolute, as though uncertain whether to come over to me or not. I had no desire for an interview with him, however, so I hurried past him, on which he continued on his way, still shouting and striking about with his club. When he had disappeared over the fells, I made my way down to his cottage, determined to find some clue to what had occurred. I was surprised, on reaching it, to find the iron- plated door flung wide open. The ground immediately outside it was marked with the signs of a struggle. The chemical apparatus within and the furniture were all dashed about and shattered. Most suggestive of all, the sinister wooden cage was stained with blood-marks, and its unfortunate occupant had disappeared. My heart was heavy for the little man, for I was assured I should never see him in this world more.

There was nothing in the cabin to throw any light upon the identity of my neighbours. The room was stuffed with chemical instruments. In one corner a small bookcase contained a choice selection of works of science. In another was a pile of geological specimens collected from the limestone.

I caught no glimpse of the surgeon upon my homeward journey; but when I reached my cottage I was astonished and indignant to find that somebody had entered it in my absence. Boxes had been pulled out from under the bed, the curtains disarranged, the chairs drawn out from the wall. Even my study had not been safe from this rough intruder, for the prints of a heavy boot were plainly visible on the ebony-black carpet.

IV--OF THE MAN WHO CAME IN THE NIGHT

The night set in gusty and tempestuous, and the moon was all girt with ragged clouds. The wind blew in melancholy gusts, sobbing and sighing over the moor, and setting all the gorse bushes agroaning. From time to time a little sputter of rain pattered up against the window-pane. I sat until near midnight, glancing over the fragment on immortality by Iamblichus, the Alexandrian platonist, of whom the Emperor Julian said that he was posterior to Plato in time but not in genius. At last, shutting up my book, I opened my door and took a last look at the dreary fell and still more dreary sky. As I protruded my head, a swoop of wind caught me and sent the red ashes of my pipe sparkling and dancing through the darkness. At the same moment the moon shone brilliantly out from between two clouds, and I saw, sitting on the hillside, not two hundred yards from my door, the man who called himself the surgeon of Gaster Fell. He was squatted among the heather, his elbows upon his knees, and his chin resting upon his hands, as motionless as a stone, with his gaze fixed steadily upon the door of my dwelling.

At the sight of this ill-omened sentinel, a chill of horror and of fear shot through me, for his gloomy and mysterious associations had cast a glamour round the man, and the hour and place were in keeping with his sinister presence. In a moment, however, a manly glow of resentment and self-confidence drove this petty emotion from my mind, and I strode fearlessly in his direction. He rose as I approached and faced me, with the moon shining on his grave, bearded face and glittering on his eyeballs. "What is the meaning of this?" I cried, as I came upon him. "What right have you to play the spy on me?"

I could see the flush of anger rise on his face. "Your stay in the country has made you forget your manners," he said. "The moor is free to all."

"You will say next that my house is free to all," I said, hotly. "You have had the impertience to ransack it in my absence this afternoon."

He started, and his features showed the most intense excitement. "I swear to you that I had no hand in it!" he cried. "I have never set foot in your house in my life. Oh, sir, sir, if you will but believe me, there is a danger hanging over you, and you would do well to be careful."

"I have had enough of you," I said. "I saw that cowardly blow you struck when you thought no human eye rested upon you. I have been to your cottage, too, and know all that it has to tell. If there is a law in England, you shall hang for what you have done. As to me, I am an old soldier, sir, and I am armed. I shall not fasten my door. But if you or any other villain attempt to cross my threshold it shall be at your own risk." With these words, I swung round upon my heel and strode into my cabin.

For two days the wind freshened and increased, with constant squalls of rain until on the third night the most furious storm was raging which I can ever recollect in England. I felt that it was positively useless to go to bed, nor could I concentrate my mind sufficiently to read a book. I turned my lamp half down to moderate the glare, and leaning back in my chair, I gave myself up to reverie. I must have lost all perception of time, for I have no recollection how long I sat there on the borderland betwixt thought and slumber. At last, about 3 or possibly 4 o'clock, I came to myself with a start--not only came to myself, but with every sense and nerve upon the strain. Looking round my chamber in the dim light, I could not see anything to justify my sudden trepidation. The homely room, the rain-blurred window and the rude wooden door were all as they had been. I had begun to persuade myself that some half-formed dream had sent that vague thrill through my nerves, when in a moment I became conscious of what it was. It was a sound--the sound of a human step outside my solitary cottage.

Amid the thunder and the rain and the wind I could hear it--a dull, stealthy footfall, now on the grass, now on the stones--occasionally stopping entirely, then resumed, and ever drawing nearer. I sat breathlessly, listening to the eerie sound. It had stopped now at my very door, and was replaced by a panting and gasping, as of one who has travelled fast and far.

By the flickering light of the expiring lamp I could see that the latch of my door was twitching, as though a gentle pressure was exerted on it from without. Slowly, slowly, it rose, until it was free of the catch, and then there was a pause of a quarter minute or more, while I still eat silent with dilated eyes and drawn sabre. Then, very slowly, the door began to revolve upon its hinges, and the keen air of the night came whistling through the slit. Very cautiously it was pushed open, so that never a sound came from the rusty hinges. As the aperture enlarged, I became aware of a dark, shadowy figure upon my threshold, and of a pale face that looked in at me. The features were human, but the eyes were not. They seemed to burn through the darkness with a greenish brilliancy of their own; and in their baleful, shifty glare I was conscious of the very spirit of murder. Springing from my chair, I had raised my naked sword, when, with a wild shouting, a second figure dashed up to my door. At its approach my shadowy visitant uttered a shrill cry, and fled away across the fells, yelping like a beaten hound.

Tingling with my recent fear, I stood at my door, peering through the night with the discordant cry of the fugitives still ringing in my ears. At that moment a vivid flash of lightning illuminated the whole landscape and made it as clear as day. By its light I saw far away upon the hillside two dark figures pursuing each other with extreme rapidity across the fells. Even at that distance the contrast between them forbid all doubt as to their identity. The first was the small, elderly man, whom I had supposed to be dead; the second was my neighbour, the surgeon. For an instant they stood out clear and hard in the unearthly light; in the next, the darkness had closed over them, and they were gone. As I turned to re-enter my chamber, my foot rattled against something on my threshold. Stooping, I found it was a straight knife, fashioned entirely of lead, and so soft and brittle that it was a strange choice for a weapon. To render it more harmless, the top had been cut square off. The edge, however, had been assiduously sharpened against a stone, as was evident from the markings upon it, so that it was still a dangerous implement in the grasp of a determined man.

And what was the meaning of it all? you ask. Many a drama which I have come across in my wandering life, some as strange and as striking as this one, has lacked the ultimate explanation which you demand. Fate is a grand weaver of tales; but she ends them, as a rule, in defiance of all artistic laws, and with an unbecoming want of regard for literary propriety. As it happens, however, I have a letter before me as I write which I may add without comment, and which will clear all that may remain dark.

"KIRKBY LUNATIC ASYLUM,
"September 4th, 1885.

"SIR,--I am deeply conscious that some apology and explanation is due to you for the very startling and, in your eyes, mysterious events which have recently occurred, and which have so seriously interfered with the retired existence which you desire to lead. I should have called upon you on the morning after the recapture of my father, but my knowledge of your dislike to visitors and also of--you will excuse my saying it--your very violent temper, led me to think that it was better to communicate with you by letter.

"My poor father was a hard-working general practitioner in Birmingham, where his name is still remembered and respected. About ten years ago he began to show signs of mental aberration, which we were inclined to put down to overwork and the effects of a sunstroke. Feeling my own incompetence to pronounce upon a case of such importance, I at once sought the highest advice in Birmingham and London. Among others we consulted the eminent alienist, Mr. Fraser Brown, who pronounced my father's case to be intermittent in its nature, but dangerous during the paroxysms. 'It may take a homicidal, or it may take a religious turn,' he said; 'or it may prove to be a mixture of both. For months he may be as well as you or me, and then in a moment he may break out. You will incur a great responsibility if you leave him without supervision.'

"I need say no more, sir. You will understand the terrible task which has fallen upon my poor sister and me in endeavouring to save my father from the asylum which in his sane moments filled him with horror. I can only regret that your peace has been disturbed by our misfortunes, and I offer you in my sister's name and my own our apologies."

"Yours truly,
"J. CAMERON."